Pyrrha's Journey

Rehema Marie

ISBN print: 979-8-9899938-0-2
ISBN ebook: 979-8-9899938-1-9
Library of Congress Control Number: 2024911114

First edition June 2024.
Edited by Darcy Greenwood
Edited by Andrea Hope
Cover Art and Design by Cora Hays
HPH Logo design by E Olson

Published in the United States by
Hyacinth Publishing House, Hancock, MI 49930
https://hyacinthpublishinghouse.com

This story started as a poem:

When hope is cruel
And mercy lost,
Tiger valley
Herculean pass.

FINDING YUHT

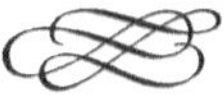

Pʏʀʀʜᴀ ʜᴜᴍᴍᴇᴅ ᴀs sʜᴇ ᴍᴇᴀɴᴅᴇʀᴇᴅ ᴀʟᴏɴɢ ᴛʜᴇ ɢᴀʀᴅᴇɴ ᴘᴀᴛʜ through the grey dawn light. Today was her fifteenth birthday, and she hoped to begin her magical journey into adulthood. She walked from the twin cottages to the smoldering fire ring in the front yard. She pushed her red curls out of her face and straightened her long tunic as she sang, "I have wakened in Thy shelter, O my God, and it becometh him that seeketh that shelter to abide within the Sanctuary of Thy protection and the Stronghold of Thy defense."[1]

The birds flitted and twittered about the Tock family's homestead searching for a morning meal. Pyrrha knelt at the ashes of last night's bonfire and raked the blackened earth looking for tubers, some potatoes or taro, still baking in the coals. She placed a few nuggets on a flat stone nearby. The warriors of Copperton were returning in twos and threes, staggering back over the mountains from their disparate outposts along the borderlands with Ironweald. The Tocks' property would be one of the first welcoming havens on the southern edge of the rugged boundary. The passing soldiers trudging their final miles home from the five-year-long war would appreciate a healthy bite to eat as a token of hospitality.

Copperton and Ironweald had once been friendly outposts in the northern mountain ranges. They had been mining towns separated by a wall of towering peaks. On one side, copper was chiseled from the ground; on the other side, iron was blasted from the rocks. As years passed, the towns spread into their opposite valleys. Farmers grew food to support the populations and industrialists built factories to supply necessities. In time, both small towns had become city-states and then territories. With independence, they ran their affairs as separate countries. The Tock family had been in the mountains from the beginning. Pyrrha had never remembered a time when there was not a smoldering conflict between the neighboring nations.

Pyrrha sang a prayer as she worked. "Illumine my inner being, O my Lord, with the splendors of the Dayspring of Thy Revelation, even as thou didst illumine my outer being with the morning light of Thy favor."[1]

From the road, the pair of cottages barely showed between the cedar boughs and maple branches that camouflaged the compound year-round. Their simple architecture and natural paint blended into the landscape. The homes were not extravagant. Pyrrha lived in the older one with her grandfather, Grand Tock, and her parents, Dr. Rahd and Mama Jojo. The newer one housed Uncle Marz, Auntie Farz, and cousin Woods. They looked as impressive as they were—bungalows with a few rooms for living and wraparound porches for fresh air. Of course, there was electricity and plumbing, which had been installed generations ago. Yet, from afar, it seemed that the Tock family followed the traditional ways since their homes always looked dark, and the path to the watering hole was well worn.

Pyrrha poked the ashes, looking for hope. Grand Tock had not yet returned from his wartime mission, despite the nightly fireside vigils. Every day they relit the fire so it could burn until the next dawn, yet every morning, they awoke to silence instead of the familiar snoring of her grandfather in bed. He was the glue that held the family together with his abundant love. Too many nights ago, he had departed on his secret assignment from Duke Zachariah. No one understood why Copperton's ruler had requested a grey-bearded elder instead of a youthful conscript for that quest. But, then again, only Grand Tock knew the details of the royal summons.

Pyrrha studied the burnt logs in the fire pit to glimpse her fate—tigers chasing smoke and dragons dancing on water. Muck! Had she not learned that reading her own fortune was gibberish? Few were wise enough to see their fate and follow their destined path without trepidation changing their course. The way forward was clouded for one's own protection. Maybe it was true that uncertainty propelled action while naïveté inspired courage.

A woodpecker knocked and a squirrel pranced among the trees, yet the nearby roadway was still devoid of creaking bikes or carts. Pyrrha stood, bringing herself up to her full height, which was still as short as a sprig. She looked back at the matching thatched-roofed cottages—no one else seemed to have awoken yet after the long night of fireside tales.

Pyrrha continued with her morning chores. First, she must fetch water; after breakfast, she would rekindle the garden fire that was a beacon to bring her grandfather home. She picked up two empty buckets by balancing the shoulder pole across the flat of her neck. This old way of collecting water left her hands mostly free and her mind mostly empty, allowing her feet to follow the circular path around the homestead.

Pyrrha reached the deep well and drew water without even a splash. This liquid tasted so much sweeter than what was pumped through the cottage pipes into the kitchen and bathroom, so, of course, Mama Jojo preferred it for her morning coffee. Dr. Rahd enjoyed it with mint leaves.

Despite the peace pact between the two warring nations of Copperton and Ironweald, Pyrrha was as alert as she was wary. The conflict had begun before she was born, when the mineral rights treaty was renegotiated, but the real fighting had started after the drought, when water resources were redistributed. On too many mornings during recent years, the signs of a wounded soldier or an enemy spy had stopped her in her tracks and forced her to be on guard to confront trespassers. Tock's Land was too near the uninhabited forests on the border with Ironweald, so the creatures that passed through were not always tame. Thus, she treaded lightly and breathed into the present moment, paying attention to the feelings within her and without. She carried her grandfather's darts in the folds of her cloak, close to her bosom yet within easy reach, to feel safe under his protection.

This section of path dipped near the main road, yet it was hidden in foliage. Off the path, down the slope, among the leaves, nearly out of view, a man lay sleeping. Pyrrha paused. She placed the full buckets of water upon the dust without a sound. He was tall with broad shoulders. He wore metal armor, leather boots, and a woolen cap, which could hardly contain his black curls. At his side, yet still looped about his frame, was a bag filled with bulky supplies, and hidden in the leaves at his fingertips was the hilt of a blade. He was unlike anyone she had ever seen—confidently self-possessed even as he slept. He did not wear the common soldier's garb, so he could be a fleeing spy.

Pyrrha, without thinking, did what she always did—she climbed up an overhanging tree and with perfect precision pinned him to the ground with the darts gifted from Grand Tock. Then, she waited. She studied his demeanor for clues as to whether he was friend or foe. This trespasser on her family's land seemed to be holding secrets he did not want to reveal since he had not rested with the other soldiers, as expected, at the welcome fire in the garden. His dirt-stained clothes and unshaven face hinted at a very long journey, yet his stately demeanor radiated a depth of character. Such details tantalized Pyrrha as she lay in the branches above, peering down at his sleeping form, and wondering who he was. It was not long before the unknown friend stirred from his slumber. He looked around, aware that he was no longer alone.

"Good sir!" whispered Pyrrha from the tree branch above.

"Dear lady!" replied the stranger pinned to the ground like an insect on display in a museum. "What a spectacular welcome!" he said in a perfect north-country drawl. "It's been a long way home. Do you have a cup of water for this lost soul finding his way north?"

"Don't move, good sir."

"If only I could!" The man chuckled at his precarious predicament.

Pyrrha thought about the difficulties of trust; then, she went on with the traditional greeting to see if he knew the proper response. "Good sir, whose son do we have the honor of hosting?"

"I am Yuht of the Mountain. I am making my way back from the last battle." As he talked, he slowly wiggled his hand to reach the glint of metal.

Pyrrha did what she had been trained to do by Grand Tock. She threw a dart, pinning the collar of his shirt to the dust.

"Aiya!" exclaimed Yuht. "You have drawn blood."

"Well, I told you not to move. I see your knife in the leaves, and I'm sure you are trained to use it if you hide it so perfectly within reach."

"My dear lady, what can I tell you that will allow you to trust me and enable me to return home this fine day?"

"What is the name of the mountain with five peaks?"

"Mount Gaea."

"What is the river that can go everywhere and nowhere?"

"River Libertad."

"Where can you find both black pearls and red coral?"

"The Ocean of Wisdom…and…the Duke's crown."

"Who are you?"

"I'm Yuht. I live on the mountain north of Newcomen. I am making my way home."

"Who are your people?"

Yuht did not reply to her question. He just smiled with a sparkle in his eyes. He kindly asked, "May I have a cup of water? It has been a long way home from the last battle, and I am thirsty."

Pyrrha slowly climbed down from the tree and backed up the hill toward the path without breaking eye contact with Yuht. She picked up the two buckets of water by replacing the pole on her shoulders and glided back into the gully to sit beside the soldier.

As she looked upon his face, she heard his voice in her head: *Who are you? Why have we never met before?*

She examined his face, but his lips had not moved—a channel of telepathy seemed momentarily to open between them. It was peculiar to have this happen with a stranger; she had only communicated like this with her family in times of great need. She leaned into the unexpected and spoke through her mind.

I am Pyrrha. This is Tock's Land. It was gifted by Duke Zachariah to Grand Tock for charting the Duke's View.

As she stared into his eyes, she communicated with his soul.

You are Grand Tock's granddaughter?

Yes.

The tiger girl?

Yes.

The Duke is lucky to have such a loyal lady living in this land and guarding this realm.

Pyrrha was speechless. She slowly pulled out the darts from Yuht's shirt cuffs and pant hems.

Thank you. Yuht communicated with his eyes.

Finally, Pyrrha withdrew the final dart, which had pinched his collar and pricked his neck. She extracted a handkerchief from her pocket and wetted it with the well water.

I'm sorry. She cleaned the nick on his skin. *I did not mean to hurt you.*

It is like a kiss. Yuht smiled.

He sat up slowly. He held the handkerchief to his skin with one hand while he sipped a small bowl of water with the other.

"The Duke is lucky to have such a warrior," Yuht said. "Those small darts you have are potent protection. You had me completely immobilized."

Pyrrha blushed. Roses. Potent perfume emanated from this soldier's very veins. The fragrance overwhelmed her. The war had dimmed her memory of blossoms, but she was suddenly in the middle of a garden surrounded by a colorful array of roses, all smiling down on her and bathing her in joy.

"I have been in the war these last five years. I have worked deep in the mines discovering vast new lines of knowledge. Through it all, I have not been injured. It is ironic that today, the first day home, the first day of peace, I am wounded by a friend." Yuht spoke without remorse; instead, he expressed deep pleasure. "Please gift me this handkerchief and the dart that scratched me as a keepsake."

"Ahhmm," Pyrrha stammered. Who was this man to trespass on her family's property and to ask for one of Grand Tock's precious darts gifted by Jupiter the Giant? Yet, she could not help herself under his gaze. Something gave way deep inside her.

Yes! It is yours. She nodded her consent.

"By my ancestors," Yuht solemnly swore, "the bounty of your gift will come back to you one-thousand fold."

This formality made Pyrrha laugh nervously, and reply as one always did. "May this gift be worth that much to thee."

With that, Yuht placed the offending dart in his breast pocket and securely tied the handkerchief around his neck to stay the trickle of blood. A rustling in the trees ended the sweet tenor of their rendezvous.

Woods, Pyrrha's older cousin who lived next door, interrupted the conversation. His gruff morning voice called out, "Good sir, whose son do we have the honor of hosting?"

Pyrrha's bright voice answered, "This is Yuht of the Mountain." She quickly changed her tone when she saw Woods' raised arrow across his angry face. "He means us no harm."

Yuht's calm voice interjected, "I am making my way back from the last battle. For one night, I rested upon Tock's Land. This morning, my dear lady gave me some clear water from the deep well. Now, I am refreshed enough to be on my way home."

Woods lowered his arrow an inch, but he did not let down his guard. Under the rim of a cap, his sky-blue eyes brewed grey as storm clouds.

Yuht moved with slow grace, narrating his intentions. "Thank you for this fine water!" He put the bowl on the ground. "I will be setting off for the mountain north of town now," he said cautiously. "Let me gather my things…" he said as he picked himself up and arranged his bag on his hip. "May I pick up my knife and tuck it in my belt?" he asked.

Please. Pyrrha nodded her assent.

"Goodbye, my dear lady!" Yuht said when he was ready to set off. Then, he touched his hand to his heart in a cordial salute and bowed his head with a nod toward Pyrrha. "Goodbye, sir!" he grunted in Woods' direction and jutted out his chin.

Then, Yuht turned and lumbered up the steep embankment to the road toward town and the hills beyond. In silence, Pyrrha and Woods watched him walk away. He did not look back. Finally, Yuht disappeared between the leaves of the trees and behind the roll of the hill, and the scratch of his boots on the ground faded from ear.

"Who was that?" asked an exasperated Woods.

"Yuht of the Mountain," replied Pyrrha airily.

"I mean, *who* is he? *Who* do you know from the *mountain*?"

"Well, you and I don't know every rock and tree in this land."

"Uh, but we know every mountain, and all of them have names."

"Forgive him his secrets…. During the war, we have all had so many…. He is likely not used to speaking openly anymore."

"You are too trusting!" Woods huffed. "Just look at what he was wearing! That breastplate alone is worth the price of your family's cottage. And his leather boots—most soldiers returning home have nothing more than cloth slippers or straw sandals."

"Oooh, Woods, I never knew you to be so excited about men's fashion," Pyrrha replied.

Woods rolled his eyes.

As they had been talking, they had walked the long path around Tock's Land to arrive back at Pyrrha's front door. Woods put the buckets down on the stoop before turning to cross the garden to the cottage he shared with Uncle Marz and Auntie Farz.

"Thank you!" Pyrrha shouted at his back. Then, she whispered to herself, "Thank you for keeping an eye on me, guarding me from unknown friends, and carrying my burdens." She was grateful for his protection despite his stubborn, overprotective ways.

As Pyrrha entered her family's small cottage at the edge of the forest, her mind raced around the chance encounter with the unknown friend. On the dawn of her fifteenth birthday, the day of maturity, she had suddenly met someone who had captured her attention. Yet she had more questions than answers—curiosity tumbled around her head while desires stirred her heart.

FIRE STARTER

Fire starts with a spark—it needs power to burn and oxygen to breathe. Without this trinity of heat, fuel, and air, the fire goes cold. Pyrrha sang as she worked, preparing anew the bonfire for Grand Tock's vigil:

Build the fire twig by twig, stick by stick, log by log.
Frayed paper, shaved wood chips.
Autumn leaves, balled hair.
In the fire ring!
Hiss, crack, sizzle, wheeze.
Hum, fizz, whistle, creak.
Make the fire sing!
Build the fire twig by twig, stick by stick, log by log.

It was Pyrrha's favorite childhood song. Her grandfather would hum it on summer evenings in the garden as they prepared for barbecues and s'mores. Grand Tock's green eyes would dance while his silver mustache and beard glimmered in the firelight. He smelled spicy like jing—the medicinal root the family farmed on Tock's Land. Grand Tock would steadily puff on his pipe, making tendrils of tobacco smoke play like ghosts swirling into the spirit world.

When the kindling was set and the logs were laid, he would stroke her auburn hair and sing in baritone, "Look Pyrrha! Your hair is the color of flames. Now, strike the flint and make a wish."

So she did. The pyramid of kindling would ignite into a golden red with streaks of blue. All night, Grand Tock and Pyrrha would tend the fire, adding logs and fanning the flames to keep it hot enough that the smoke was only a whisper wafting her wish to heaven.

Everyone had been praying and dreaming of the war's end. Today, on her fifteenth birthday, as Copperton welcomed the warriors home, Pyrrha struck the flint, lit the bonfire, and made the same wish as always, "May I be worthy of my family's name, live up to my family's legacy, and become like Grand Tock—a hero of Copperton."

Pyrrha watched the tiny spark catch the nest of leaves, hair, chips, and paper. She blew gently on the kernel of heat until the twigs and the kindling turned red. She fanned the breeze into the pyramid of branches. When the flames leaped high, she carefully balanced a few split tree stumps over the hotbed of coals. In a few hours, the fire would settle; then, she could stack on more fuel to make the bonfire blaze. Each neighborhood had prepared an open bonfire, causing the landscape to look like rubies strung along the necklace of roadway home. This fire was the beacon for soldiers trekking home. Tonight, the family would again wait around the flames for Grand Tock's return. They hoped his secret mission would allow him to return with the other warriors.

The air smelled like mowed lawns and new flowers, fresh baked bread, and ginger ale. The jingle of wind chimes and children's laughter added festive cheer. Yet the day was full of awkwardness as everyone buzzed around in disbelief—the peace treaty between Copperton and Ironweald was so new. The two countries had been friendly long ago, when they overflowed with float copper and iron ore deposits. Eventually, claims ran to dust and slag. Industry slowed, and money became scarce. Longstanding disagreements about new technology, living standards, and environmental health divided the once similar countries. War was the inevitable conclusion. Ironweald wanted to prove iron was stronger than copper, while Copperton invested in alchemy to change copper into gold.

Of course, the war was more complicated—for many years Ironweald's rulers had been mistreating their peoples with cruel laws and high taxes. Many had fled north to Copperton to live more freely and gain prosperity under the reign of the beneficent Duke Zachariah. Though he was not perfect, he was renowned for being kind, just, and gracious. He took leadership as an honor bestowed by the Great King of old. Thus, he was determined that his family remain stewards of the land while he added democratically elected members to the Duke's Court advisory council to represent the people's concerns.

Pyrrha looked around the yard to see what chores were still to be done. Woods was across the garden by the shed, stacking another wheelbarrow heavy with freshly chopped logs. He stood lean and tall swinging a large axe with grace and precision. For more than an hour now, he had been lumbering to and fro, silently supplying her with materials as she built the family fire. He was a helpful neighbor, a good friend, and though they were not related by blood, she called him cousin.

Uncle Marz had helped Grand Tock so much over the years —a servant who became like a son—that her grandfather had gifted him a plot of land next to his own home. Together, they had worked side by side to build the second cottage among the trees. Thus, a debt of gratitude bonded Uncle Marz to Grand Tock and his descendants. Uncle Marz and Dr. Rahd had grown up as brothers; her uncle ran the family jing farm, which enabled Dr. Rahd to live in the world of books and theories. To honor this, to show her respect, Pyrrha always used familial terms of endearment for Uncle Marz and Auntie Farz and, in return, they treated her as an adopted daughter. Much of the time, they looked after her more than her own parents.

The focused tasks were a godsend for Pyrrha and Woods from the nervous ticks and jitteriness which infected every limb. They were antsy with anticipation for the evening festivities, for the soldiers coming home, and for the possibility to see Grand Tock again and hear his newest tales. Pyrrha was also enlivened by meeting Yuht—the unknown friend, the stranger with secrets. His dark eyes and confident shoulders were seared into her mind's eye.

The yard had been raked clean of the early autumn leaves that had fallen on the green grass. The gravel drive had been leveled with bags of pebbles to even the grade and fill the holes. Mama Jojo's black curly hair and colorful dresses had not been seen all day, nor had Dr. Rahd's copper beard and silver spectacles been spotted on the property. Who knew where Mama Jojo was expelling her boundless energy or where Dr. Rahd was squirreled away reading while everyone else was busy working? Pyrrha did not ask, nor did she await her parents' return since they were often missing for large parts of the day and night, pursuing their own concerns. They each usually managed to find their way home when something important was about to happen—like her birthday party, like the end of the war, and like the bonfire for Grand Tock's return.

Pyrrha helped Woods with all the chores assigned by Uncle Marz and Auntie Farz. Uncle Marz's round face and bald head would appear out of nowhere to shout new tasks in his deep, husky voice while Auntie Farz's petite frame and dark eyes would search for them in the yard so she could murmur her next set of instructions at close range. It seemed the jobs would never end; just as one task was completed, and Pyrrha and

Woods were leaning against a tree to take a breath, Auntie would step out on the cottage porch and stretch in the sunlight before singing her next request, while Uncle would stomp around from behind the house, scratch the stubble on his chin, unfurl his frown, and yell another to-do item.

By midafternoon, Pyrrha was bored with preparations and wanted the festivities to begin, so she snuck up on Woods and tapped him on the shoulder. When he swept his head around, his hair moving like wheat in a field, she thrust her garden rake handle into his chest as a fencing foil.

"On guard!" she asserted pressing her weapon forward.

"Ready," Woods countered lifting his broom handle to cross swords.

"Allez!"

They lunged and thwacked poles, hopping about the grassy field they had just mowed and cleared of debris for the evening's celebration.

Pyrrha thrashed her sword like a cornered tiger swatting with a fistful of claws. She smiled, showing off her gapped front teeth and pink tongue. Woods casually blocked her straightforward attacks with graceful strokes over and under, right and left. The rake and broom swiped and smacked, hit and whacked —punctuated by grunts and giggles. They shuffled across the yard, gliding forward and sashaying backward in practiced combat. Woods, two-and-a-half years older and supposedly wiser, towered over Pyrrha. His arms stretched a few inches longer, but his short-handled broomstick maintained a well-matched competition. Crack, slap, knock, bat. They swung their wooden swords in defense of their pride. Inevitably, the loser would be tasked with the most dreaded chores yet to be assigned.

"Enough violence," barked Uncle Marz from the cottage door. "The war is over. The time for fighting is done!"

The thumps and thuds and shouts and shrieks had awoken

him from his afternoon nap, his respite from preparations. He scratched the nonexistent stubble on his head while surveying the youth tearing about the garden.

"You have energy, Woods and Pyrrha? Then, get the old bikes and ride to town to fill Auntie Farz's grocery order."

Pyrrha and Woods did not need to be told twice. They dropped their gardening tools in the shed, picked up hats to cover their hair, and went off to find the bicycles. No one wanted Uncle Marz in a foul mood for the evening's fireside chat, as he had prepared a special retelling of some of Grand Tock's epic adventures to entertain the troops and fill their hearts with pride. They all secretly hoped the tale would attract Grand Tock—calling him home as they repeated his name and remembered his honors. He was not only beloved to the family; he was a national hero whose bravery and inquisitive spirit had enabled Copperton to double its size as well as its resources.

Receiving Auntie Farz's instructions, Pyrrha and Woods pedaled toward town on the rusty bikes that had once been red and blue. Both had woven baskets tied to the handlebars, and a wooden crate fastened atop the rear fender to be filled with goods. It was a serviceable mode of transportation. It was sufficient to carry all the foodstuff they needed to buy in Newcomen, the capital of Copperton. Woods rode like the wind as his long legs accelerated him forward. Pyrrha followed focusing on her pace—breath, pedal, heartbeat.

Remember to breathe, Grand Tock's voice boomed in her head.

Obediently, she breathed in the fresh air of peace and freedom, the aroma of sunshine on fields ripe with crops.

Remember to breathe deeply. His voice was clear as if he was biking next to her. She gulped in the air, but she choked on whiffs of cow manure and crushed weeds.

Keep breathing! Grand Tock's voice insisted.

She concentrated on the air as it went in-n-out and in-n-out and in-n-out of her lungs. She paid attention to pedaling her feet up-n-down, up-n-down, up-n-down. She listened for her beating heart as it thumped, thumped, thumped in her chest. The rhythm of inhalations and exhalations kept her energized as she steadily pushed the bike up the incline toward town. This breathing practice—this foundational meditation training—helped settle her spinning mind that constantly anticipated what could possibly go wrong.

"Hey!" she called to Woods ahead on the road. "Slow up, would ya?"

He skidded to a stop at the top of the next knoll. "You can't keep up, lil' warrior?"

She scowled at him. "It's my birthday! You have to be nice to me."

"I am nice to you…always."

She smiled because it was true. Woods was always much nicer to her than she was to him. He treated her like a little sister; he taught her to do all the things he had learned a few years before. When they had both caught their breath, they pedaled on at a more leisurely pace, chatting as they rode to town.

"So, do you feel different?" Woods asked. "Now that you are fifteen and all."

"I guess…I'm supposed to be an adult today!"

On her fifteenth birthday, she was recognized as an adult, who had all the obligations of abiding by the laws, but without quite all the responsibilities of full adult citizenship.

"Hahaha!" Woods laughed throwing his head back over his shoulders and letting his bike zigzag as he chuckled at the idea. "Naw, it doesn't happen so quickly. You need a few days yet to grow into a proper adult."

For the next three years, she would be practicing at adulthood much like a toddler riding a bike with training wheels. Woods, a few years older, was eagerly preparing for his eighteenth birthday; he had been readying himself to enroll in the militia. This was her dream too—to protect Copperton from Ironweald's greedy land grabs.

"Yeah, but according to the Duke, I'm a young adult now," Pyrrha retorted.

"Yes, honor the Duke and he will honor you."

"That's your dream! Be honored with serving Copperton in a few months when you turn eighteen."

"It was…but now the war is over!" Woods said. "So I don't know if I'll become a soldier immediately."

"Are you sad about that?" Pyrrha pried.

"Ya know…" Woods frowned. "I think you have more of the Grand Tock spirit than I do, lil' warrior," Woods replied. "I was planning to be a soldier, but maybe I'll be an explorer instead."

Pyrrha grinned and let her teeth show. Pyrrha and Woods had spent all their free time during the last five years training to defend Copperton—shooting arrows, throwing darts, reading maps, and climbing hills. Grand Tock had taught them everything he knew. They created obstacle courses in their backyard on the land beyond the view of the homestead and out of earshot of Auntie and Uncle. They played war. Sometimes, they even tracked real spies who had crossed the border, but by nightfall Grand Tock would insist on calling the land-guards for assistance.

"You like Uncle Marz's gift, eh?" Woods asked admiring the pendant of a diamond-eyed golden tiger hanging on a black cord fastened around Pyrrha's neck.

"It's the best gift I've ever received," Pyrrha replied with misty eyes. She touched her new necklace and tucked the valuable treasure beneath the collar of her blouse as they pedaled toward town. It was a symbol of the nation as well as her childhood adventure with Grand Tock. "Maybe if I keep the tiger close to my heart, it will give me the courage of Copperton."

"You've never lacked for courage," Woods laughed thinking

of the morning visitor. "I think a little less courage might keep you alive longer."

"Act first; think second…I can't help myself…even when I try, I think about what I did after the fact!"

"Maybe make it a rule—Thou shall not pin mystery men to the forest floor!"

Pyrrha scowled at Woods. Her pulse quickened in her chest thinking of Yuht's dark eyes and curls. She took the boost of excitement cursing through her blood and raced Woods on their bikes for the next mile.

The announcement of the war ending was bittersweet news. At once, Woods and Pyrrha were relieved and unmoored. They were delighted that the fighting would end and that Grand Tock would come home, but all their future plans to become valiant soldiers and defend Copperton disappeared in the mist of a peaceful future. They longed to hear of Grand Tock's secret adventures during the last year, but they were sad that their time had not yet come to prove themselves as worthy warriors and protectors of Copperton. The war had been terrible, but the predictable problems seemed more normal than the pleasantries of peace.

The rocky road bumped Pyrrha and Woods out of their thoughts.

"We should ride single file," Woods suggested. "You go ahead—"

"Yeah, so you don't zoom off and leave me in the dust!" Pyrrha interjected.

"We'll slow up for all the people about."

"It's so busy!"

"More people than we have seen in a minute…"

"We'll head for the square?"

"Got it."

The traffic thickened as they approached the old part of Newcomen—a mule here, some horse-drawn carts there, and, out of nowhere, a few motorcycles zoomed by. The clatter of hooves on the brick road set the rhythm; the merchants' voices melodiously combined; the bells and horns accentuated the ambient song. The country was dancing in harmony to the anthem of peace.

As Pyrrha and Woods neared the marketplace, the curved country road straightened into a city street; the grassy embankments grew into cement sidewalks. Timber ranches morphed into brick townhouses; barbed-wire pastures rolled into picket-fenced gardens. The landscape became dense with buildings and people as they entered Bell Tower Square, the center of town, market plaza. They rode single file with the front tire of Woods bike overlapping the back tire on Pyrrha's frame.

Colors! The town folk were dressed in their finest clothes—pink dresses, red bowties, glittery ribbons, and leather shoes. The lampposts were draped with yellow flowers and blue flags while the houses flew red and green banners. Wherever they looked, their eyes were overwhelmed with joy. Yesterday had been black and white, but today rainbow colors bloomed.

Pyrrha and Woods dismounted and walked their bikes through the crowded streets; their heels clicked lightly on the newly patched brick road. The shopfronts showed the owners' wealth in the facades from humble to prosperous—wood, cement, brick, and marble. Traditional family businesses were in timber sheds attached to the front of generational homes. Groceries were housed in large cement blocks with wide glass doors; whereas, the dress and hat shops lived in the brick buildings that lined the main thoroughfare. The grandest establishments in old town were the banks carved like marble mountains into the foundation of the city blocks—seeming to be as old as the rocks from which they were built and just as dependable.

The smell of fresh pretzels and spicy mustard drew Pyrrha's attention to the street vendors flaunting delicious treats not seen in many years. Woods found a bench in the center square, and they leaned their bikes against the backrest. This was their special place. It was comforting to be surrounded by the din of shopkeepers, under the chiming bells, next to the cooing pigeons.

Best of all, laid before them across the plaza floor was Uncle Marz's mosaic map of the country of Copperton; it depicted all of Grand Tock's early adventures in skillful detail. To the north was the Ocean of Wisdom, which threw coral and pearls on the beach with every crashing wave. To the south, Ironweald's pollution was so thick that the land was only shown in greyscale. In the middle—the pride of all—were the mountains and forests, the lakes and the streams of Greater Copperton and the Duke's View. Pyrrha and Woods admired it all. As Grand Tock's custom required, they did not leave the bench until they glimpsed the many secret symbols hidden in plain view by Uncle Marz's artistry—the x marking Jupiter's Cave, the slash of Tiger Valley, and the diamond for Tock's Land.

Pyrrha blinked back memories. The smells were dizzying, so she arose and followed her nose to the sorbet vendor selling fresh squeezed mango essence over cups of shaved ice. She bought two cold treats to share before they divided up Auntie Farz's shopping list.

"So…what do you want to do?" Woods asked as he looked over the list.

Sugar and butter from Pat's Grocery on the top of the hill. Marshmallows at Bonkers, and some chocolate too. Rye bread from Nisu Bakery with the poodle sleeping near the door. Brats and tofu sticks at the one-armed butcher's stall. Beets from Farmer Saari's cart on the way home.

Pyrrha grinned, "I'll get the sweet stuff from Pat's and Bonkers."

"Alright, I'll get the bread and brats—" Woods conceded.

"Remember tofu for me," Pyrrha added.

"Of course," Woods winked. "We'll meet at Saari's to pick up the vegetables."

"Yup! Race you to the finish," Pyrrha smiled. It made her happy to return to the routine of shopping in the bustling town.

"See ya!" And, Woods was off on his bike skirting the crowds to save time.

During the war, this shopping excursion had been a rare treat afforded by an all-to-temporary ceasefire. Pyrrha meandered through the streets to find the required shops and pick up the delightful treats. With the merchandise safely stowed in the front basket and the back crate, she worked her way toward Farmer Saari's cart on the road leading out of town.

"Good afternoon, dearest Granddaughter of Tock!" burped a slimy voice nearby.

Pyrrha looked around, trying to recognize who spoke. A shiver ran up her spine and her shoulders clenched when she saw Old Snark with his wheelbarrow of secondhand medical supplies.

Being polite as trained, Pyrrha nodded, "Fine day, isn't it?"

"It is always a beautiful day when my eyes are graced with the sight of you, dear lady," Old Snark replied. "Before you pedal off like the wind, here is a small token for your fifteenth."

Surprised that an acquaintance remembered her special birthday, yet her parents had not, Pyrrha paused and reached out for the small bundle.

"Thank you, Uncle Sn… Duceau!" She stammered trying to be courteous and not use his snarky nickname.

Then, she tucked the gift away, likely a book by the size and weight of things, and headed to meet Woods. She rode quickly. She breathed steadily, pacing herself. Pedal, pedal, breathe. Pedal, pedal, breathe. Pedal, pedal, breathe.

Woods was paying Farmer Saari for a few pounds of produce when she skidded to a stop on the dirt road.

"Hiya, Pyrrha!" Farmer Saari nodded. "Woods here tells me it's your birthday. Well, happy birthday!"

"Hello, Uncle Saari," Pyrrha smiled. "Thank you, Uncle! It's a good day."

"For such a special day, the day you become an adult," Farmer Saari said, "I gave Woods an early pumpkin for your evening meal." The farmer blushed. "I'm sorry it is not more, but I trade in vegetables, and the early pumpkins are sweet this year."

"That is so thoughtful, Uncle Saari!" Pyrrha nodded her head and put her hand to her heart in a nod of gratitude. "Thank you." She had always liked Uncle Saari, as he was kind and generous to all who crossed his path.

When they were on their bikes heading home, Woods teased Pyrrha for taking too long with her errands, "Awe! Don't look so dejected. You can't win every time."

"Oh, actually, it's not that. I was delayed by Uncle Duceau!"

Woods scowled. "What did that old crazy want?"

"He gave me a book, I think, for my fifteenth!"

"How odd…" Woods mused.

"Well…yes…Woods, I have a question."

"Ask already—"

"Is it weird that distant uncles give me gifts on my fifteenth, but my parents are nowhere to be found?"

"Yes, but…"

"Spit it out—"

"Pyrrha, your parents aren't the most attentive or responsible guardians."

"Hahahahahah! Now, that is an understatement."

Woods gave Pyrrha a weird look. "You aren't supposed to laugh at that."

She winced. "I'm stitched funny." She always laughed at hard truths and cried at jokes—like the signals for pain and joy were tightly spiraled around each other triggering giggles and tears at all the wrong times.

As they rode their ladened bicycles home, they set a steady pace to pedal without breaking a real sweat. With the right tempo, they would not be tired for the late-night bonfire. If they rode steadily, they would have enough time to unpack and shower, and Pyrrha could then re-braid her hair before the neighbors gathered to hear Uncle Marz's epic stories about Grand Tock's adventures. Nothing. They wanted nothing to break the magic in the air—the war was over; Pyrrha was fifteen; Yuht lived on the mountain. This year would bring new experiences beyond her wildest imagination.

FINDING THE WAY HOME

IT WAS DUSK. THE SHADOWS OF TREES REACHED DOWN THE GRAVEL driveway to the garden where the family sat around the campfire enjoying the golden light before sunset. Auntie Farz poked at the potatoes in the coals; Woods rested across a long bench admiring the first stars visible in the night sky; Pyrrha watched the treetops dancing in the breeze; Mama Jojo hummed an old tune under her breath; Dr. Rahd looked up from his book in anticipation of the fireside tale.

"Tonight, I will tell you a story," Uncle Marz said in a low rumble. "But first, we must commemorate Pyrrha's fifteenth."

Woods sat up and looked toward his cousin. "Well get up already and make your fifteen rounds around the fire!"

"Do I have to?" Pyrrha protested.

"Up with you already," Auntie Farz insisted.

Thus, Pyrrha commenced the birthday tradition; once around the fire for each year of life, and one sincere thank you for each person present.

"Best to start now, before we have more company," Woods prodded.

Pyrrha skipped around the fire ring a few times to get a rhythm and iron out her thoughts.

"Mama Jojo, thank you for giving me life, and Dr. Rahd, I'm grateful for all you have taught me from your great studies of the books of old," she said on her fifth trip around the fire.

After a few more circles, she complimented Auntie Farz, "Thank you for always welcoming me home with delicious meals and warm hugs."

"Woods, I appreciate your ..." she paused to find the right word, "practicality."

Everyone laughed.

Finally, on her last trip around the fire, she stopped in front of Uncle Marz. "I'm grateful for your stories that remind me of our great legacy."

Everyone smiled. Pyrrha took her seat again on the bench.

"Tonight," Uncle Marz spoke. "We will keep our fire burning to light the path for the brave soldiers as they find their way home. To entertain, to keep us awake, I'll tell you of the great warrior, Tock, the giant tamer and the tiger slayer."

"Uncle Marz, this time can you start at the beginning and not skip a step?" Pyrrha asked.

"As you wish! You are the keeper of his spirit, so we shall re-walk his path as he walked it," Uncle Marz sang in his melodious voice. "When Tock was a mere lad, not much older than you are now, Pyrrha, he embarked on a great adventure. However, he did not know that cool summer morning when he went out to the farm that it would be anything other than a typical day of harvesting jing in the woods on the edge of the mountains. He wore a simple tunic and trousers and carried a pouch filled with a few early apples, late berries, and a loaf of bread. As he walked the well-worn path to the jing patch, he hummed the old walking tune."

At this song's mention, Mama Jojo piped up so all present could hear her haunting rendition of "Ode to Walking to Work on an Early Morning." Everyone drummed along on the benches to the pace of a groggy stroll.

After a brief spell when the song had run out of rhythm, Uncle Marz continued. "When Tock neared the jing patch, he noticed some worrying signs—the woods were unusually quiet without birds or animals chattering; trees were knocked down across the entrance to the clearing; and then, a shadow passed over the sun. Just as he was able to catch a glimpse of his once well-ordered rows of jing upended and his neatly kept tools thrown about, he felt the bottom of his stomach go upside down. He was picked up off the ground and thrown into a sack. All was black."

The crackle and the hiss of the fire filled the air as everyone peered off into the darkness just outside the circle of light. There had been movement from the main road down the lane. Their first visitors were here.

"Good sir!" Woods called in a deeper voice than necessary, standing up and touching his bow beside him.

Pyrrha reached for her darts too. Yet, Uncle Marz, Auntie Farz, Mama Jojo, and Dr. Rahd sat calmly unmoved. Their age had given them patience to react as the situation required, not hastily before a muscle needed to move. They trusted the wary of war to bring people in peace.

"It's been a long way home," whispered a disembodied voice from the edge of the clearing beyond the firelight. "Do you have a morsel for these lost souls finding their way north? We could smell turnips roasting from a mile away."

"Anyone seeking his North Star is welcome here," replied Dr. Rahd.

With a shuffle here and there, two seats upon the logs were made for the disheveled men in thread-bare uniforms with thin straw sandals tied to their feet. Auntie Farz passed over hot roasted potatoes skewered on sticks, while Pyrrha ladled dippers of fresh water into small bowls.

Mama Jojo began to sing the eating song. "The fowls of the air and the beasts of the field receive their meat each day from Thee, and all beings partake of Thy care and loving kindness."[1]

Oh, how Jojo would sing even if she could never remember the whole song, but it did not matter because the unknown friends who had just joined this company of neighbors picked up the tune in much stronger voices than their tiny frames seemed able to contain, and the three of them mumbled and hummed their way through to the end.

"Good sirs! Whose sons do we have the honor of hosting tonight?" asked Dr. Rahd with professorial interest. "I always like meeting the living descendants of the genealogies that I have studied in the university library."

"I am Emerson of Riverside and this is Neilson of Riverway. We are making our way back from the last battle. We were fortunate that peace descended like a fog and prevented us from another day of fighting. We have been gone these last few years helping in the mines collecting what knowledge we could, but our bodies are now weak from the effort of overthinking minutia."

"Dear unknown friends," Dr. Rahd interrupted, "you are speaking gibberish. Do you need a place to rest for a few hours before walking the last track home?"

"Yes," replied Emerson simply.

"We are grateful for the light you shine and the hospitality you extend," Neilson added.

Dr. Rahd led them to the far side of the fire circle where a straw bed was covered by a rug the color of the sea. Woods passed them a few more sticks of roasted taro and turnips, while Mama Jojo ladled out generous portions of water infused with jing juice to wash the food down.

Once everyone was settled in comfortably, Uncle Marz restarted the story. "Dear guests! Tonight, I share the story of Grand Tock and Jupiter the Giant. One summer morning many moons ago, Tock went to his jing field. He arrived to discover it torn apart, but before he could do a thing about it, he was thrown into a sack and blacked out."

The guests nodded at the beginnings of this familiar tale.

Uncle Marz spoke, "It was a bumpy ride being carried in a big bag. Tock would wake from the discomfort of the jostling, but quickly he would catch an overpowering whiff of that very familiar scent of jing and fall back asleep. This went on for miles and hours. In his groggy state, he struggled to get fresh gulps of air. When he would wake for a brief moment, he would hold his knife and attempt to cut the bag open to escape. The burlap was coarse, so it was difficult to make an incision, but Tock persisted. Wake. Stab. Smell. Sleep. Wake. Stab. Smell. Sleep. Wake. Stab. Smell. Sleep. This pattern went on in a desperate strike at freedom. Suddenly, the sound of ripping cloth brought a rush of cool mountain air and a hard thump on the ground. This time when Tock came to, he let out a scream as fear immobilized his body. Before him sat something he had never seen—an extra large, rocky mountain of a human.

"The giant had burly hair that grew out of his head, chest, and arms like a real jack-pine savage. He smelled of moss and coal with a whiff of jasmine, and when he spoke, Jupiter the Giant's voice roared and splashed like a hundred-foot waterfall dancing over a cliff.

"'Hi, little man!' said Jupiter the Giant.

"'Hi!' Tock responded with his hoarse voice.

"'Well, your little trick has really slowed us down! Now, we must spend the night under the constellations before reaching home.'

"'You are taking me home!'

"'Hahahaha!' Jupiter laughed until the sound ricocheted off the surrounding hills and cliffs to fill the valley with thunder. After a time, he said, 'Sorry, little man, I'm afraid that you will never go home now that you have seen a giant.'

"Well that is how Jupiter the Giant had understood the conversation. Tock heard the conversation very differently. It went more like this:

"'Rooooooaaaaar!'

"'Hi!'

"'WhaaaaaRAAAAyeeee.'

"'You are taking me home!'

"'Hahahahaha!' Silence. 'WoRoooooaaaaarYeeeee.'"

"Tock sat up on the grey ground, slowly massaging his limbs awake while drinking in the dewy air. He thought of running, but he could not stand. Jupiter the Giant, the mammoth of a man, delicately strung a fine bone needle with a spiderweb. The large hole in the bag melted together like wax with each of Jupiter's stitches. Within an hour, the sack was mended. When Tock examined the cloth, he could not even see where the slice had been made by his blade. Jupiter did finer needlework than any grandparent's embroidery. Then, each and every piece of jing was carefully picked up and placed back in the bag. Clearly, Jupiter cared for each chunk of root as if it were a precious diamond.

"'Little man,' said Jupiter, 'we will walk until we find a cave to shelter in for the night.'

"Tock only heard a roar. He was so frightened that he didn't know what to think, so he imagined that the giant had said something like, 'I think you will taste very good boiled in a stew with this jing.'

"Jupiter picked up the bag and slung it over one shoulder and then picked up Tock and perched him on the other side. Tock did not fight this arrangement since he knew he was out muscled, and he was still hungover from the aroma of jing. Instead, he came up with a strategy. Tock would try to stay alert. He looked around to figure out where he was and what he could learn for his eventual escape.

"First, he focused all of his attention on his captor, Jupiter.

From his perch, Tock smelt woodsmoke in Jupiter's tousled hair; he felt strength in his stiff shoulders; and he sensed sure footedness with his lengthy stride. The landscape was familiar but different. At home, the trees were mostly birch, oak, and maple with a few pines, and cedars for good measure. Yet here, they were in a slightly different forest mix. There was a greater and greater concentration of firs and pines than leafy trees. The tall, straight, red and white trunks towered above them before the first branches of needles yawned out in upward spirals. The ground was empty of undergrowth and was covered instead with mosses, dried needles, and cones.

"Tock looked to the mountains to see if he could catch the glimpse of any landmark outlined by the silhouette of the peaks. As they crossed over the next mountain pass, Tock looked back and strained his eyes against the setting sun, and he saw a troubling sign. Gaea, the five peaks that made up the voluptuous body of the reclining goddess, was the farthest set of mountains to his west. Normally, this was in the far northeast. If this landmark was correct, and who knew if it was the same outline from both sides, he estimated he was several days journey from home and had gone farther afield than anyone he had ever known.

"Instead of panicking, Tock decided to follow the ancient ways of being. Of course, he had hated these mindfulness lessons in school and at home, but he had learned their value when farming jing as his attention to detail had helped his family increase their crop yield and then their wealth. Tock focused on being present in the moment and making a mental map of his situation. He studied the terrain. He watched the giant. He relaxed into his predicament and conserved his physical energy for what was yet to come.

"Time went by in a quick, quick, slow fashion as is common with mindfulness. He focused on breathing out, slowly lengthening his exhale to steady his nerves. With each inhale he would try to count to four, but with the exhales he would draw them out to six counts or more. This uneven breath, with short inhales and long, extended exhales, had a way of forcing his body to slow down. Inevitably, his mind wandered. A small bird would serenade the world with a new song, his heartbeat would flutter, and so his count would be broken. With a sigh, Tock would refocus on his quickening breath and start the long exhales and short inhales again, counting the seconds of the breath to regain control of his body and emotions. Before he could believe it, the time had flown by; the light was nearly gone from the sky. Jupiter stopped and stooped into a low rock enclosure.

"'Little man, we are going to stop here for the night,' said Jupiter. 'I'm going to keep you in this cave while I go out to get us something to eat. These mountains aren't safe. I am the least dangerous beast in these woods. If you want to be helpful, you can build up a small fire for us to keep warm.'

"Unfortunately, Tock did not understand a bit of this. He just heard 'Rooooooaaaaar Yeeeee HOOOO...' as Jupiter pointed to a pile of sticks in the back of the cave. Then Jupiter left him in the rocky cavern placing a spiderweb net over the small entrance. When Tock felt he was completely alone with the giant far enough away, he tried pushing on the webbing over the doorway to get out, but he just bounced off it. Tock walked to the back of the cave, turned around, and ran full speed at the net covering the cave door. He flew through the air and stuck briefly to the webwork before being placed gently upon the floor. This was unexpected and fascinating. What a special silken mesh net. He tried his knife and found that his sharp blade did nothing to the webbing either. It did not go through it, nor did it stick to it. Instead, the strings just hugged the sharp blade like a dear friend and released the metal with a gentle shake of the hand. The unusual material was lightweight and transparent and yet strong and durable. Tock played with it for a while trying to understand its secrets, but it remained elusive, so he could only imagine it to be of some kind of magic he had not yet witnessed.

"As purple skies outside turned black, it became cooler and damper in the cave, so Tock found the small pit next to the pile of wood and built a fire. He watched the smoke follow the wall up, slide along the roof, and exit by the door like a well-guided guest. He was impressed by the simple design that made a groove into a chimney to escort the smoke out of the cavern. Time passed and a cold chill shook him from his nap of boredom, so he added more kindling and logs to the fire until it roared and warmed the rock walls all around him.

"Eventually, Jupiter returned with a bunch of tubers and moss. He wrapped the green around the gold and then buried them in the coals with a long stick. Tock knew what that meant —their meal would not be ready for hours, so they would go to sleep and wake up to a delicious breakfast. Before falling asleep again by the fire, Jupiter passed Tock a pouch filled with jing water. That was the last thing he remembered."

"Uncle Marz, that jing juice is potent stuff!" Woods interjected.

"Yes, indeed, son! That is why we only put a drop of jing juice in each of the soldiers' cups."

Auntie Farz interrupted, "This is to help them heal, as they sleep for only a short while before they make their final trek home to their families. They must be forced to rest, or they will not have the strength for their family reunions." As she spoke, she compassionately gazed upon the sleeping faces of Emerson and Neilson sleeping.

Mama Jojo nodded and began to hum a sleeping tune. "This, Thy servant, seeketh to sleep in the shelter of Thy mercy, and to repose beneath the canopy of Thy grace, imploring Thy care and Thy protection."[2]

When the song faded to the chorus of rustling leaves in the

canopy, Uncle Marz scratched his bald head, wrung his thick hands and went on with the story. "Tock and Jupiter awoke the next morning and ate a healthy breakfast of taro sweetened by moss. Then, Jupiter packed up the cave, threw the bag of jing over one shoulder, hoisted Tock onto the other shoulder, and began another day of walking.

"Two things became apparent to Tock. One, this giant was extremely talkative. And two, he seemed to be rather friendly. He did not seem like he was going to eat him anytime soon. All morning Jupiter regaled Tock with stories of the mountains, trees, and animals all around. Unfortunately, Tock was completely oblivious and just heard a giant roaring and pointing and laughing and roaring again. However, Tock tried to understand pieces of this animated monologue. He knew he was trapped in this situation, and though not resigned to acceptance, he felt his only hope was to learn how to communicate with his captor. He also knew that he couldn't have any more of that liquid in the pouch. It was more potent than any reduction he had ever drunk before. It would put him directly to sleep again, and he wanted to be able to remember the road home when he had a chance to escape.

"Tock and Jupiter moved across the land at an astounding speed. First, giant strides are at least ten times the length of an average person's stride, and Jupiter walked the pace of thunder rolling across the land. This worried Tock because in his estimation, they had traveled in two days what would take him a month on his own. Furthermore, this was unmapped territory outside the realm of the Duke's family's influence, so no search party would be willing to go after him even if they could have tracked this giant's soft tread."

"Jupiter the Giant had been walking for two days carrying Tock on one shoulder and a bag full of jing over the other. Before nightfall on the second day, their pace slowed, and they turned away from the straight north compass route, wound down and over a stream, and climbed up a small embankment. Jupiter whistled. The sound of hooves stamped the path ahead. A black horse emerged from around a corner galloping at them full speed. It skidded to a stop at Jupiter's heels, so he pet the horse like it was a favorite puppy. It was a normal sized horse that only looked small beside the giant. Jupiter tied the burden of jing onto its back like it was a beast of burden. The horse trotted ahead contentedly swishing his tail; he led them to a cliff face covered by leafy vines. Jupiter parted the curtain of vegetation and a beautifully arranged home appeared.

"Of course, everything was sized for giants. Jupiter watched Tock take in his dwelling—the fine woodworking, the delicate glassware, the colorful paintings, and the intricate fixtures. Jupiter was always happy to see others delight at how civilized a giant's abode could be. At just the right moment, Jupiter parted the silk tablecloth covering the end table to show Tock a human-sized bedroom complete with a four-poster bed, rocking chair, armoire, and standing mirror. Tock had his private tent, outfitted like a dollhouse, in the middle of the giant's living room.

"Grand Tock began living with Jupiter in the cave. This arrangement was not easy for him to stomach, as he knew that despite the allure of silk, art, and food, he was a prisoner. Yet, Tock was pragmatic. He needed to learn enough about where he was to sort out how to get home, and he needed to maintain his strength and gather resources to make the long journey back, so he decided to make a friendly alliance with his captor, and learn how to converse with him in the language of giants. At the very least, if he could understand the giant, his day-to-day existence would be more tolerable.

"Thus, Tock began learning Giant. It started with simple nouns; he would point at a piece of furniture, then Jupiter would roar, Tock would mimic the roar, then Jupiter would laugh uncontrollably for a minute before repeating the word.

This pattern of point and repeat gave Jupiter endless hours of amusement and Tock plenty of time to learn. Jupiter had been alone for so long that he did not mind the childish interactions. Tock pointed at the horse.

"'Heima!' Jupiter exclaimed while the horse whinnied and pranced happily nearby.

"'Hey-ma,' Tock repeated as he pointed to the horse as dark as coal.

"'Hei—ma,' Jupiter enunciated slapping Tock on the back for his good try.

"Tock was a quick study. Sometimes Jupiter would also want to learn to pronounce a word or two from Tock, but the giant was impatient and had terrible enunciation, so he gave up quickly. Tock, however, was determined. He moved from learning simple nouns to simple sentences like 'I'm hungry' and 'the apple is on the table.' These phrases greatly improved daily communication and thus relations, but they were no use when Jupiter went off and told a story of something or other.

"Time in the cave had a quick, quick, slow pace—some days sped by with a week of work suddenly over, while other days dragged on hour by hour and minute by minute. They would get up in the morning, eat a cold morsel from last night's dinner, and then they would go out to the jing patches. Yes, this giant had come to steal Tock's family jing for a reason. His jing patch was in total disarray. It had been eaten through by a terrible infestation, so most of the jing lay withered and dried at the roots. Jupiter had wandered far and wide to find a new strain of jing that was hardy enough to regenerate his crop and improve his yield. Thus, with great sympathy, Tock worked side by side with Jupiter to replant and replenish his gardens.

"They weeded out the bad crops and burned them; they planted the new jing; they spliced different varieties of jing together to experiment with new strains; but most importantly, Tock introduced Jupiter to the methods of pest suppression used by his ancestors and taught to him by his mother and grandfather—planting garlic, rosemary, basil, mint, and marigolds—as these were excellent deterrents for many bugs and animals. The fragrant nature of these plants repulsed many pests, so they arranged them in rings around each jing patch and gently laced some repelling plants within the patch as well. An added benefit, these herbs could be used in many medicinal concoctions or to flavor a stew."

"Tock had been living in the giant's cave for many weeks and had gotten into the rhythm: waking, working, eating, sleeping, waking, working, eating, sleeping. But this day, when he awoke, things were different.

"Jupiter was not in the cave, as usual, preparing their rice porridge gruel. Instead, the normal clanging of pots and spoons was replaced by the thud, thud, thud of a hoe breaking ground in the garden. Tock scrambled out of bed and scurried out of the cave to find Jupiter uprooting the jing patch and packing the medicinal clumps into burlap sacks for travel. Though the high mountain valley had perfect growing conditions, the two-month old crop was a bit small to harvest.

"'What's happening?' asked Tock in his simple language.

"'We're going for a walk today,' proclaimed Jupiter.

"'Where?'

"'Over the peaks, a few strides away, there are Rrrraor.'

"'What are Rrrraor?'

"'Hahahahahaha…I haven't taught you that word yet.'

"'What will we do with it when we find it?'

"'No more questions little one. We must prepare to go.'

"Jupiter packed supplies for a week-long journey in his back-pack. He prepared a longbow and arrows—sharpening the arrowheads and straightening the feathers. Tock got out his own backpack, a pair of pants, and a jacket—all new. Jupiter had taken some bits from his old garments and stitched them together into warmer clothes for his guest. Tock had been woefully unprepared for the weather in the northern highlands, which were a season cooler than the lowland climes. The two packed extra clothes, a blanket for sleeping, nourishment for the road, and whatnot. Then, when they were both ready, they set off. Jupiter put Heima in her pen, pet the horse one last time and signaled for her to stay. Then, he put on his backpack. Over one shoulder he slung his bow and quills while on the other he let Tock perch. Off they went.

"From the first step, Jupiter climbed snaking paths that wound up the steep sides of the valley toward the high mountain pass. He walked along cliff faces with one hand on the mountain wall while his outside foot moved precariously close to the edge of the ledge. He stopped at springs to refill their waterskins and rock outcroppings to rest and take in the views. Surprisingly, Jupiter was quiet as they went; he mumbled under his breath, or he hummed a low tune, but he concentrated on his plans too much to chat idly. Instead, he seemed to prepare every step for what lay ahead. Jupiter stopped abruptly. He quietly swung Tock and his quills to the ground. He crouched low, putting his hand above his eyes to block the sunlight and improve his vision. Then, Jupiter pointed at a smudge in the sunlight.

"'Rrrraor!' Jupiter whispered under his breath.

"'Rrrraor?' Tock repeated as he looked far across to a point on the next mountain.

"There, on the far slope, stood a wild cat, a mountain lion, no, a tiger. The majestic animal prowled back and forth, pacing as if daring the world to see his elegance. Then, he stretched his paws up onto the rock face and scratched the mountain to make his mark before disappearing like a ghost.

"'Tiger!' said Tock.

"'Rrrraor.' said Jupiter as they continued on their way.

"Late in the afternoon, they rounded a rocky outcropping on the far side of the canyon. This was the place where the tiger had been only a few hours before. A musky stench scented the air and brought tingles to Tock's toes. They paused and examined the rock face, looking for markings. There, at Jupiter's eye level, were hundreds of scratches made over many years, like a tally of time. The grandeur of a wild animal claiming its territory and staking its worldly property caught Tock by surprise. But there was no time for staying to contemplate the meaning of tiger customs. Daylight was as precious as the sun's arc was long. The golden orb hung one fist above the western horizon—so in the next hour or so, they would need to make camp.

"Their path led to a high plateau that seemed to stretch on for miles. They walked across the moss and rocks until they found a grassy spot that had a clear spring which flowed to a cool pond. This is where Jupiter decided to make camp. Tock did not like this exposed high plane, as it felt like he was in open view of many tigers. He would have preferred a safe cave to hide inside. He liked the place even less when he went to the water's edge to refill their waterskins. There were footprints of a cat.

"Tock stretched out his fingers as wide as he could and placed his hand next to the paw print to measure the size. His hand seemed tiny in comparison. The tiger's toes and claws stretched beyond his fingertips. Tock returned to camp and told Jupiter of his discovery, but the giant only smiled and nodded. That night, the two of them made a small fire, reheated some potatoes, and looked at the stars—their closest companions. When Tock got sleepy, he took out his blanket and curled up next to Jupiter. At least, this giant was safer than a tiger.

"On that morning, so many mornings ago…Grand Tock and Jupiter awoke on the mountain plateau with a light headache from the altitude squeezing the air out of their lungs and the cold biting the hair on their heads. It made them grumpy as they went about the tasks necessary for the day. Tock filled their waterskins at the pond encircled by tiger prints as Jupiter paced with impatience. He wanted to get on with things before the sun really cast enough light to see the trail. Jupiter destroyed camp and threw a scrap of bread to Tock before barreling off toward the next valley on the far side of the flat expanse. Tock held the bread in one fist and ran after Jupiter to not be left behind. After a hundred paces, or a mile, at the cliff's edge, Jupiter stopped and waited for Tock to catch up. He lifted him to his shoulder to ride for a while.

"They descended switchbacks that only goats could see. They picked their way among boulders and shrubs until the landscape's rocky edges were veiled with grasses and herbs. Gradually, as they ventured down the hillside, the scrubby bushes became taller. Near the top, the greenery was waist-high on Jupiter, while at the bottom of the cliff face, the vegetation grew shoulder-height. There, in the middle of the valley pass, was a tall tree whose wide branches twisted toward the mountaintops as its broad leaves seemed to slap the air with disagreement. This gnarled, ancient maple was their destination."

"As Tock and Jupiter descended, their alertness heightened. The signs of life, the feeling of being watched, was omnipresent. Tock from his perch on Jupiter's shoulder keenly scanned the surrounding mountainsides for patterns of movement, but all was still except the breeze rustling the leaves and the beating of their hearts in their chests.

"When they reached the old maple at the center of it all, Jupiter swiped Tock from his shoulder and tied him to the base of the tree. The action was so gentle and knowing that Tock sat in shock—bound, unable to move. The spiderwebbing was soft while the bark was stiff. He set about to protest, but before a holler left Tock's lips, he saw a fierce grimace cross Jupiter's face. The giant had intentionally cut his finger and was squeezing droplets of blood in an arc encircling the base of the gnarled tree where Tock was tied. Without so much as a look in the direction of the tree, Jupiter took a long swig of jing juice and retraced his steps up the rocky escarpment they had just descended together.

"Tock was frozen with fear and befuddled with binding. After all of this time with Jupiter, Tock had began to hold some trust for him despite knowing he was a kidnapped hostage. The giant had fed him, clothed him, taught him, and even entertained him. It had not escaped Tock that he was a prisoner, but he had been treated as an honored guest at the home of a lonely recluse. Except for snatching him unwillingly from his home—which was a horrible injustice—Jupiter had never been violent or aggressive. And yet, there sat Tock—tied to a tree in the wilderness beyond any point of return. His only companion for the last few moons had secured him to a tree with an unbreakable thread and left him stranded without a word while tigers were on the prowl.

"*Save your strength,* thought Tock. *Assess your situation and be present in the moment.*

"He dug into himself and all his mindfulness training to find the tools that would best help him survive. Truthfully, in a moment of danger it was never pertinent to chew on how and why things turned out as they had. There would, hopefully, be many warm nights by the fireside to untangle that mess of could ofs, should ofs, and would ofs. But first, he must survive.

"*What do I know?*

"He was likely a thousand miles from home, with the nearest safe destination being Jupiter's cave. He had no food or supplies, as everything useful was in Jupiter's bag. However, he held two things on him of value—a waterskin and a knife. Tock wriggled about to free his hands. It took some time and patience, but with effort, he touched both items to confirm that they were still on his person. Feeling them and using them were two different matters. He slowly slithered against the spiderwebbing to gain some mobility. But, it would take awhile before he could grab, flex, stretch, or swing.

"The wind shifted, and a musty stench filled the air. Tock's attention darted from ledge to shrubs to grass to ledge again. He saw gold and black. Something was stalking the perimeter of the valley. A wild predator had sniffed Jupiter's blood and was on the prowl to investigate. Tock sat helplessly exposed in the middle of nowhere, tied to a wretched tree like a sacrificial offering to the gods of old.

"Far off on the outer rim of the mountain pass was movement, but before Tock could focus on the shape, it was gone again. Then his right eye caught yellow, and awhile later, his left eye glimpsed death. A tiger was circling in very wide arcs around the valley surveying the scene, as if trying to sniff out the trap. Slowly the tiger's tracks spiraled down the slopes and around the valley floor. Each loop seemed to take eons, which left too much time to ponder his demise.

"Tock did not want to die in fear. He did not want his last breath to be a primordial scream. This was not what he had imagined as a young man—no, he had dreamed of growing old or at least dying in battle as a warrior; never had he thought he would be dinner for a wild beast. This fate was not his destiny. He beseeched God for assistance.

"'O Thou the Merciful One! O my Lord! Make Thy protection my armor, Thy preservation my shield...'[3] Tock prayed with all his heart.

"He summoned his heart to calm and his mind to open to the possibilities all around him. He sniffed the air and tasted the copper tinge of hardy grass that had not felt rain for many days. He heard the air serenade the landscape with an unwelcome cackle. He felt the gruffness of the ancient tree bark on his back and under his legs, as the trunk and roots unwillingly held him in place. He saw the shadow of a tiger on the far ledge.

"Amber streaked past Tock. Thud! A mighty beast lay limp at his feet. On the ground in front of him, a beautiful being lay with an arrow piercing her breast. The tiger was dead with such a perfect shot that little blood oozed from the wound. Jupiter raised his head from his hunter's hide where he had been waiting for the tiger to take the bait.

"'What?!' muttered Tock. This realization of the gruesome plan was quickly followed by another concern. How had the tiger he had been diligently tracking descended into the valley so quickly? Such a feat would be nearly impossible to accomplish unnoticed. This female tiger must be the mate. So, where was the male tiger now that this one lay in a lifeless heap?

"A rustling of leaves was followed by the musty stench of wilderness. He knew before he moved his eyes upward that another tiger was very much alive above his head in the branches. Death quaked his soul. Sorrow rolled out of his pours. He looked into the brown eyes of the captivating creature perched among the foliage.

"'Go!' Tock whispered.

"The tiger looked at the ball of fur fallen upon the ground willing it to move. A tiger's tear dropped upon Tock's forehead. The water seared him with pain.

"'Go!' Tock screamed as Jupiter's arrow whistled through the leaves and pierced the bark of the millennium branch. When Tock looked again, the elusive tiger was gone, and only the acrid iron smell of blood from a fresh kill filled the air.

"Shock caused Tock to forget the unimportant details, so he never told the rest of the story in quite the same way.

"Jupiter strung up, gutted, and skinned the tiger, taking special care with the valuable hide. The muscle was protected as much as possible, but it was clearly a secondary concern. The pelt was treated with jing juice to preserve the fur and make it last for generations to come. Then, the meat was smoked over a small fire so it could be eaten through the next leg of the journey. The edible innards were placed in a stew to sustain Jupiter and Tock while they camped on the valley floor.

"It was not a safe place out in the open of the mountain pass.

The second tiger was never far away, but always out of sight, and beyond the range of bow and arrow. The fresh carcass attracted scavenger birds and animals of prey, which were happy to feast on another's demise. To protect them, Jupiter stretched the webbing into a huge tent over the skinning and smoking operation. The lattice of delicate strings kept the scavengers out but also allowed the wind to blow through and take away the stench of fur, flesh, and fire.

"For many days they stayed in that treacherous mountain pass, and for many days Tock and Jupiter did not speak. Tock had been immediately untied from the tree and free to roam around the valley, but with a vengeful tiger prowling nearby, it was hard to plan an escape. Yet, Tock still made preparations. He ate his fill at meals and squirreled away food for traveling, taking extra portions of dried meats or crackers whenever Jupiter was otherwise engaged. He practiced knife throwing to increase his chances of survival. But most of the time, he planned his escape—retracing his steps up the cliff, across the plateau, and through the mountain passes back to Jupiter's cave. There, he could restock supplies and ride the black horse Heima home to his family's cottage in Copperton.

"One morning, it snowed. The white flakes floated gently down, melting when they hit the ground. By afternoon, Jupiter was silently taking down camp, packing his backpack, and making ready to leave. The end of their time in the valley was near.

"'Lil' man, this is where our paths part,' Jupiter said sullenly. "You can go home to your people, and I must return to mine."

"Tock's heart raced with joy, fear, and anticipation. He was a free man now, but he must traverse a vast wilderness alone to return home.

"'I will give you some things to pay you for your services. You rescued my jing fields and helped me slay a tiger. This is no small feat for a little man," Jupiter continued.

"Tock was speechless as the giant pulled out a petite leather satchel from his large canvas backpack.

"'First, I will give you this pouch which will always carry everything you need and never weigh more than you can handle. Next, I will give you a map of this land between Copperton and the Ocean of Wisdom. This shall help you get home and return again if that is your choice. Third, I will give you the Stymphlaian bird feathers which are the most deadly throwing darts in the natural world. Fourth, I will give you a spot of webbing to protect you in the wilderness. Finally, when you get to my cave, you may take Heima, my horse, and all other little people possessions which you can carry off over the mountains.'

"This was a lot of information for Tock to take in, so he looked up at Jupiter and began to cry. These were not tears of gratitude or fear, of which he felt both, but these were the tears of a great release—days of sorrow over the majestic dead tiger, days of exhausting exertion on this recent excursion, months of anger about being held captive against his will. All of Tock's emotions poured out of him into a puddle on the ground. Jupiter sat quietly as Tock rocked back and forth howling. The giant was not indifferent, just restrained about comforting a little creature he could crush with one hand.

"When Tock's tears slowed and he was able to blow his nose and wipe his face dry, Jupiter said, 'If you are willing, I will take you, as my friend, to the Ocean of Knowledge and Understanding. It is just on the other side of that ridge. There you may submerge yourself in the salty waves and wash away your cares. You may walk upon the sandy beaches and collect all the coral and pearls you can carry. From here, for me, it is less than an hour walk downhill, but it will take you an extra day when you climb back up the mountain to return home alone.'

"Tock looked at the bag of holding and all his new supplies.

He looked at his feet and his giant companion. Then, he surprised himself and said, 'Let's go swim in the ocean.'

"Jupiter the Giant lifted Grand Tock on his shoulder for one last trip. They climbed over the next rise of hills and took in the view of the ocean laid out below them. With care, Jupiter meandered his way down the steep track that led to the sea. He slowly descended into the sweet, salty air that arose in a mist to meet them."

"The end!" Mama Jojo announced. "That story always makes me cry."

Everyone else around the fire was silent, still absorbed in the tale.

"It's bittersweet," Auntie Farz finally mustered.

"Yes, his story is the history of our family's change of fate," Dr. Rahd stated resolutely as the great professor he was.

The visitors were softly snoring on the marine blue rug. The evening's peace descended all around as the fire glow illuminated rosy cheeks.

"Well, folks! Is it past our bedtime? Should I pause the storytelling for this evening?" asked Uncle Marz. "We can tell other stories tomorrow night."

A round of heads bobbed and a few people rubbed their eyes. Pyrrha got up from her seat on the hard log and stretched out the kinks in her back.

"Good night!" she said to her parents.

"Happy Birthday," Mama Jojo and Dr. Rahd said in unison.

"Dream of tigers!" she whispered to Woods as she slapped him on the back.

"See you in the morning!" she said to Uncle Marz and Auntie Farz.

After everyone mumbled good-night replies, she made her way back toward home just down the path from the circle of friends. Woods followed after, shuffling to the matching cottage. The older folks and the visitors stayed around the fire, resting in a friendly embrace of its glow.

When Pyrrha got inside she prepared a pot of sleeping tea for her parents. Then, she washed her face, combed her hair, put on pajamas, and plopped into bed. She slipped under a summer quilt for comfort as the evening had cooled. She admired her grandfather's antique furniture, gifted to him by Jupiter the Giant—the canopy bed stood strong, the armoire glowed in the lamp light, the mirror reflected shadows of colors, while the desk and chair rested assured in their elegance. She looked up at the ceiling and waited for sleep to descend.

It had been a grand evening with so many unknown friends visiting their bonfire to share a morsel of food and sip jing juice. Uncle Marz's version of Grand Tock's adventures were always disconcerting, because she knew so much more about the events than what he could summarize. Her grandfather had told her these tales himself, playing out each character with actions and accents. More importantly, he had taken her on horseback rides and hikes to camp in the places described in the tales. A shiver shook her as she touched the scar from the gnarled maple tree in Tiger Valley. Haunted by her own memories of another time in that mountain landscape, she closed her eyes and let the stories play out in her dreams.

THE DREAM

THE GREAT SEER, GREAT-GRANDMOTHER ETHEL SAT ROBED IN purple and infused with frankincense. She was her young, vibrant self with her red curls framing her face and flowing down her back. She hunched over the glowing orb, which changed colors as firelight flickering red, blue, and gold. Pyrrha sat out of body, hushed by curiosity and concern at what the crystal ball might reveal. It was as quiet as cotton balls, cool as winter's breath, and smoky as dusty candles. With practiced magic, Great-Grandmother Ethel turned from the light of the globe and reached under the table to pull out a small filing box filled with a long deck of cards stretching into history. With reverence, she began to turn over each card from the stack and read the cards aloud one at a time. This was no ordinary Tarot deck; it was an index of Pyrrha's life—each important event was written clearly, carefully on a plain, white three-by-five card and placed in a filing box.

Great-Grandmother Ethel read aloud each moment in Pyrrha's life. "The birth of a princess…Speaking the first word —'Tock'…Learning to walk along the well-worn path… An accidental poisoning from unattended bottles of jing juice…"

As she read, the room began to fill with other souls. Great aunts and uncles, lost cousins and friends from the world beyond the veil all crowded into the mystical tent.

Great-Grandmother Ethel continued to read, "Traveling with Grand Tock through the mountains to the sea…The year of silence, speaking without words… Singing the bird calls… Starting at Copperton Training Academy…"

More people arrived. Great-Grandmother Ethel's lilting voice, which called out the memories on the cards, began to deepen into a husky baritone shrouded in mystery. The robed being at the table behind the crystal ball was no longer familiar.

Death stood cloaked in a gown of midnight blue, surrounded in an aura of finality. The dark voice read Pyrrha's past. With each card, he took a little more life from the maiden.

"Finding the first spy trespassing on Tock's Land…War with Ironweald…"

This was how it was going to be—Pyrrha's loved ones from the afterworld would all come to comfort her as her life flashed before her eyes in the final hour of her earthly existence. Death unheralded had come to her in a dream from which she would not awaken.

Yet, destiny can change in an instant, or maybe fate caught up to the moment. Darkness cloaked opaque stopped reading from the deck. Death fixed Pyrrha in a meaningful glance and with words that pierced into her heart in an explosion of light said, "This one is out of order."

With that, he abandoned the cards of Pyrrha's life experiences and placed the last one on the table. He vanished from the room without another word.

Slowly, as they had come, the spirits of relatives past and friends gone before left one by one. Finally, only Great-Grandmother Ethel remained. She looked into the crystal ball to see the future, but the firelight had turned to smoke and the way forward was obscured. Then, Great-Grandmother Ethel touched her heart and bowed her head to say goodbye and excuse herself. She returned into the world beyond, where the living could not go.

Pyrrha—in the dream—reached out; she picked up the fateful card on the table that had prevented her death and extended her life.

It read, "Meeting Yuht."

Pyrrha awoke disoriented in her bedroom. The vision of Great-Grandmother Ethel, Death, and the deck of cards was seared in her mind. Her heart raced. Her life had flashed before her eyes, yet somehow her death had been forestalled by meeting Yuht. Who was the man Yuht to have such power? His strong shoulders and energetic eyes made her cheeks flush, her lips smile, and her heart skip.

Everything she knew about dreams overflowed her mind—sometimes they are visions of reality stripped of time and place; sometimes they are symbolic re-imaginations of things hidden in the heart; yet, sometimes they are a gibberish of fears, wants, people, and things that occupied the recent days. Knowing what kind of dream she had had would help her know what to do. But, like the crystal ball, her mind was muddled.

Pyrrha pulled out her book of prayers. She had painstakingly copied her favorites in a thin volume to carry with her wherever she would go. She opened to a prayer revealed for dreams. It was to be said after awakening from a nightmare. So, she began to chant:

"O Thou by Whose name the sea of joy moveth and the fragrance of happiness is wafted!

"I ask Thee to show me from the wonders of Thy favour that which shall brighten mine eyes and gladden my heart. Thou, verily, art the All-Bounteous, the Most Generous."[1]

She repeated the precious prayer more than a dozen times until her heart calmed, her eyelids drooped, and sleep came to comfort her. She repeated it until she could no longer move her lips. Meaning and purpose would come in time. Eventually, she would understand—who was Yuht and how was he a catalyst pushing her destiny into the world faster than anticipated.

WOODS WHISPERS

Each day was filled with news and activity. Just a day earlier, late in the afternoon before sunset, the castle bugles had trumpeted out a great welcome, and Royal Mountain had raised a flurry of flags for the Marquess's return home from the war. The son of the Duke had been gone these last five years supervising the frontlines. In celebration of his safe homecoming, it was announced that a fair would be held before the Feast Day. Everyone would come from far and wide to trade their goods.

Woods sat at the kitchen table eating breakfast. Auntie Farz always made simple things elegant—the yogurt was sprinkled with thimbleberries; the pancakes were dressed in a juneberry syrup; the tea was presented with warm foamed milk. A sprinkle of care made each meal deliciously colorful.

"Son, why the long face?" Uncle Marz asked Woods across the table.

Woods looked at his father—well the only father figure he had ever known, the only father he could remember. They were a family that had found each other, one generation after another. Grand Tock had found Uncle Marz and adopted him as a son, Uncle Marz had found Auntie Farz and married her, and together they had found Woods, who they brought up as their own child. The love they shared was strong because it was a choice—given freely and returned honestly. They were a found family; no one looked like the other, but under their skin they were compatible —complimenting and encouraging each other through life.

"It's Pyrrha, isn't it?" Uncle Marz asked between bites of pancakes.

"She has been so…insufferable since…"

"She found the soldier sleeping in the leaves?" Auntie Farz inquired.

"Uggghhh…All she talks about is Yuht, Yuht, Yuht."

"Ah!" Uncle Marz nodded.

"She hates boys," Woods exhaled. "She has only ever considered them cockroaches in the kitchen."

Auntie Farz raised her eyebrows and scratched her wrist. "Let's not talk of insects in the house." She shook her head, "Just the thought makes me itchy."

"Well, Woods! It's not like you to be easily annoyed," Uncle Marz remarked.

"He is a stranger. Something about him makes me uncomfortable," Woods exhaled.

"From what you said, Yuht is no boy," Uncle Marz observed. "He is most definitely a man returning home from the long war."

"Uh, Uncle! But, who is he?" Woods poked with his knife at the last few bites on his plate.

"That's a good question," Uncle Marz replied. "I've some ideas, but we won't know anything for sure until the fair."

"Ugh…He'll be there?"

"Well, if he isn't a spy that slithered away south, then, yes," Uncle Marz paused for emphasis. "Anyone who is anyone will be there. We all want to celebrate."

"And see old friends…" mused Auntie Farz. "And restock the

pantry...and buy something nice." She was looking forward to the festivities of traders coming from far and wide.

"What should I do?" Woods asked.

"Nothing!" Uncle Marz answered honestly. "Nothing, except help me get ready for the fair. There are so many things to prepare."

"And be patient with Pyrrha," Auntie Farz added. "She relies on us...and especially you...Often, you are the only one she talks to."

"But she isn't acting normal," Woods sighed. "I catch her staring into space like a star gazer."

"Well," Auntie Farz smiled at Uncle Marz.

Uncle Marz returned the happy gaze.

"What!" Woods looked at his parents. "Are you making fun of me?"

"Ahem!" Uncle Marz coughed. "Sorry, son, it's just—"

"It's just," Auntie Farz interrupted. "Pyrrha is distracted."

"Yup, tell me about it," Woods agreed.

"Besides this," Auntie Farz continued. "Pyrrha is anxious for Grand Tock to return from his latest expedition."

"Aren't we all!" Woods exhaled.

"Yes, but..." Uncle Marz broke in. "Pyrrha and her grandfather have a different bond."

"Blood, you mean," Woods sighed.

"No," Uncle Marz countered. "Pyrrha and Grand Tock have always been linked by the tiger...That expedition changed them both...and not necessarily for the better."

"Well now," Auntie Farz cut in. "We all have our pasts."

"Yes we do," Uncle Marz agreed and took the hint to end this conversation. "It's hard to understand how fallen leaves of years gone by feed our future lives."

With that, Auntie Farz and Uncle Marz closed the topic of discussion. Yet, the three of them still sat around the table, nibbling on the berries and yogurt that were still unfinished. Woods looked all tossed up like hay after a storm.

"There is something else, isn't there, Woods?" Auntie Farz inquired with a gentle nudge.

Woods glanced between Auntie and Uncle; there was so little that he could keep from them. He could never quite smooth his brow flat enough to hide his emotions.

"Do you think the war is really over?" Woods asked. "Do you think the cease fire will keep?"

"It's hard to say—" Uncle Marz started.

"I hope so!" Auntie Farz exclaimed.

"What is it?" Uncle Marz asked.

"Will I have to enlist in the militia?" Woods faltered.

"We don't know," Uncle Marz answered honestly. "You know it has always been our rule to be completely honest with you."

"And neither of us like war one bit…" Auntie Farz added. "It disrupted both our childhoods and now yours too."

"But if I'm not a soldier," Woods mustered. "How will I prove I'm not a Weald. How will I show my Copper?"

"You do not have to prove that you are a citizen of Copperton—because it is a fact," Uncle Marz countered. "You are Copper through and through."

"But…I don't look like I belong! I have Ironweald skin, hair, and eyes." Woods shook his golden hair that was three shades lighter than anyone around. He beseeched his parents with his grey-blue eyes that looked like the sky before a summer rain.

"Love," Auntie Farz chimed in. "Copperton is much more diverse than—"

"Look at me! I don't even look like you, my parents." He stretched his gangly limbs that were longer and leaner than anyone he knew.

"Something else is bothering you here," Uncle Marz astutely observed. "Do you think you will win glory if you go off to fight in a war?"

An awkward silence permeated the room. Even the fire seemed to stop crackling.

"Well..." Woods coughed. He had no real reply. He knew that his parents were right that war was something to be avoided, yet after five years of imagining his future as a soldier, he was unable to envision a peaceful life afterward. He had not thought about how he would live once the war ended. He had not imagined another profession. More importantly, how would he become distinguished like Uncle Marz or Grand Tock without an adventurous expedition?

"Woods, there is more to be discussed here, but..." Uncle Marz switched topics. "There's a list of chores to be done that isn't getting any shorter despite the hours of sunlight passing by."

"Alright..." Woods sighed knowing the busy fussing would be a good distraction.

"But first, the dishes," Auntie Farz smiled encouragingly at the men at the table.

Uncle Marz and Woods picked up the breakfast plates and cleared the table. Woods washed the pottery while Uncle Marz put away the leftover food. The family was egalitarian—everyone did their part and each did a little more to make things run smoothly with an extra dash of love.

When the morning meal was cleaned up, Woods went outside to start on Uncle Marz's endless to-do items. They had been making wooden sculptures, toys, and housewares for the last several years. Whenever they found newly fallen trees in the forest behind the house or neighbors asked for help chopping down broken branches, they stockpiled the raw materials. The plethora of supply gave Woods and Uncle Marz plenty to whittle, carve, file, and sand into wares to be traded in town.

Uncle Marz had taught Woods everything he knew about being a craftsman and artisan. It was never a lesson with textbooks and lectures; it was an apprenticeship in life skills. They would work side by side; Uncle Marz would praise that which was praiseworthy and ignore that which was not; he would only scold Woods when he was in danger of getting seriously hurt. Gradually, Woods grew adept at mimicking techniques while adding his own decorative flair. He was growing into a young man that Uncle Marz was proud to call his son.

Woods went to the back storage shed and found a ladder to climb up into the rafters where he uncovered boxes of finished woodwork that had been stored away for just such an occasion as the fair. With care, he brought down each box and carried them to the front garden. There, Uncle Marz sorted through the pieces and chose only the best ones to bring to town. Carefully, he arranged two piles—one for merchandise and another to be saved for another day when a final alteration or embellishment would make it ready to be sent out into the world.

Then, Woods helped Pyrrha with her jing juice cart. First, they wrestled the dilapidated bicycle wagon out from the shed and cleaned it. Recently, it had been used for hauling wood and storing gardening supplies, so it needed to be mended and painted before all else. Woods managed to repair the wobbly wheel in under an hour while Pyrrha brushed the cart with a few coats of purple stain to brighten up the naturally elegant frame. As they worked, they chatted.

"Did you sleep well last night?" Woods asked.

Pyrrha looked up from their work with tired eyes. "No!" she said. "No! I don't mean to be rude, but I'm tired."

"You look like you were haunted by a ghost."

"Eh? You aren't far off," Pyrrha replied. "I dreamed…no nightmared…that's not a word…anyway…of Great-Grand-mother Ethel. She came to visit me with Old-Man Death."

"Death?" Woods questioned. "Was he hooded in black and all that?"

"Yes, that Death," Pyrrha sighed. "But he wore midnight blue!"

"That's still terrible."

"He gave me quite the fright," she coughed. "At least Great-Grandmother Ethel was a comforting sight."

"She has been gone a few years now," Woods remembered. "Has it been ten?"

Pyrrha paused and counted her fingers. "Yeah, since the fall after the tiger."

"You mean the autumn—"

"Well, the tiger fell…and I fell too."

"You always had a dark sense of humor."

Pyrrha grimaced. "What am I supposed to say?"

"I don't know!" Woods countered. "Sometimes you are proud you killed the second tiger, but other times you seem sad or angry."

"Well, its all mixed up."

Woods looked up from fixing the cart wheel to see if he could read Pyrrha's expression. He did not want to stop her flow if she wanted to speak about the past—especially with Auntie Farz's encouragement to listen still ringing in his ears.

"Sometimes, I blame myself for taking the life of that majestic creature—even if it was in self-defense."

"Hmmmhm," Woods nodded to keep her speaking.

"Sometimes, I am angry that Grand Tock so foolishly let me follow him on his expedition."

"Yup," Woods agreed.

"Sometimes, I think it's just the Will of God, my destiny…for bad things to happen to me, around me, in my life, all the time—"

"Heh!" Woods interrupted. "Let's not make the tiger thing about everything!"

"Sorry," Pyrrha moaned. "I got grey; I had a bad dream last night, and I don't know what it means."

"Do you want to tell me about it?"

"Ah, nooo…I mean yes…I mean…Yuht's in it, so it would annoy you."

Woods tensed. All the muscles in his body just clenched at the sound of the stranger's name. Yet, Auntie Farz's words extolling compassion propelled him to be patient. "If you want to talk about it…"

Pyrrha glanced up from the work. "It's alright! I mean the dream just made me think about fate, destiny, and my future."

"Do you believe in fate?"

"Yeah, like, I don't know," Pyrrha fumbled for words. "What about you?"

"It has been a good thing for me…I don't know what would have happened if fate hadn't united Grand Tock and Uncle and Auntie and I."

"Well, yeah that is a good fate…" Pyrrha smiled.

"My life started off on the wrong foot," Woods continued. "But, it has been getting better ever since I joined the Tock clan."

"Hahaha!" Pyrrha laughed. "I don't remember a time that you weren't a Tock."

"Well, mostly I don't either," Woods smiled. "When the flash-backs come, I remind myself that it was long ago and far away."

"I forget that you came from Ironweald."

"Mostly I do too…except when strangers suspiciously look me up and down."

"Yeah, your hair is a bit…colorless for these parts."

"Like un-toasted bread, like milk without coffee, like bland oat porridge—"

"Hey, you said it not me!"

"Not all of us can have fire-tiger blood like you!"

"Hey! Be nice."

"Sorry!"

Pyrrha grinned. "So what else does Uncle Marz have for us to do today?"

"You really want to help me with his never-ending lists of chores?"

"Since you fixed this cart, I'm mostly done with my stuff," Pyrrha sighed. "That is until Mama Jojo and Dr. Rahd return from their...wherever they are!"

"Where are they?"

"Hm..." Pyrrha shrugged. "I guess Dr. Rahd is at the library, but Mama Jojo...who knows."

"Ha! Hem!" Woods coughed. He did not want to say anything disparaging of his adopted family. "So, we have some oiling to do. All those pieces that I pulled out of the shed need to be glossed and shined for market."

"I'll grab some rags and get a stool as this job might take awhile."

"Good idea! Meet you back here in a few minutes."

For the next two hours, Woods and Pyrrha sat side by side on stools in the front garden, cleaning up the wares to be sold on market day. They played word games and made up riddles as they worked on oiling the sculptures, toys, and housewares.

Woods enjoyed these moments with his cousin when they were talking. He liked being the older cousin who was strong and confident, yet caring and wise. With Pyrrha by his side, he knew where he belonged—in the Tock clan, a warrior in a family of warriors.

MARKET DAY

THE DAYS OF PEACE HAD A QUICK, QUICK, SLOW PACE TO THEM. IT had only been two nights since the bonfire, but the time had gone by in a flash. Pyrrha had dreamed of far-off lands enveloped in fog where tigers and dragons and lakes and gardens came in and out of view. She had also dreamed of Yuht's dark eyes smiling at her and telling her secrets without words as they sat together in the pavilion next to the lake on Mount Omega. When she awoke, all of the visions vanished and she was left with the dry taste of morning breath in her mouth. She opened her eyes with a hope that the new day would bring Grand Tock down the lane home, but still he had not yet come.

Pyrrha prepared for the fair. Everyone would come from far and wide to trade their goods. It would be a chance to sell the family's jing juice and buy many delicacies in short supply during the war—honey, oil, flour, and salt. Simple things that gave flavor to life. Of course, Pyrrha was anticipating buying finer things too like chocolate, cloth, and a colorful vase to match the wildflowers in the yard.

As it had been a few years since the last great gathering of merchants, most of Pyrrha's time was spent preparing the jing cart for the fair. She dug into the store of jing juice and dusted off the best bottles from three years known for their special characteristics—the year of the flood where the jing was especially watery and made a very light juice good for sweet drops in a baby's bottle, the year of the drought where the jing was small and coarse which made a spectacularly rich syrup that soothed late-winter coughs, and this year's early harvest which she affectionately named Peace because it brought a rejuvenating sleep upon all who sipped it.

As she worked, she thought of Yuht—like a hummingbird flitting around a bird feeder. Without warning, his dark curls would come to mind or his strong shoulders covered by that royal breastplate. Most unsettling would be his deep voice ringing in her ears.

Who are you? Why have we never met before?

Each time he came to mind, she blushed and shook off the moment, so he would temporarily fly from her mind. For each jing juice bottle, she found a perfectly painted label from among Dr. Rahd's collection of watercolor practices. Since his brain stroke a few years back, the eminent professor had become a prolific painter—occasionally his work was spectacular, but often his colorful practices of brushstroke techniques were piled on his workbench awaiting further details. Then, a touch of inspiration would turn mediocrity into artistry.

Pyrrha leafed through the pages of flowers created by a flurry of chaotic splatters while cleaning the color palette. There were plenty of summer designs to make ninety-nine similar yet unique decorative labels. When the cart's contents were finally assembled for market, she would ask for Mama Jojo's blessing. But, first she had to find her.

Mama Jojo was not amongst the other villagers gossiping and adding their own news. She was not sympathetically listening to grieving widows and mothers whose husbands and sons would not return home from war. Pyrrha finally found

Mama Jojo in the hut beside the jing field talking to a butterfly while trying out new recipes of pickled jing, which smelled terribly bitter. Only after some convincing, Mama Jojo agreed to come home and assist with the final preparations for the fair.

Every major undertaking must be blessed by the matriarch; each day needed a sacred prayer to encourage unfailing providence and to eschew unnecessary misfortunes. So, Mama Jojo chanted:

"I am but a poor creature, O my Lord; I have clung to the hem of Thy riches. I am sore sick; I have held fast the cord of Thy healing. Deliver me from the ills that have encircled me, and wash me thoroughly with the waters of Thy graciousness and mercy, and attire me with the raiment of wholesomeness, through Thy forgiveness and bounty."[1]

The last thing Pyrrha added to the cart was Grand Tock's tiger paw. This was his symbolic gift to her as a talisman of courage that represented both his first adventure with Jupiter the Giant and his second expedition with Pyrrha. The tiger paw elicited memories of two tigers killed in one place decades apart. She never thought of it as a lucky charm like a rabbit's foot. Instead, the soft fur and the sharp claws embodied her grandfather's heroic spirit; thus, it gave her comfort and confidence as a warrior in training. She placed the tiger paw inside the cart out of sight but where she could touch it when she needed to hold someone's hand. It would give her courage at the fair in the dizzying crowds of unknown friends.

On the morning of the fair, Pyrrha awoke and dressed with a giddy anticipation and gummy anxiety. She wore a simple, blue skirt and matching blouse that modestly highlighted the curves in her figure yet allowed a freedom of movement that guaranteed comfort throughout the eventful day. She tied up her long red hair with a delicate cord that disappeared into braids. She finished her hairstyle with a few flower pins. She wore a brushing of coal around her green eyes and a dab of color on her lips. Before leaving the house, she picked at a breakfast of toast and peanut butter, and she sipped at a cup of coffee with frothy milk. However, nerves kept her from finishing the meal.

Then, a clanging erupted outside the front door. Woods was waiting for her with his tricycle cart, so she packed her coffee in a thermos, put her toast in a bag, and joined him and the long procession of horses, carts, bicycles, and cars heading toward Bell Tower Square.

Despite the large crowds of people making their way to the town center, everything ran quite orderly. When they arrived at Uncle Marz's mosaic map, each merchant was assigned a specific section based on what they were selling. Pyrrha was sent to the north of the square with the others selling medicinal herbs and family remedies, while Woods was in the east with those specializing in small household items and toys. To the west was the food market, where fresh fruits and vegetables could be found, while the south was reserved for larger items like furniture and bicycles, as trucks could easily drive in and unload there.

The fair was bursting with excitement. The townsfolk and neighboring villages had all come to celebrate. Tock Family's Jing Juice and other herbal remedies were selling well. By noon, there were only a dozen bottles remaining. Pyrrha had already had a chance to take a few laps around the fair and buy a few delights, as Dr. Rahd and Mama Jojo had come in turns to watch over the cart. Pyrrha was in such high spirits that she was not even annoyed that Dr. Rahd would undersell the merchandise and Mama Jojo would give it away. They both had an uncomfortable relationship with money—hoarding and spending without much attention to the economics of running a small business and providing for a family. But, somehow, their balanced thriftiness and generosity of spirit was rewarded, as they never lacked for necessities.

Just after lunch, when the sun was high and bright, but still not too hot for a summer's day, a commotion erupted in the south of the square. A large car had driven slowly into the middle of the festivities, and quite a big deal was being made of the occupants as they emerged and moved slowly from stall to stall admiring the goods on display, while greeting and talking to everyone about.

Whispers reached Pyrrha that at the center of the storm of fascination was Marquess Yuddha, who had just returned from the war, and who would soon take the throne as the new Duke of Copperton, when his father retired to the title of Archduke. He was escorting the Marchioness Juno and their two young sons, aged four and five, on the first public outing of royals in years. The youngest boy, it was said, had stoically awaited his father's return to finally be introduced, as he had been born nine months after the Marquess had left for war. The crowd's excitement and enthrallment were contagious.

"Marchioness Juno has such a beautiful dress! Do you see how it changes from black to green as she walks in and out of the sunlight?" a young seamstress said, admiring the elegant fabric from afar.

"Oh, how the Marquess has grown up during the war. He looks more and more like his distinguished father, though his dark eyes mirror the wisdom of his mother Duchess Zaynah," the old bookbinder commented.

The cooing over the youngest royalty, Sir Ian and Sir Jacob, turned to outright laughter as the two boys ran through the fairgrounds playing pirates, clowns, dragons, and horses. The delighted onlookers would give them props for their make-believe games as they passed by each stall.

Woods appeared out of nowhere and whispered in Pyrrha's ear. "You will never guess who just showed up!"

"Who?"

When she turned to hear the reply, Woods had already

slipped back through the crowd to man his own cart a few sections away.

"Dear lady, what do you have here?" said an all-too-familiar voice.

Pyrrha turned and gazed at Yuht dressed as a celebrated prince. His face was clean shaven and radiated joyous affection. His dark emerald suit slimmed his broad shoulders and highlighted his brown eyes and dark curls. On his lapel was a glint of metal—her dart was mounted and pinned as an ornamental war medal among the other ribbons signifying honors bestowed.

"Yuht!" she exclaimed.

"Dear lady, I am Marquess Yuddha," he coughed. "It is a pleasure to meet you at the fair." He surreptitiously tapped his hand to his heart and nodded his head.

"The pleasure is all mine," Pyrrha said as she curtsied deeply.

They would pretend that this was their first introduction.

"What are you selling?"

"This is Grand Tock's Jing Juice. It can heal almost any ailment."

"Ah well, I was attacked by a highway robber on my way home from the war, and I got a little scrape on my neck that is not seeming to heal." Yuht smiled as he slowly pulled at his collar to reveal an inflamed red scab where her dart had nipped his skin.

"Oh! That doesn't look good. I know just the thing to soothe it." Pyrrha reached for a bottle of Peace, carefully opened it, and added a dried purple flower, a tiny twig, and some seeds. She closed the bottle and shook it until the color changed to match the emerald green of his jacket.

"Oooohhhh!" gasped the crowd of onlookers.

"Place one or two drops on a cloth each morning and evening and dab the wound," Pyrrha instructed as she gently handed Yuht the bottle. "This should bring you peace—for that is what it is called."

"Thank you!" Yuht said, taking the medicine. His hand chastely avoided hers as he reached for the bottle. "What do I owe you?"

"Please take it as a gift from the highwayman, as she knew not what she did."

Fortunately, no one heard this last comment as the crowds parted with much ado. There among the hustle and bustle emerged Marchioness Juno with Sir Ian and Sir Jacob in tow.

"My dearest Yuddha, I thought I lost you," Juno's sugar-sweet voice crackled. "What is this young lady here selling?"

"Medicine. Juno. Medicine." Yuht smiled while showing her the bottle of Peace with the golden label.

"My dear girl!" Juno's syrupy voice drawled. "Do you have something to keep me looking young and beautiful for the coronation ceremony?" Her voice was light, yet she evaluated Pyrrha harshly with cold eyes.

"Actually, I do have something fit for such an occasion," Pyrrha replied courteously. She reached deep into her cart and pulled out a small red vile no larger than her pinkie finger. "This orchid juice will keep your skin fresh. Just use a drop to wash your face each morning and evening. However, be careful, as more will cause some serious long-term side effects."

"Oh, I'm so honored with your gift," cooed Juno. She swiftly snatched the bottle and hid the natural potion in the folds of her dress.

Yuht looked from Pyrrha to Juno and back again before subtly touching his hand to his heart and nodding a farewell. As he strolled away, rose blooms perfumed the air. Pyrrha was left in a cloud of flower blossoms. The crowd moved on following the Marquess, Marchioness, and little Sirs as they toured the rest of the fairgrounds.

Uncle Marz stood next to Pyrrha gazing after the crowd.

"Have you heard the Marquess' story of the highwayman who gave him that nasty cut?" he inquired. "Supposedly, Marquess Yuddha was ambushed while he slept along the roadside on his way home from the last battle. The highwayman was chased off by a young lad with a bow and arrow. When the Marquess tried to thank the boy, the boy ran off into the woods too. Of course, there is a reward out for the hero and a punishment for the highwayman, if they can be found."

Pyrrha listened wide-eyed and mouth agape. No words came in response. Uncle Marz's knowing expression and devious grin was unsettling. Of course, Woods had told him the story of finding the hidden soldier sleeping on Tock's Land. But, had he noticed Grand Tock's dart displayed so prominently upon Yuht's lapel and realized the highwayman was Pyrrha and the young lad, Woods? Before she could ask her uncle, he was gone—off to stroll the fairgrounds.

After the hubbub of the royal visit died down, the shoppers began to thin, so the merchants started packing up their stalls in preparation to make their way home before sunset. Woods counted and packed his remaining bowls and toys. Pyrrha wrapped the last few bottles of jing juice in cloth and secured them in a box, so they would not break or spill on the ride home.

Old Snark found Pyrrha at her cart as she secured the last few items. This day at the fair, he had been selling cleaning supplies and bootleg moonshine in the shadows of a shed beyond the properly assigned stalls.

"It was a good day today, eh?" Old Snark enquired.

Ever polite to her elders, Pyrrha summoned a kind reply, "Yes, I'd say. I think I sold ninety bottles of jing juice and some other herbal remedies as well."

"That is a good bit of fortune," replied Old Snark. "And Marquess Yuddha was quite taken with your emerald balm. From one alchemist to another, that was a great trick of yours to add the twigs and seeds to change the color to match the royal green."

"Thanks!" Pyrrha blushed.

Old Snark was no fool with the chemistry of herbs, though he did not always use his knowledge for the most noble pursuits. He might mix up a mean batch of Joy or a dusting of Life to keep those who needed it distracted by mirages. Though, his alternative uses of knowledge were not Pyrrha's concerns.

Old Snark prattled on. "You must have had a blessing from Jojo and a wink from Grand Tock to have such a good selling day, eh?"

Pyrrha could not help but smile at the old neighbor, as he knew her family well from years of observation. She mostly thought he was harmless, but she grew weary of his chatter and wanted to shoo him away.

"Do you still have that tiger paw from Grand Tock?" asked Old Snark before she locked her cart for the day. "Can I see it?" he pried.

In her giddiness from the jubilance of the fair, she smiled at Old Snark. A small peak at her family's heirloom would get rid of her unwanted guest.

"Always!" she said. "Do you need to shake hands with Neema the Tiger to have some good fortune rub off on you?"

Old Snark sparked with delight as he cozied up to Pyrrha's cart, peeked into the open door, and slyly shook hands with the tiger paw.

"The fur is so soft and the claws are so sharp. Who would believe it?" he mumbled under his breath as he danced away. "Good day, Pyrrha! Please send my hellos to Mama Jojo and Dr. Rahd."

"May the blessings fall upon you and yours like leaves in the autumn," Pyrrha replied.

She closed the conversation as she shut the cart door and

firmly locked it. She pulled out her bicycle and hitched the cart to the frame.

Woods waited nearby. He had a silly grin on his face from socializing all day while his body twitched with the exhilaration of buying and selling so many fine things.

"Ready?" Woods asked.

"Ready!" Pyrrha confirmed.

Finally, they mounted their bicycles and pedaled together out of town. They followed the line of horses and carts making their way home for dinner.

PRIMPING FOR A PARTY

Pyrrha and Woods were in the yard weeding the garden when a bugle called them to attention. A court official atop a royal stallion stopped in the lane between the two cottages on Tock's Land. His magenta robe fluttered in the wind as he called out the invitation.

"Hear ye! Hear ye! Dear compatriots of Copperton! You are invited to the Coronation Ball to honor Marquess Yuddha's and Marchioness Juno's ascension to the throne as the newly appointed rulers of the land. Long live Duke Yuddha and Duchess Juno. Yestereve, the Royal Court accepted the retirement of Duke Zachariah and Duchess Zaynah. They will now be formally addressed as Archduke Zachariah and Archduchess Zaynah. May their elder years be graced with contentment and peace.

"At sundown, the Royal Court bestowed the responsibilities of stewardship upon the next generation—Duke Yuddha and Duchess Juno. Citizenry of Copperton, please join the royal court in honoring the great services of the Archduke Zachariah and Archduchess Zaynah, and let us celebrate the enthronement of Duke Yuddha and Duchess Juno. Tomorrow, as the sun falls into the evening sky, come to the palace for dancing and jubilation. All are welcome who celebrate Copperton!"

Then, the court official bowed down to place the royal invitation in Woods' hands. With a quick snap of the reins and a whinny from his steed, he trotted off to the next cluster of homesteads to continue the round of invitation announcements.

"We're invited to a party!?" Woods sputtered.

"Yuht is the new ruler of Copperton!" Pyrrha remarked.

"What fun!" Woods exclaimed. "So much to celebrate."

"Heh..." Pyrrha hemmed.

"Don't you want to dance?" Woods asked. "Isn't this every girl's dream to attend a ball at the Great Hall in the palace?"

"Huhhhh...if only life was some happily-ever-after fairytale." Pyrrha hit him for his sexist remark.

"But, isn't it?" Woods poked.

Pyrrha was already out of earshot stomping down the lane to the house to be alone. Before she could enter the cottage, she was greeted by Mama Jojo. The news of the Coronation Ball had awoken in her a fever of extravagance that danced across her face. She had been gone for days, but yestereve she had returned in the mood to be a helpful homebody—clearly anticipating a formal confirmation of the rumors.

"Ooooh..." Mama Jojo exclaimed intercepting Pyrrha at the front door. "We are invited to a ball. What should I wear?"

Pyrrha watched her mother push the dining room table out of the way and remove several floorboards in the kitchen corner before disappearing down a hidden stairwell into the basement.

"Pyrrha!" Mama Jojo commanded. "Come help me with these."

Pyrrha followed her mother down the stairs into the rock cellar to rediscover the treasury of long-forgotten possessions. Trunks of old things hid under layers of dust.

"What is all this stuff?" Pyrrha exclaimed. "I've never seen all these boxes down here."

"We hid them down here when the war started," Mama Jojo explained. "Some are my dowry, some are your grandparents' things, some are Rahd's books, and you know…." She held up an old, broken lamp that had faded to rust. "Some are fire hazards!"

Pyrrha took the broken light fixture out of her mother's hands. It looked familiar, like a long-lost toy. In its glory days, it had been a golden dragon dancing with a red lightbulb caught in its teeth.

"This was my nightlight!" Pyrrha remarked.

"Ahyah…put that down. I need you to carry this trunk upstairs," Mama Jojo commanded. "Maybe there's something in here for the ball."

"Really?"

"Go get a washrag from the kitchen to keep this dust in the basement where it belongs."

Pyrrha carried the dragon lamp upstairs and placed it out of sight. Then, she grabbed a dishrag, wet it under the faucet, and ran back downstairs. It took a few minutes to wipe off the years of cobwebs and powder.

"Hurry up! Bring that trunk up here," Mama Jojo called.

"Coming," Pyrrha answered.

She bent her knees and straightened her back to lift the box up the steep stairs. It was heavy for something filled with clothes, so she rested for a second on the steps to regain her balance. Once in the kitchen, Mama Jojo directed her to put the box atop old newspapers spread across the dining table. She pointed to bits of dirt only visible in the sunlight and demanded Pyrrha re-clean the chest to remove the fuzz and webbing.

"We don't want the clothes dirtied before they are even taken out of the trunks," Mama Jojo tutted as she wandered off to another room.

In time, Mama Jojo returned with some skeleton keys. The

lid creaked as she unlocked the chest and opened it wide. The box revealed a stack of carefully packed clothes, each separated from the next in its own linen garment bag. These frivolities were from a time with charming parties long before the dark days of fighting and war overshadowed Copperton.

Jojo caressed the fine fabric and pinched the seams nostalgically; they were keepsakes from her dowry. In days long past, maybe even before she had moved to Tock's Land to marry Dr. Rahd, she had been able to wear these fine gowns at celebrations and festivals. Pyrrha watched her mother carefully unpack each dress and drape it over a chair or a couch arm or furniture back until the front rooms—the kitchen, dining room, and living room—were as vibrant as a summer garden's first bloom.

"Go get the standing mirror in your room," Mama Jojo demanded. "We need to see which of these still work."

Pyrrha glided into her bedroom and pulled out Grand Tock's looking glass. Thankfully the standing mirror had wheels, as it stood nearly as tall and wide as a door and was as heavy as a mule. She rolled it down the hallway and into the living room. Mama Jojo was already out of her work clothes and trying on dresses.

"Close those curtains a bit," Mama Jojo demanded. "Marz and Farz don't need to see me in my silkies." She twirled about in a flowery spring dress. "And zip me up," she ordered.

Pyrrha moved around the room helping her mother to try on all of the dresses, pant suits, and matching shawls. She would pull a garment from its linen bag, take out any pins, unzip and unbutton it, before handing it to her mother.

Mama Jojo got in and out of dresses like she was jumping in and out of waves on the lake. She threw the unsuitable outfits into a large no-thank-you pile. The castoffs were delicious aquas and ambers, corals, and fuchsias. They were lacy and sequined, silky and elegant. Each item of apparel was more glamorous than the last, but each had a flaw that was only visible to her mother—too tight, too long, too dark, too red. Finally, Mama Jojo settled upon a midnight blue ensemble that flattered her handsome, motherly features.

"Well, what do you think?!" Mama Jojo remarked. It was more of an order than a question.

"I like it, Mom."

"Like! That is all I get. Like. This is imported silk!"

"You know what I mean. It is beautiful," Pyrrha stammered. "I'm just a bit speechless as I haven't seen this much color in years."

"Yes, long ago, before I met your father, I really was a party girl. Then, I moved here and I realized these dresses could hardly be seen outside of the palace. So, I packed them up hoping you might be worthy of wearing them one day."

"Can I," Pyrrha hesitated, "wear one of these to the Coronation Ball?"

"Well…" Mama Jojo sighed. "I want you to look just as beautiful as you can." Mama Jojo evaluated her daughter. "I want you to try and put a good foot forward representing the Tock family in front of the Duke's family and the town."

Pyrrha blushed and winced. She loved her mother, but she was never straightforward with compliments. They usually had a whipping tail that pushed Pyrrha off balance and made her question the intent.

Yet, Mama Jojo commanded the room like a fairy godmother in a folktale. She threw dresses at Pyrrha and demanded she try them on. Few satisfied her taste. Some were too big. Some were too short. Some showed too many curves while others did not accentuate enough.

"No! That color clashes with your beautiful auburn hair," Mama Jojo complained.

"Yuck!" Mama Jojo gasped. "It makes your skin look sickly like a ghost."

"Yes, that is the one," Mama Jojo cooed. "Oh! I'm going to cry!"

After what must have been an hour of fussing, Mama Jojo was finally satisfied. Pyrrha looked in the mirror. The dress gently hugged her curves yet beautifully flowed when she twirled. The color shone copper in the light and glowed rose in the shade. It was understated. It was demure. Pyrrha smiled at her mother in the mirrored reflection, amazed with the gracious gift.

"Now, clean this up," demanded Mama Jojo. "I must find Rahd's navy suit as I'm sure you must press it before tomorrow evening."

"Hhhhmmmm," sighed Pyrrha. She knew the tender mother-daughter moment could not last long. This afternoon had been the most time that they had spent alone together in weeks. It was the most sentimental thing they had done together in years.

"Oh wait!" Mama Jojo exclaimed. "Ask Auntie Farz over. I think this pantsuit would fit her."

Mama Jojo disappeared. Laid out on the corner of the sofa was a dress set with a grey jacket and pair of trousers. It was tailored with wide legs for a grandmother. The ornamental buttons and embroidered hemlines accentuated the outdated fashion choice. However, when Auntie Farz finally did try it on, it was surprisingly suitable, making her straight body flow like a curvaceous river.

As Pyrrha cleared the living room of gowns, she breathed in the perfumed garments and exhaled her emotions—giddiness about a new dress, happiness to spend a moment with her mom, frustration with cleaning up a roomful of delicate garments, loneliness when being left by herself in the cottage, and anxious excitement to see Yuht again so soon. With so many feelings whirling around inside her heart, she did what her grandfather had taught her to do so many years before.

Breathe in. Breathe out. Grand Tock's voice serenaded her in baritone.

Pyrrha found a rhythm with the whoosh and swoosh of the air in her lungs going in—and—out—and—in—and—out. As she watched her breath, her breathing slowed down. She took longer to inhale, and she allowed deeper exhales. As she relaxed her body, her emotions calmed.

Pay attention. Breath is life. It ends when we stop breathing.

Such a simple truth; such a simplified understanding, yet it was a fundamental truth. Grand Tock was right that people died when they stopped breathing.

Take a break, Grand Tock admonished. *Everything in moderation.*

Pyrrha methodically placed each party dress extracted from the basement treasure chest back in its proper garment bag and brought them into her bedroom to hang in Jupiter the Giant's armoire in hopes of more parties with pretty dresses in her future.

Until then, Grand Tock's great closet had been nearly empty with only a single woolen coat and one leather bag for traveling, but now the dresses and pantsuits competed for space on the rod. She pushed and prodded the clothing to shut the closet doors.

She hung her own dress for the ball on a hook on the back of her bedroom door. In the morning, she would steam iron it with a hint of lavender oil to release the decades-old wrinkles and the faint whiff of musty basement boxes. Then, she would press her father's suit and mother's gown as well. They would be presentable as the Tock family for the ball.

There was one last thing to do before tomorrow. Pyrrha would help Woods dye his hair. It was a precaution so that his typical Ironweald looks would not catch so many stares. His golden locks needed to be brushed brown for such a large party where he could not wear a hat to cover his hair.

These times of celebration brought up so many emotions. Pyrrha was conflicted about her family status—Mama Jojo and Dr. Rahd would get all dressed up and put on cheery expressions for the ball. The family would look unified as the respectable Tock clan especially with the gracious manners of Uncle Marz, Auntie Farz, and Woods. But all would question— where was Grand Tock, who was conspicuously absent? Usually, his jovial charm enlivened every room and his trickster spirit surprised all with laughter. Without his attendance, the Tock family would look less grand.

Then, there was Yuht—she would see him again. Her body burned with anticipation yet also twisted with anxiety. At the Ball, Duke Yuddha would stand elegantly before his country as the newly crowned ruler of Copperton. A dance might afford Pyrrha the chance to see Yuht up close and possibly learn what her fateful nightmare had meant and how their destinies were intertwined. He was married. He was powerful. He had children. He was rich. He was more than he seemed a few days ago when she met him under the trees. Dizzy with all these thoughts and feelings swirling around, Pyrrha distracted herself with preparations and chores.

THE BALL

THE AFTERNOON OF THE CORONATION BALL FINALLY ARRIVED. The road running past Tock's Land was busy with traffic. Wealthy citizens drove electric cars taken out of old garages, some well-off inhabitants hitched horses to antiquated carriages, a few poorer families pedaled bicycles slowly up the hill trying not to break a sweat in their party wear. The towns-folk who lived near the palace walked the modest incline to the Great Hall, while the country folk hopped aboard the public transportation arranged by the Royal Family.

Pyrrha, Woods, Uncle Marz, Auntie Farz, Mama Jojo, and Dr. Rahd waited patiently on the side of the main road for one of the busses. However, the first few which drove by were full to brimming at the final stop before town. So gradually, in threes, twos, and one, the Tocks found their way to the palace steps. Dr. Rahd was the first to give up waiting on the busses and head off toward town on foot.

"I'll meet you all there," he threw over his shoulder as he ambled north.

Mama Jojo, in a fit not to be left behind by her husband,

threw herself in front of a neighbor's horse and cart prancing down the lane.

"Kindly sir!" she asked sweetly. "I see you have a few extra seats in your carriage. May we ladies ride with you?"

The tuxedo-clad gentleman scooted over to allow Pyrrha a seat next to him, while Mama Jojo and Auntie Farz were offered seats on either side of the manservant driving the cab. This arrangement would normally have been unacceptable to Mama Jojo, but the senior in the carriage seemed too grumpy to talk pleasantries, while the young cabbie driving the horses was so handsome in his uniform. Mama Jojo happily sat close to him while her fine dress fluttered in the wind. Auntie Farz was just delighted to be along for the ride.

A farmer, with a rather slow cart and mule, was passing as this drama unfolded before him on the road—Dr. Rahd stomping off toward town, Mama Jojo throwing herself in front of the finest carriage, and patient Uncle Marz and cousin Woods waiting for a seat on the next bus.

"Good afternoon, Uncle Marz," Farmer Saari greeted. "Would you and your son like a ride to the palace?"

"Indeed," replied Uncle Marz.

"Thank you!" Woods graciously exclaimed.

"Mr. Saari, can we pick up Dr. Rahd along the way?" Uncle Marz requested.

Farmer Saari acquiesced with a nod. Thus, within the twinkle of an eye, Pyrrha, Woods, Uncle Marz, Auntie Farz, Mama Jojo, and Dr. Rahd were all comfortably settled in carriages and carts making their way to town. Yet, horses move quicker than mules, and cabbies drive faster than farmers, so everyone arrived to the ball at quite different times.

Mama Jojo, Auntie Farz, and Pyrrha arrived first in the gentleman's carriage. When they disembarked, they joined the flood of people taking the path from town to the Great Hall. Pyrrha felt like a fish in a strong current. People pushed around her on all sides. At first, she was flanked by Mama Jojo and Auntie Farz. The next moment, she was alone in the crowd of well-dressed citizenry moving toward the palace.

She looked above the heads. Top hats, feather bonnets, glittering tiaras, flower crowns, and silk parasols were interspersed with the bobbing heads of children catching a ride on their parents' shoulders. When she looked down at the ground, high heels, leather loafers, wooden clogs, cowboy boots, woven sandals, and tennis shoes represented peoples from all walks of life. Towns folk, gentry, farmers, soldiers, professors, and children. The old, the young, the rich, the poor. All of Copperton was coming to celebrate the Archduke's retirement and the young Duke's coronation.

This was new. She had never been to the royal residence before. From town, the home looked quaint. Tucked among the manicured gardens, it seemed like a slightly larger than average house in the foothills of the mountains. However, as she meandered up the long, winding driveway, the building grew larger and larger as she got nearer and nearer. Close up, the massive marble blocks constructing the façade were as wide as she was tall; some twenty bricks reached sixty feet tall and one hundred feet wide. What added to the optical illusion of small grandeur were the massive trees—these were not the trees of the valley grown in the last century after the lumberjacks logged too much of the forest. No! These were millennium trees that had been growing from the time before records. They were not measured in tens of feet but were easily two hundred feet tall.

Even the gardens were exaggeratedly grand. The roses were not merely the size of fists; instead, they burst forth like heads of red cabbages perfuming the whole hillside with the musk of love. The grass was not just groomed greenery; it was an emerald rug running the length of the palace grounds, wafting the essences of peace in the land. The decorations were not only ornamentations; strings of diamond lights twinkled like stars in the sky, while torches illuminated carved statues and sparkling fountains.

Pyrrha was swept forward by the crowd of attendees through the grand entrance to the Great Hall. She had lost Mama Jojo, Dr. Rahd, Auntie Farz, Uncle Marz, and Woods, but she was not alone. People were all around her. But, she did not know any of them. None were family. None were friends. None were the familiar faces from farm or town. Copperton had so many unknown friends celebrating the dukedom's emergence from the war.

This was not how she had imagined her first ball. Her nervousness surprised her. She had hoped for some companion to guide her through the customs and protocols of the dance. She had assumed Mama Jojo or Auntie Farz might lead her around the room on their arm making introductions. She put on a brave face despite the anxiety that nibbled at the edges of her stomach. She stood proud despite the discomfort that welled up among strangers in a strange place.

Though things were not exactly as she imagined, they were still beyond her expectations. She took a deep breath and assessed the palace room she had been escorted into by the crowd. She set a course to navigate the Great Hall to find someone she knew. In sweeping arcs, she circled around the room skirting the periphery of the dance floor. She glided through the ballroom admiring the art. The ceilings were mosaics celebrating the infinite variability of the number Pi. The floors were grey marble covered with ornamental rugs elaborating the complexities of geometric thought. On the walls hung oil paintings and watercolors of places near and far. The most impressive artwork was the ten-foot-tall statues on display—from every point of view they elicited different interpretations of rhyme and reason.

Yet, what filled the room with life was the orchestra serenading the crowd with cheerful melodies and the roar of families laughing, friends whispering, and neighbors chatting—these everyday sounds had been muted during the war. The fragrances of happiness had been absent too. The air was filled with the essence of almond oil, rose water, cinnamon spice, mint medley, and aroma of ambrosia. The long buffet contained baked bread, assorted cheeses, ripe fruit, and fresh vegetables. The smell of good food wafted through the crowded room tempting Pyrrha from her mission to find a familiar face. But, she persevered on her course.

While she looked for Mama Jojo, Auntie Farz, Dr. Rahd, Uncle Marz, and Woods, the diversity of people amazed her. Farmers wore khaki pants and overalls. Countryfolk wore pantsuits and sundresses. Gentry wore tuxedoes and gowns. Soldiers wore uniforms decorated with medals, while the few aristocrats donned gold and silver crowns.

After one loop around the Great Hall, she discovered Auntie Farz standing in a corner with an old friend who lived on a river a few miles from Tock's Land. On the second sweep of the room, she found Mama Jojo admiring a painting hung in the hall. When the two made their way back to the corner, Dr. Rahd, Uncle Marz, and Woods were chatting congenially with friends nearby. Each held a plate stacked high with food from the buffet.

"Pyrrha," called Auntie Farz. "Let me introduce you to Jorge's father."

Graciously, Pyrrha made polite conversation nodding and smiling at all the right times. There were awkward pauses and nervous laughs as she did not know what to say to these people whom she had not seen or talked to in many yeara.

Woods sidled up beside her and asked, "You good?"

Pyrrha gave a weak smile in reply.

"Dance?" he questioned.

Pyrrha looked at him quizzically. "Are you serious?"

"Oh, come on. It'll be better than this corner."

"It's been a long time."

"They are the simple steps we learned at school in the gymnasium," Woods encouraged.

Pyrrha looked around and thought about another hour of stilted chatter. "Sure! Let's go."

"I promise to step on your toes," Woods teased.

"Make it good, and break one," Pyrrha replied. "Then, I'll have an excuse not to dance with anyone else."

Woods led Pyrrha through the crush of attendees to the center of the ballroom. The dance floor felt spacious compared to the crowded hall. All around, young and old, fathers and daughters, sisters and friends waltzed in unison. They whirled, skipped, and hopped to the rhythm. Dresses swayed and heels clicked. Pyrrha and Woods swung around the room prancing and twirling to the orchestra's melody. Despite it being a few years since they had danced together in school, their feet remembered the simple steps which carried the beat from one waltz to the next foxtrot.

As Pyrrha danced, she synched in time with Woods. Their friendship was as smooth as their movements with the music. Without words they talked through their hands—a push or a pull, a lean or a tug. They moved forward-and-back and side-to-side, avoiding the other partners dancing nearby. And there were many—two men in tuxedos waltzed together; the sparkle of two glittering dresses caught her eye; a mother danced in a circle with her three children dressed as dolls. Then, out of the corner of her eye, Pyrrha saw a crown...no, two. She glanced at the couple who were swaying by their side. Yuht, no Duke Yuddha, led his wife, Duchess Juno, around the ballroom floor. The music seemed to accelerate in speed, like the rhythm of her heart, when the Duke nodded and smiled as he passed close by.

Woods, always the steady friend, led Pyrrha to the other side of the ballroom floor, gently guiding her through the steps. The one-two-three pattern moved her without much effort. The repetition of the school choreography came back easily. Woods was a good lead—playing it cautiously at first and then adding more turns and dips as they confidently flowed together as dancing partners. Every now and again, Pyrrha glimpsed Duke Yuddha looking her way. Sometimes, when he spun or turned, she saw Duchess Juno scowling in her direction.

An announcement came over the speaker system. "Ladies and gentlemen, belles and beaus! Find a person! Find a few! Let's partner up! Let's partner eight! The square dancing begins!"

Around the room, couples of four squared up to make groups of eight. Pyrrha and Woods found themselves in a circle with Federico, Jorge, and Emerson from the campfire a few nights past. They each had a date on their arm. Before all could be formally introduced, the caller belted out the commands to start the dancers moving round and round, so the couples nodded hello, smiled in greeting, and began the square dance.

"Circle up! Circle of eight! Bow to your corner! Bow to your date!" The caller sang the starting lines for the beginning steps.

Woods bowed to the young woman to his left, then he bowed to Pyrrha on his right. Pyrrha did just the opposite. She turned to Jorge on her right and curtsied; then, she turned to Woods and bowed humorously low.

"All join hands and circle right!"

As demanded, the group of eight held hands and pranced joyfully like a merry-go-round. The skirts swayed with the rhythm while the heels clicked in time to the beat.

"Swing your partner when you're home! Swing your partner high and low!" he sang.

When they arrived back at their starting place in the square, Woods spun Pyrrha like a ballerina. Each couple danced exceptionally as a pair.

"Head Gents! Into the center and do-si-do! Side Gents! Into the center and don't touch toes!" the caller instructed.

Jorge and Emerson went into the center and trotted around each other with a flourish and a kick. Then, Woods and Federico followed suit smiling and laughing at the chance to show off.

"Ladies, into the center, take a twirl! Together form a right-hand star!"

Pyrrha and the three other belles sashayed and spun into the middle of the circle and linked forearms to make a spoked wheel. Then, they pranced in a circle while their partners stomped and clapped emphasizing the swing.

"Pass your beau and grab the next! Don't be shy! Swing your best!"

Pyrrha marched past Woods and winked. Then, she took Emerson's outstretched hand. In this mixer dance, she would switch partners every few calls. She would move around the square to also dance with Federico and Jorge in turn. Round and round, the squares whirled. In and out of the center, the ladies and gents played. They swung with their partner and the next in a daisy-chain, moving from circles to squares to partner twirls.

The music played on. The calls for the dance rang out in quick progression. With each call, there was a flurry of steps to follow. There was never a dull moment, and never a lag in the fiddler's pace. Each dancer made a few missteps, but no one broke a toe, so it was a fun mixer on the whole. By the end of one song, Pyrrha had danced with everyone in her circle of eight as a partner and as a date. She had been swung, twirled, curtsied, and whirled, with a do-si-do and a happy star.

When the next song started, there was barely time to think. Woods and Pyrrha nodded to each other to stay on the floor and join the next square dance. Jorge and his partner stepped away, and a new couple joined to make the circle of eight complete. Everyone shuffled round so the newcomers could take the place of honor as lead dancers.

There, next to Pyrrha, was Yuht taking Jorge's place. Emerson and his date stood respectfully opposite the Duke and Duchess, while from the other side Federico bowed and his lady curtsied. Once again there was no time to spare before the caller began the second dance.

"Circle up! Circle of eight! Bow to your corner! Bow to your date!"

Pyrrha curtsied respectfully to Duke Yuddha, nodding her head low to hide her blush. Yuddha smiled affectionately down upon her as he bowed with deep respect. Then, she turned to Woods, giving him a wooden-doll bow at the hips.

"All join hands and circle right!"

Pyrrha and Yuht were suddenly holding hands. His fingers embraced hers in a gentle hug. His grasp was firm. His clasp was electrifying. However, there was no time to pause as the music moved along, Pyrrha forced her feet to step in time to the rhythm.

"Swing your partner when you're home! Swing your parter high and low!"

When she arrived back at her starting place in the square, Woods guided Pyrrha in a simple twirl as a pair. He spun her slow taking special care.

"Head Gents! Into the center and do-si-do! Side Gents! Into the center and don't touch toes!"

Duke Yuddha and Emerson went into the center and trotted around each other with a flourish and a kick. To see the crowned ruler dance with grace gave Pyrrha a moment of pause. Then, Woods and Federico did the same smiling stiffly, as they knew many people in the Great Hall were watching and commenting on their skills as they danced next to the Duke.

"Ladies, into the center, take a twirl! Together form a right-hand star!"

Pyrrha and Juno sashayed into the center with the two other belles to link forearms and make a spoked wheel. Juno's eyes pierced like spears as she smiled like a princess ascending the throne.

"Pass your beau and grab the next! Don't be shy! Swing your best!"

Pyrrha glided past Woods and grasped Emerson's outstretched hand. They were switching partners with each turn, so it was a relief that she had another round to practice with Federico before she met Duke Yuddha for a dance.

Pyrrha looked over at Woods, who was awkwardly dancing with Duchess Juno. Woods was not assured of his footing with a woman of such position. He guided her with a light touch, meekly leading the aristocrat by the hand through the caller's commands, hoping she would acquiesce. Both Woods and Juno were delighted when the next turn came around and she was off to dance with Emerson and Pyrrha paired with Federico.

Those calls went by in the blink of an eye and once again the announcement came to change partners.

"Pass that beau and grab the next! Don't be shy! Swing your best!"

Yuht's outstretched hand grasped hers. He pulled her close wrapping one arm around her waist for a close swing. Roses. Smiles. Serenity. The Duke of Copperton was dancing with her. He led her through the steps guiding her movements with grace. The man from her dreams. Her feet followed the rhythm as her heart raced ahead.

Yuht bent close to her ear and whispered, "I'm so happy to dance with you tonight—"

The caller interrupted, "Join hands in a circle of eight! Circle round and don't be late!"

Pyrrha joined hands with Yuht and Federico and glided around the circle as if floating on air. Yuht held her hand as delicately as a bouquet of flowers. He gazed upon her like she was a rare orchid in full bloom.

"Head Gents! Into the center and do-si-do! Side Gents! Into the center and don't touch toes!"

Pyrrha watched Yuht's strong shoulders and straight back as he do-si-doed with Emerson, and when he returned to her side, she gladly let him sweep her up in his arm and give her one last swing while Woods and Federico took their turn in the center of the square.

"Ladies, into the center, take a twirl! Together form a right-hand star!"

Pyrrha, Juno, and the two other belles sashayed into the center to make the spokes of a wheel. The four men stood on the sides of the square clapping along. Juno's manicured nails dug into Pyrrha's forearm as they trotted in a circle as a star, yet all the while the Duchess smiled benevolently.

The caller sang the last steps. "Pass that beau and go on home! Don't be shy! He's the one you know!"

Pyrrha slumped into Woods' arms for the final partner twirl at the end of the song.

"Thank you, dancers!"

When the song ended, all the couples on the dance floor bowed and curtsied to the Duke and Duchess. Pyrrha blushed so deeply that she was unable to raise her head to meet Yuht's eyes.

She yanked Woods' hand to signal she wanted out. He guided her from the ballroom floor, as she floated in the memory of Yuht's embrace with his lips near her ear. At the edge of the hall, she took a moment to catch her breath and regain her composure. When she was ready, Woods led her back to the corner of the Great Hall to rejoin Mama Jojo, Dr. Rahd, Auntie Farz, and Uncle Marz, who were happily chatting with neighbors and making plans to go home.

The family made their way outside and found the bus waiting half-empty at the end of the palace drive. It was still early in the evening and many revelers were still out enjoying the summer party. But, the Tock family had had their fill of eating and dancing. It was more socializing than they had had in years.

On the bus, each person sat alone on their own bench. Copperton was veiled by nightfall as the bus trundled along the dirt road out of town. The world passed by in the shadowy light cast by the moon and clouds. Darkness brought speculations—Had she really danced with Yuht? Had he chosen their square to dance with her? As her dream foretold, was her fate somehow tied up with his? Then, there was Juno, the jealous wife. The pieces did not fit together.

Where was Grand Tock when she needed someone to talk with? Her parents were too aloof to discuss these kinds of complicated emotions, while her aunt and uncle were too busy to have time for her concerns. There was Woods, but everything about Yuht made him angry. His jaw tightened and his shoulders stiffened whenever Yuht's name was brought up in conversation. Maybe she would figure it out on her own. Maybe in the next few days things would become clear.

"Tock's Land," the bus driver hollered. "Last call for Tock's Land."

Her family had all disembarked. It was time to go home. She stood up and walked off the bus. She would put her emotions to rest for the night. Tomorrow would bring something new.

THE FIRST MOUNTAIN

The days after the ball passed at a quick, quick, slow pace. Pyrrha shuffled around the house and the yard, doing chores close to home. Woods needed help in the garden and Auntie Farz invited Pyrrha for dinner. Yet, the days and nights moved like a fog which obscured her view of the way forward.

It was inky dark when pounding rattled the front door. Who could be knocking at three o'clock in the morning? Through her dreams, Pyrrha's conscious mind told her to wake up and get the door. She knew Mama Jojo was sleeping out in the jing fields and Dr. Rahd was deep in the stacks of the community library.

She slid out of bed and into a pair of slippers and threw a shawl over her shoulders, more for modesty than warmth. She walked through the house to the front door, turning on enough lights to illuminate her path but not blind her sleepy eyes. On the front stoop, she was greeted by three police officers, two women and a man, in perfectly pressed uniforms with calm faces. These were not the gruff and tough street police, nor were they poorly trained militia; these were the well-respected intelligence agents sent for special missions which required tact and discretion.

"Are you Ms. Pyrrha Tock?" the older woman, Captain Mahoney, queried when the door opened.

"Yes. I am Pyrrha Tock." She had learned at a young age to always be respectful of such officers, to answer their questions efficiently without adding any information. She had also learned to be calm despite the anxiety that agitated her every limb. "What brings you here before dawn?"

"You must come with us," the older woman continued.

"Can I report to the station in the morning?"

"No."

"May I know the reason that I must go with you?"

"You will be fully apprised of the situation when we take you in."

"Am I being arrested?" Pyrrha inquired.

Captain Mahoney replied, "I am not at liberty to say."

"May I change my clothes instead of wearing my silk pajamas?"

The three officers scowled amongst each other, looked at her pink pants and camisole, and wordlessly came to a decision.

"Yes, you may change, but Sergeant Kyhn will accompany you. In addition, please grab your papers," commanded Captain Mahoney.

The young female officer nodded and moved forward to escort her while she changed. Pyrrha and Sergeant Kyhn left Captain Mahoney and the male police officer standing outside the front door under the porch light. They moved carefully through the dimly lit house to the bedroom in the back of the cottage. As Pyrrha walked, she thought about her situation. She was alone at home and the police had come to take her somewhere. Many questions ran through her mind—Was she in trouble? Was her family in trouble? Why would they not tell her anything?

Then there were the more pragmatic concerns—she needed to dress wisely for she did not know where she was going nor how long she would be gone. She had grown up hearing too many of Grand Tock's great adventures where he had left the house abruptly, so he was woefully unprepared with insufficient clothing and insufficient supplies. Thus, she slipped clean work pants over her silk pajama bottoms and pulled out two pairs of thin wool socks from the dresser drawer to put on. With these layers, she would remain warm if she stayed outside on this cool summer evening. On top, she also overdressed adding a shirt and wraparound sweater over her camisole and bra. It seemed like a lot of clothes—especially for the summer—but the extra padding and warmth felt like a comforting hug in the uncertain situation.

As she dressed, Sergeant Kyhn stood nearby averting her eyes from Pyrrha's body. However, she was not being polite. Instead, she scanned the room to create a detailed mental map of all she saw, from the wall hangings to the carved furniture. Under such scrutiny it would be difficult for Pyrrha to write a note to tell her parents of the circumstances, so she decided to leave several unusual signs to help them realize that this was not a normal absence from home.

After dressing, but before leaving the bedroom, she took the flowers out of the vase on the bedside table and nonchalantly placed them on the bed before walking to the fireplace and throwing the water on the coals then returning the vase to the bedside stand. The noise of hissing ashes caught Sergeant Kyhn off guard.

"What are you doing?" Sergeant Kyhn admonished.

"Oh, sorry! I put out the fire," Pyrrha replied.

"Enough of this nonsense. Get your documents, so we can be on our way."

"Yes," Pyrrha nodded.

She went to the old desk in the living room and bent down

to open the file drawer. She briefly thought of writing a note on the floor, but there was no pen within reach, so instead she left the desk drawer open with the empty folder resting on top. Surely these small signs of disordered mess around the house would be a clue for her parents, if they were not too self-absorbed to notice.

As she stood up and turned around, she waved her documents and asked, "Do I need more than my passport and residence card?"

This question and sudden movement interrupted Sergeant Kyhn's scan of the kitchen and dining room.

"No, those documents are sufficient," replied Sergeant Kyhn.

The two emerged on the front stoop.

Captain Mahoney looked at Pyrrha's outfit and grunted to the young male colleague, "Officer Stone, bind her hands. Then, escort her to the car."

The early morning was quiet; all of the night owls had gone to bed, but none of the early birds had yet awoken. Pyrrha looked across the garden to Uncle and Auntie's home hoping to see signs of life, to witness her leaving. But, the house was dark and the curtains drawn. However, there, among the trees, bushes, and flowers was an extra shadow. Someone was hidden in the shade of black.

"Whippoorwill, whippoorwill," came the studied call of the little bird.

"Ah-hem!" Pyrrha coughed.

"Whippoorwill, whippoorwill."

"Ah-hem-huh-hoo!" Pyrrha coughed louder. Then, she covered her mouth and face with her hands to hide the glint in her eyes.

Woods was amid the trees at the edge of the garden, watching the night's activities. His imitation birdcall was alerting her that her absence would not go unmarked. If it had been any other time, she would have responded with her own bird call. She would have hooted like an owl as she so often did when they met unexpectedly along the road, in the forest, or by the fields.

"In!" ordered Captain Mahoney as she opened the rear passenger door of the plain black car.

Sergeant Kyhn was at her side with a hand on Pyrrha's shoulder encouraging her down into the backseat while simultaneously raising her hand above Pyrrha's head to protect it from being knocked on the top of the door frame. Captain Mahoney slid into the front seat, and Officer Stone took the wheel of the car. Before they set off, Pyrrha's seatbelt was fastened around her and she was blindfolded. That was the last thing she remembered.

IMPRISONED

The second time Pyrrha awoke that morning, it was still dark—not a natural dark of the cottage before sunrise, but the dark of a dungeon room deep underground with insufficient windows to let in sunlight. She felt sluggish and slow. Her mind and her body could not sort out where she was and how she had gotten there. The last thing she remembered were the police escorting her into the car and Woods' birdcall. Once in the backseat, it had all blurred to a blackout. After the blindfold was on and the engine roared, she had tried to count the turns and remember the route, but she could not focus and quickly lost track of the way. When they had left the edge of the village and started uphill, there was nothing to remember until she awoke in this dark cavern.

In this kind of situation, it would be easy to get scared and to loose one's wits, so Pyrrha played an old game passed down from Grand Tock—What do I know? The rules were simple. Clearly state all of the things that were known for sure, and then from those factual details of hard reality try to unemotionally piece together the puzzle at hand. So what did she know?

It was cool, but not cold. A musty odor permeated the air. It was dark, but not pitch black. Some light, air, and noise were coming in from a small window high on the far wall, so she could see the outline of things. She was in a kind of cage about nine feet by nine feet with a stone wall on two sides and metal bars squaring the other sides. The cell was clean but old and a bit dusty from disuse. There was a simple iron bed with cotton padding, wooden table and chair, a tile sink, and a porcelain toilet. Her hands were no longer tied together.

Next to the cell, but well out of reach, was a thick metal door that seemed to go out to a hallway or stairwell—she guessed this from the distant voices and sounds that ricocheted in muted tones off hard walls. Her cell was in one corner of an enormous stone room, which extended into darkness, as her echo seemed to just fade away in the blackness of space. She had never been in this room before. The size of the rocks in the walls and the size of the room were larger than any normal place in the whole of Copperton.

She was hungry, so she must have been here for many hours. There were no bumps, bruises or cuts on her body, and her clothes were not dirty—only rumbled and wrinkled from sitting in a car and sleeping on a cot. Her documents were missing along with her precious darts, which she had secretly slipped into the folds of her sweater while Sergeant Kyhn had turned away as she had dressed.

Pyrrha tried to puzzle together a story. However, she could not think of any logical reason that she would be in trouble with the secret police. Instead, her mind wandered to imaginary situations where her mother or father had accidentally done something wrong and she was picked up in their stead because they could not be found—wherever they were. Then, she wondered if she was being charged as the highwayman that had attacked Duke Yuddha.

This idea made her face blush. Just thinking of Yuht laying pinned to the forest floor near her home and then discovering later that he was an aristocrat made her body tingle with embarrassment at her naiveté. Then, she warmed with titillation remembering his kind words at the fair and his graceful dancing at the ball. She beamed just thinking that such an important person knew her by name and always seemed happy to see her. But, he also filled her with questions. Did he really care for her in some special way, or was he just being polite as a prince?

Maybe she had misread the situation. Maybe he was upset with her. Maybe the police were spies from Ironweald who had captured her…Unfortunately, this train of thought—thinking about the facts of her current situation—had led to rumination, which produced anxiety and frustration. It was time to play another variation of the game—Tall Tales.

To distract herself from catastrophic imaginings, she played into her fantasies and invented outlandish scenarios, one more unlikely than the last. She was like Grand Tock on his first expedition; this was the beginning of her own adventure where these police were really the helpers of Jupiter's descendants who had been sent for her as the carrier of her grandfather's spirit. They needed her, as only she could be trusted, to assist with a secret mission—as her grandfather could not be found. In another story, Yuht strolled into her imagination as her prince in shining armor to slay a dragon and rescue her from this captivity. His dark eyes pierced through the unlit room and made her heart quicken like bat wings in a cave. Finally, she thought of reality again and only one memory from the previous evening brought her comfort—Woods standing among the trees calling out to her in secret.

She heard Woods' voice through the language of the whippoorwill. *I have witnessed you leave in the night, so I will find Mama Jojo in the jing patch and Dr. Rahd in the library and tell them what happened. Then, we will consult together with Uncle Marz and Auntie Farz and make a plan to find you.*

All of these ideas swirled with her imagination until she just had to stop and breathe—in-and-out, in-and-out, in-and-out. She had to breathe in a methodic, meditative practice counting the length of her inhales and exhales to calm her mind and soothe her anxiety as she waited for whatever next thing that was to happen.

This strict meditation required her full attention and blocked out everything else. Yet, as with all meditative practices, once she was lulled into the repetition, her mind wandered. This time, she was spirited away to the Ocean of Wisdom. She saw grey skies and whitecaps from a brewing storm. The enormous waves danced in the wind rolling toward a distant shore and crashing with thunderous applause. Thus, her breath became like her thoughts—deep, yet choppy.

How long she lay on the cot trapped in her mind, it was hard to say, but her meditation was interrupted by footsteps softly padding down stairs. The sound of clanking keys rattled the lock. Then, the metal door creaked opened and in came a splash of light followed by Sergeant Kyhn. The sight of a familiar, though placid, face was a relief. Pyrrha could not help herself from smiling when Sergeant Kyhn slid a plate of hot mush through the bars in front of her. Next, the guard stepped to the other side of the jail cell and slid a folded robe on the table. Lastly, she flipped a small switch next to the door which illuminated the prison in a grey glow.

"First, eat. Then, change," Sergeant Kyhn commanded. "I will be back in thirty minutes, so you should wash your face and look presentable for your trial."

"What do you mean?" Pyrrha asked.

"This is not the time for questions, tiger girl," Sergeant Kyhn barked.

"Is my trial about the tiger?" Pyrrha asked despite her trepidation.

"Is there another crime we should charge you with?"

Sergeant Kyhn retorted before walking out, shutting and locking the dungeon door.

Pyrrha's tongue froze; her body stilled. The metallic clangs reverberated through the room. The hard steps echoed off the stones. Would she be prosecuted for something that happened so long ago? Grand Tock's mission to slay the tiger had somehow become her burden again.

Despite the uncertainty, Pyrrha was hungry, so she ate. The food smelt edible and even tasted as potato-carrot-taro mash should. Within a few minutes, the plate was empty. Next, she looked at the clothes placed on the table. There was a white silken inner robe and an outer black cotton robe with a wide grey belt. These were the traditional garments of the olden days; she knew how to wear them from her childhood games playing dress up with neighborhood friends. She took off everything but her undergarments and put on the penguin wear. She washed her face and combed her hair into an elegant topknot like the warriors of old. Then to pass the time, she made the bed, folded her own clothes in a neat pile, and placed them on the cot. She straightened up the whole cell to distract herself from whatever was to come next.

Before long, steps were heard from beyond the door, the rustling of keys, and then Sergeant Kyhn entered followed by Captain Mahoney and Officer Stone—the three police who had come to her home the night before.

"We are taking you to your trial," Captain Mahoney announced in her matter-of-fact, do-not-ask-me-questions tone of voice.

"But, I have not yet been charged with a crime," Pyrrha replied.

"All in good time. All things good and bad happen in time."

She was speechless. How could Captain Mahoney glibly recite philosophical truths and make it sound like nonsense?

"Let's go!" barked Officer Stone. "We cannot keep the Duke's Court waiting."

Pyrrha's shoulders fell. The moment of truth—she was in the basement of Duke Yuddha's palace. The stones were the right color; the room was the right size; the sounds were the right distance from Newcomen. Her innards wobbled, yet she tried to control her hands from noticeably shaking. She did not want to meet the Duke as she was—dressed in humiliating garments. Yet, there seemed to be few choices. Three expertly trained palace guards were ushering her from her chambers and encouraging her forward.

Pyrrha acquiesced. She passively followed the three police out of the cell to the metal dungeon door, to the base of a long stairwell. She paused. Her heart caught in her chest. She was beneath the Great Hall in the passageway below the ballroom where she had danced with Yuht only a few days before. She looked at the steps absorbing the truth—she had been confined under the palace by someone she thought she loved. How did she not know?

Each step brought up new revelations and new questions— Who was Duke Yuddha? What was her crime? How would her dream of fatefully meeting Yuht play out in real life? The puzzle made less sense as more pieces were unveiled. She missed Grand Tock and wished for his wise counsel and mischievous flair. Would she ever be able to see him again?

WOODS UNCOVERS THE RIDDLES

WOODS AWOKE TO THE SOUND OF A LOW HUM. IT WAS NOT UNCLE Marz's snoring, nor thunder rumbling over the hills. It was unnatural—a pitch-perfect machine agitating the dark morning air. Woods slipped from his bedroom and tiptoed down the hall, listening to the sounds about the house. Uncle Marz and Auntie Farz were breathing in that measured way of deep dreams. The yard chirped and buzzed with insects that never rested. The leaves teased secrets across the canopy. Yet, the manufactured hum insistently murmured its presence. What's more, there were shuffled crunches of gravel.

Woods slid near the wall by the living room window to spy on the neighboring cottage. Pyrrha should be home alone tonight, as her parents, Mama Jojo and Dr. Rahd had been conspicuously absent of late. With the front stoop light on at Pyrrha's home, a black car and uniformed attendant could be seen pacing the lane by the front garden.

This had never happened before. Woods watched while trying to wake his sleeping mind. Nightmare or not, he willed his body to the backdoor and out among the trunks of trees that separated the two homes. He was propelled forward by curiosity and fear.

The mosquitoes buzzed at his ears and nipped at his skin, yet he did not swat or scratch. There was a whiff of car exhaust and wood smoke playing in the air. Woods felt the grass and sticks under his bare toes; he treaded with measured steps to not attract attention. Through Pyrrha's kitchen windows, Woods noted movement. There was at least one, if not two, more uniformed individuals inside the house.

The door opened and a commanding woman demanded attention. "Officer Stone, bind her hands. Then, escort her to the car."

The man standing in the lane rushed to follow orders. Pyrrha emerged from the house surrounded by three guards, yet she seemed self-possessed and alert to her surroundings. Her eyes scanned the garden and paused where she saw Woods' shadow among the trees. This was his moment to rescue her, yet the trained guards would easily overpower two unarmed youth. So, instead of freeing her, he would give her hope. He must let her know that her departure did not go unnoticed.

"Whippoorwill, whippoorwill," Woods called out like the bird.

"Ah-hem!" Pyrrha coughed.

"Whippoorwill, whippoorwill."

"Ah-hem-huh-hoo!" Pyrrha coughed louder.

Before Woods could communicate anything of use, Pyrrha was encouraged down into the backseat. Officer Stone marched around to the driver's seat to take the wheel, and the other two women took their places in the car. With the crunch of gravel under the tires, the black car left the yard and turned onto the main road toward town.

Woods waited in the garden, listening to the world. He felt his surroundings. After what seemed like a long time, he concluded that no other people had accompanied these strangers onto Tock's Land. With trepidation, he ventured across the garden and slid in through the backdoor of Pyrrha's cottage.

He moved slowly—listening, feeling. He checked and rechecked that there was really no one in or outside the house. As he scanned each room, he noticed Pyrrha's unusual messages. In her bedroom, she had pulled the wildflowers out of the vase on her bedside table and thrown the colorful blossoms on the unmade bed. She had splashed water in the fireplace drowning the grey coals in liquid. In the living room, the desk area was a mess—a drawer was pulled out and file folders were left out and open. Without disturbing anymore dust, Woods snuck out of the house the way he had come and returned to his family's cottage.

A small candle burned in the kitchen. The sound of a kettle singing with hot water greeted Woods as he entered the house. He turned off the stove and inched to the living room door to see which of his parents had awoken and would catch him returning from outside. Uncle Marz sat in a recliner looking out the windows at the garden.

"That was mighty dangerous of you to venture out with the unexpected visitors," Uncle Marz scolded Woods without looking at his son.

"Sorry!" Woods mustered as he examined his dirty toes.

"Well, make me some tea already," Uncle Marz chided. "Then, dust off your feet and come tell me what you found in Pyrrha's abduction."

Woods nodded and returned to the kitchen. He selected two ceramic mugs from the cupboard, pinched in a spot of mint, and poured boiling water over the leaves. While the water infused with flavor, he brushed his dusty feet with a rag by the door. Then, he returned to the living room to sit with his father.

"I'm sorry I went out there—"

Uncle Marz raised his hand and silenced Woods. "It was dangerous…but…who was here?"

"I don't know."

"What did you see?"

"There was a black car and three uniformed guards—one man and two women."

"Do you know where they are from?"

"No… but they spoke like you and me," Woods replied. "Not like Wealds."

"Describe the uniforms."

"All black—even the details. The fabric was sturdy yet flexible. The jackets buttoned up to the collar, and the man's pants were straight with a crease down the front middle of the leg. The two women wore skirts to the knees and some kind of black leggings. They all wore leather dress shoes that seemed comfortable, yet formal."

"Were there markings on their clothing?" Uncle Marz was leaning back in the chair with his eyes closed imagining the scene. "Were there any pins or patches?"

"No…just some braided black ropes on the shoulders." Woods searched his memory for more details. "And, the car didn't even have a plate number."

"That's odd."

"There were many things that were strange." Woods added. "They were very well-mannered, but also impatient and short-tempered."

"I don't follow."

"Like they stood perfectly erect and held their hands at their sides, but they barked orders, and looked grumpy."

"How did Pyrrha look?"

Woods swallowed. There was a lump in his throat thinking about this cousin. "Pyrrha…" his voice wavered. "She looked remarkably calm…"

"So they took her away?" Uncle Marz confirmed. "Where did

they go?"

"It is hard to say," Woods replied. "They turned toward town not south."

"Hmmm…" Uncle Marz held the cup of tea in his hands. He seemed to be warming up while awakening his senses. "You went into the house, didn't you?" It was a reprimand as much as a question.

"Yes…I waited and watched…then I went in through the backdoor."

"Oh…" Uncle Marz sighed. "I guess Jojo and Rahd aren't there, are they?"

"No," Woods shook his head. "I stayed in the shadows and didn't touch anything.

"Well, what did you see?"

"Pyrrha intentionally left messes all about—"

"Don't give me your opinions. State the facts!"

"In Pyrrha's bedroom, she threw some flowers on the bed."

"What kind?"

"A sprig of forget-me-nots lay separate from the rest of the stems."

"That's a sign," Uncle Marz smiled. "Keep going."

"She put out the fire with the flower water."

"And…"

"The water was poured out to make the letter V."

"That is the symbol for help." Uncle Marz encouraged. "What else?"

"In the living room, she left the filing cabinet open with the folders in a mess."

"Wise girl," Uncle Marz took a sip of tea and visibly relaxed. "Which folders?"

"The family documents like passports and ID cards."

"Is there anything else?"

"I called out to her before she left."

"What!" Uncle Marz bolted up in fear. "How were you not arrested?"

"Whippoorwill, whippoorwill," Woods sung like the little bird in the living room.

"Oh," Uncle Marz slumped back in his chair. "I suspect the guards were too busy to realize that your call was not a real bird."

"They paid no attention...but I think Pyrrha got it because she looked in my direction and coughed."

There was noise from the back of the house. "What's happening?" Auntie Farz mumbled. "Is there a bird in the house?" She shuffled to the sofa and slumped down rubbing her eyes awake.

"It's Pyrrha," Uncle Marz said. "They have finally come."

"What?" Woods looked between his parents. "You knew this was going to happen."

"No..." Uncle Marz paused. "We just aren't completely surprised after the dancing at the ball."

"Uh..." Woods blushed at his naiveté. "You think Yuht kidnapped her."

"No," Auntie Farz tried. "The Duke—please respect his title— we do not think he would order this kind of arrest."

"You think it is an arrest!" Woods gasped. "What did Pyrrha do?"

"We..." Uncle Marz censored himself. "It is not wise to speculate about what has happened or will happen next. We must collect the facts."

Silence descended. Auntie and Uncle did not speak. Only inhales and exhales could be heard in the dim light of the living room. The quiet lasted for such a long time that Woods suspected his two parents had fallen back asleep in their seats.

"We should make a plan," Uncle Marz finally said.

"You're awake?" Woods asked.

"When the sun comes up, I'll inspect the house again with

the help of sunlight. Woods, you will go to find Dr. Rahd in the library. And, Farz, can you look for Jojo?"

They each nodded in agreement.

"Breakfast?" Auntie Farz suggested. "It'll be hard to go back to sleep."

"Why not," Uncle Marz agreed. "We need the energy."

"I'll make coffee," Woods offered.

They bustled around the kitchen preparing the morning meal, and they scuttled around the house preparing for the day. When first light broke, they were fed and dressed. Each went their separate ways to discover what they could.

Woods covered his head with a hat and took a bicycle from the shed before pedaling through the cool morning air toward the library in town. The doors to the main reading rooms would likely just open when he arrived. It baffled him how Dr. Rahd had charmed the head librarian into letting him spend the night on so many occasions. Or, did the caretakers just forget about Dr. Rahd hidden behind shelves, silently absorbing the messages on each page?

Woods rode toward old Newcomen. He stayed on the unpaved road on their side of the river. As he passed each bridge, he admired their architecture and remembered his childhood, before the war, when these abundant crossovers were just limited to two. In the dry season, many a child hopped rocks across the wide shallows and many adults rigged wood planks to traverse the trickle of water. However, when the snows melted off the mountains in the spring and the thunderstorms brought rains in the summer, everyone had to travel miles to the foundation bridges to cross the raging river that swelled with abundance.

As he approached the town, the track became wider so two

carts could pass, and the space was necessary, as people were going here and there about their morning errands. Woods weaved among the traffic, slowly maneuvering between the distracted pedestrians and restless cab drivers. The brick roads led past the banks and shops to a pillared mammoth of a building that was the city library. Woods parked his bike in the designated area, and slowly climbed the wide front steps toward the mahogany front doors.

Every time he approached this building, he imagined that it had been built for giants, since the doors were three times the height of the tallest person in Copperton. The cavernous front gallery was lined with shelves of books, yet in the middle there was always a stack of unsorted materials awaiting official placement. Several librarians were always on hand to read, categorize, and shelve the new additions, yet the pile of books seemed never to diminish.

At this early hour, the library was still quite empty. Very few people milled about or sat in the comfortable armchairs with their feet upon stools reading. Woods meandered through the main hall, treading softly so as not to attract attention. His goal was the far staircase that led to the dusty archives in the basement, where the oldest collection of rare books was housed. He was not in humor to make pleasantries with the librarians.

"Who do we have the honor of hosting today?" came a hushed whisper from his elbow.

"Good morning! It's Woods from Tock's Land."

"Oh Woods, how you have grown," replied the head librarian. "I didn't recognize you with your hat hiding your golden hair." She wore her pink hair in spikes and accentuated the color with a purple dress. When asked about her fashion choices, she would regale her audience with the book-of-the-week and the character who she had decided to impersonate. Woods could not quite place this newest costume, but he did not want the half-hour explanation that ended with a book to read in hand.

"I'm almost done with my studies. Only a few topics left—"

"Yes! Yes! What a great time to go out into the world when peace abounds. You can do anything."

"I suppose I could…" Woods sighed because this question of his future path—not in the militia—troubled him more than he wanted to admit.

"We are always looking for librarians to sort the books," she nodded at the pile in the middle of the room.

"Thank you." Woods politely acknowledged her idea, then changed topics. "I'm looking for Dr. Rahd. Is he here?"

The head librarian pulled a face. "Well, I just got here, and I haven't seen him yet, so…"

"I'll check the usual nesting sites."

"He is so diligent researching this latest fascination."

"With respect, Ma'am" Woods bowed his head and touched his hand to his heart politely before pivoting and hurrying toward the stairs.

The curving stairwell twisted round itself as Woods descended into the library's dungeons. Dim lights lit the way, casting curved shadows that accentuated the shapes of dust motes and stretched the length of time.

"Achoo!" Woods sneezed at the underground air.

"One hundred years!" Came the reply from deep within the basement. Of course the full saying was *May you not get ill; may you live one hundred years*, but few people said the whole sentence.

"Dr. Rahd?" Woods called out tentatively as he did not want to disturb the other researchers.

"Here." A nearby voice coughed.

"Where?"

"Mythology."

Woods tried to locate the voice behind the shelves, but the

wall of books obscured his view. He wandered down and around looking at the scant signage for titles that might hint at folk tales and legends. A warm glow from an added lantern encouraged him toward to a particularly cluttered table at the end of a long bookshelf. Behind the stacks of books and scrolls, sat Dr. Rahd nestled in his research.

"Dr. Rahd?" Woods hesitated.

"Ah!" He looked up from his reading, glassy-eyed and pensive. "Woods? What brings you here?"

"Um…" Woods faltered looking at his uncle's wrinkled brow and pursed lips.

"What is it?" Dr. Rahd asked placing his open book upon the table and marking the page with a scrap of note paper.

"It's Pyrrha," Woods started. "She was taken away last night in a black car."

"Ah, how interesting," Dr. Rahd said distractedly. "I'm reading about Hercules right now."

"Um…" Woods swallowed his words. They seemed to burn in his throat.

"Hercules is an ancient warrior, you read his stories in school right? Well, as you know he was born with strength beyond measure, and as a young man he was assigned ten tasks after he committed a great wrong."

"Uncle?…" Woods interrupted with frustration. "Pyrrha…"

"Most of us interpret these as physical feats that he accomplished—you know, he is written in most myths as lacking in all other capacities besides strength." Dr. Rahd tapped his head and said, "Not the fastest mind in the land, they say."

"Dr. Rahd…" Woods tried to contain his irritation without being rude.

"However, I have now realized that Hercules was surmounting spiritual hurdles as well as completing physical labors. You know like traversing the seven valleys or…"

Woods reached out and grabbed Dr. Rahd's arm. The physical connection broke the professorial rambling. "Sir, Pyrrha is gone."

"Well, do you know where she went?" Dr. Rahd asked with all logic and no emotion.

"No! That is why I am here." Woods voice simmered. "She was taken away in a black car without markings, so we do not know where she went."

"Did you follow the car?"

"No, I couldn't. It was dark and…"

"Unfortunately, I was here last night, wasn't Jojo at home?"

"She was not."

"I suggest you find Mama Jojo. She might know something," Dr. Rahd recommended. "I'll be home by sunset, so hopefully Pyrrha will wander back by then." He opened his book to the marked page and settled into his reading again. Thus, the conversation was abruptly closed.

"Thank you for your time," Woods bowed his head, but he did not touch his heart. Then, he excused himself. It took great self-control not to stomp back upstairs and slam the stairwell door.

Woods snuck out of the library avoiding any further encounters with any friendly neighbors or unknown friends. He took his bike and walked through the streets absorbing his conversation with Dr. Rahd. Pyrrha's parents were so distracted by their own concerns. As his anger seethed with the reality of things, he jumped on his bike and sped toward home.

He arrived panting. He had pushed himself hard the entire route. This helped relieve his frustrations from the convoluted conversation. When he reached the house, he was tomato-faced and breathless.

"Oh, Woods!" cooed Mama Jojo from the garden, where she was sipping tea with Uncle Marz. "Come join us," she beckoned with her hand.

Woods nodded in acknowledgement. He rolled the bicycle to

the shed and trudged back, trying to make haste yet still catch his breath from the trip to town.

Mama Jojo intercepted him on the path. "Woods, I came home immediately when Auntie Farz told me the news." She grabbed his hands and gazed into his face. "I had a dream last night." She paused. "Rrha will be sent on a mission to fight a dragon."

"Is that metaphorical?" Woods interrupted without trying to be rude.

"And you! You are so important!" Mama Jojo continued without taking a breath or breaking eye contact. "You will be the light-bearer. You must carry the torch to ignite a…" Her eyes were filled with tears and her chin wavered as she swallowed her last words in a few dramatic sobs.

"Thank you…" Woods acquiesced.

"Jojo," Uncle Marz guided her by the elbow back to a seat in the garden.

Then, Uncle Marz motioned for Woods to go into the house. Woods obliged. He retraced his steps to the back door. Auntie Farz was waiting with several dishes on the table. For a pre-lunch snack, they would have lettuce root in a spicy vinaigrette and lettuce leaves smothered in peanut sauce. These were tiny delicacies that might soothe over his frustrations from talking to Pyrrha's parents.

Wordlessly, Auntie Farz consoled him with understanding. She patted his arm and served him a generous portion. Woods accepted these affections and waited for his mind to make sense of all he had learned.

THE DUKE'S COURT

Officer Stone, Sergeant Kyhn, and Captain Mahoney marched Pyrrha toward the trial room. They plodded ceremoniously up the stone stairwell to emerge from the dungeon. As they ascended, the coarseness of the rock walls below became smoothed marble above; the cool cellar air warmed to a summertime breeze; and the electric lighting gradually faded into natural sunbeams. They strode down the broad palace halls in a formal parade of tedious grandiosity. Officer Stone led the way, carrying a standard with the emblem of the Duke's ancestry. With each step, from behind Sergeant Kyhn's head, Pyrrha saw snatches of the evergreen velvet flag swaying on a wooden pole. Captain Mahoney followed behind as the proud overseer of this entourage.

They entered a reception room designed to entertain hundreds of dignitaries; it was much like the ballroom but decorated more seriously. Their steps no longer echoed on hard floors; they slid over silk carpets that wove the story of mystic gardens. Finally, the four arrived at a single chair placed in the middle of the room facing three platforms with two thrones on each—six members of the Duke's Court would preside over her case. The center platform was elevated above the right and left, much like an awards podium in a sports ceremony for first, second, and third place.

"Sit!" grumbled Captain Mahoney.

Pyrrha sat. The three palace guards stood behind at attention. Nothing happened. They waited. Time was inconsequential. Pyrrha listened to her senses to absorb every detail. The light moved the shadows by degrees across the floor. Faint steps pattered and curtains swished far off, but the noise and movement dissipated to naught. A light breeze, with the scent of lavender and rose, wafted through the hall, and the standard flag danced.

"All rise—" called a disembodied voice from on high.

Pyrrha, the only one seated, stood.

Six elegantly dressed figures entered the room. They glided without haste like butterflies crossing an open field. Their robes fluttered, showing layers of embroidered color. With choreographed tradition, they took their assigned places. First, Lord Yuri and Lady Eliza hovered across the reception room and stood humbly upon the simplest platform nearest the door. They looked contented as if it was their highest honor to sit on the Duke's Court. Next, Archduke Zachariah was accompanied by Archduchess Zaynah to the second highest pedestal of honor. He hobbled and lurched forward while she floated beside her ailing husband anticipating his tread, balancing his moves, and guiding his steps. Finally, Duke Yuddha escorted Duchess Juno to their formal positions in the center, above the rest. They were stiff with formality and blank of expression; they appeared out of body as these posed stances seemed so unnaturally natural.

Pyrrha went clammy. She froze in fear, like a trapped animal. She was not prepared to see Yuht in his ceremonial robes in command as Duke. She had never dared to think he was the one behind her arrest. Yet, now he stood as the leader of all of Copperton presiding over her trial.

"The Duke's Court is convened!" sang the voice from above.

In a gentle wave of deference, the three couples sat upon their thrones. Pyrrha stood looking at the assemblage of nobility before her, not knowing what was yet to unfold.

"Sit!" hissed Officer Stone. His hand was upon her shoulder, pushing her into the simple wooden chair.

"The trial shall commence," announced the voice.

Pyrrha looked from one face to the next for clues of what was happening. She looked at Duke Yuddha and Duchess Juno to see if they gave any sign of recognition, yet none acknowledged her presence as they gazed into the middle distance as if there was some rare personage seated several rows behind her.

"Lady Eliza, you may read the testimony," commanded the voice.

Eliza stood and reached into the folds of her maroon gown for a scroll. She carefully unfastened it and methodically unrolled the document. "Ms. Pyrrha Tock has been found to be in possession of part of a dead, endangered species. The paw of a precious mountain tiger was discovered in Ms. Pyrrha Tock's Jing Juice cart. This talisman is forbidden under the Duke's Law. Possession of old religious artifacts is unlawful. Possession of an endangered animal is illegal."

"Are you serious?" murmured Pyrrha, rising in protest.

"Order!" demanded the disembodied voice.

Captain Mahoney was quick to her side, settling her back into her chair with two firm hands on her shoulders. In a whisper she said, "Quiet."

Pyrrha glanced from face to face to find any glimmer of explanation. The Archduchess Zaynah was solely focused on keeping her husband sitting formally upright in his chair while Archduke Zachariah's eyes wandered and hands trembled persistently. She studied Duke Yuddha. His strong shoulders were set resolutely; his hands were ceremoniously clasped; and his face was blank as a mask. Every time she tried to catch his eye, he looked in another direction, skirting the room with his gaze. The Duchess Juno beamed like a flower in bloom—she smiled down beneficently, like a portrait hanging in a gallery, while Lord Yuri and Lady Eliza looked like favored puppies heeling at their master's feet, waiting to carry out any command.

"Lady Eliza, you may continue reading the testimony," prompted the voice.

Eliza composed herself and began again. "After an inspection of Ms. Pyrrha Tock's residence, the tiger paw was found along with a complete tiger pelt, several teeth and claws, as well as other animal hides."

This time Pyrrha sat calmly with Captain Mahoney standing ready to force her down.

The voice on high spoke. "The evidence is overwhelmingly against Ms. Pyrrha Tock. There is no verbal testimony that can explain away the facts of these items in her possession. These are in direct disobedience to the Old Religions Act and the Endangered Species Act."

Pyrrha cleared her throat to answer, but now Sergeant Kyhn was at her side as well, whispering in her ear, "You have no right to speak in these chambers."

The room was silent as everyone seemed to be holding their breath waiting for the next step in the proceedings. Pyrrha slowly exhaled deliberately pushing out all of her frustrations; then, she tried to inhale hope and goodness to settle her mind, but anger poured out instead.

Why? Pyrrha's mind screamed. *Why is this happening to me?*

I don't know. Yuht's voice answered in her head.

She looked at Duke Yuddha. His eyes sparked with recognition of their connection.

How can't you know? Pyrrha concentrated on communicating. *But...Juno called the trial.*

It is your court. She took deep breaths to control her shaking frame.

"Lord Yuri, the verdict please!" requested the evanescent voice.

Lord Yuri stood and picked up a scroll that had been hidden beside him in his chair. With flair, he held the top of the scroll and let the page of text roll down ceremoniously. "Ms. Pyrrha Tock is convicted of the murder of an endangered animal and antiquated witchcraft. The sentence for these two crimes..."

The room hummed with expectation.

What? Pyrrha's mind raced. *Grand Tock was sent to kill the tiger.*

Is that true? Yuht asked.

Ask Duke Zachariah! He made the court order.

Duke Yuddha and Pyrrha looked at the frail man on the throne. They both averted their gaze when Archduchess Zaynah felt the heat of their inquiry.

"Ahem!" Lord Yuri cleared his throat, sensing he had lost his audience. "The sentence for violating the Duke's Laws—is death."

"Ahhhhhhh," gasped Archduchess Zaynah, seemingly unprepared for this outcome.

"Ahm!" coughed Duke Yuddha.

Pyrrha slumped low in her chair as all energy drained from her toes into the silk carpets, down through the marble floors, and into the earth below the palace foundation.

"Take the prisoner away," ordered the voice from on high.

Without ado, Sergeant Kyhn and Captain Mahoney each took one side of Pyrrha and lifted her from under her armpits and dragged her out of the trial room, through the long passageways, down the stairwells, and back to the dungeon cell.

Pyrrha did not move of her own accord. She let them pull her along as she stumbled under the weight of the sentence. Nothing. She thought nothing. She felt nothing. She was numb.

122

JUSTICE WITHHELD

HOW MANY HOURS HAD PYRRHA LAIN ON THE COT BEHIND BARS IN silent shock? The sun was close to setting, but the dim lightbulb hanging from the stone ceiling kept the room from complete darkness. Staring at the rock wall, tracing the joint lines with her eyes, she tried to piece together what had happened to get her imprisoned and on death row.

She thought back to the adventures with Grand Tock in the Duke's View as a child. Those memories were fraught with contradictions—there was her loving grandfather teaching her the ways of the wild world, yet there was also the person Grand Tock, with his own human foibles. For years she had kept the events of the tiger attack hidden in a black box in her heart, because she blamed herself.

Well, it was her fault because, as a curious and inquisitive child, she had disobeyed Grand Tock's instructions and snuck into his bag to accompany him on a secret errand for Duke Zachariah. That journey, filled with unexpected complications, had placed her in the face of death, roaring at her as a tiger. Her instinctive action, without time for thought, lead to a decade of regrets. Taking the life of a majestic creature was one mistake she wished to avoid again, so she had sworn to protect animals by becoming a vegetarian and refusing to eat their meat.

Her mind jumped to the day at the fair, which had been a flurry of excitement—she was shocked to learn that the soldier Yuht was, in fact, Marquess Yuddha, the soon-to-be new ruler of Copperton, and that he was married to Juno, the intimidatingly glamorous Marchioness. The day of the fair had been such a celebration as Pyrrha had sold several months worth of jing juice in a few hours, and she had been able to purchase such rare delicacies as had not been seen in many years. Yet, this had led to her unguarded interactions with Old Snark. She had never trusted him. The fair air had made her giddy to the point of distraction. When he had asked to shake hands with the tiger paw, she had not thought better of the peculiar request, even though later she questioned how he even knew of its existence.

But still, how had killing Neema the Tiger become her crime? This had been the order given to Grand Tock by Duke Zachariah. This tiger had been on the prowl for decades looking for Grand Tock and Jupiter the Giant to avenge the death of his partner. When he could find no trace of his original tormenters, he began to attack villagers who had set up new homesteads in the Duke's View—the wilds north of the traditional lands of Copperton. When Duke Zachariah heard these reports, he immediately sent for Grand Tock to finish the project he had started and kill the rogue animal who had acquired a taste for human blood.

Dinner came. She did not touch it, nor did she even roll over to see who had brought it to her cell; instead, she studied the rough marble wall and imagined animal faces in the pockmarks and landscapes in the contours of the rock. She thought about meeting Yuht on Tock's Land—what an electrifying connection. When he stared into her eyes, they communicated without sound and syllables—in the past, she had only done this with her family in times of great need. At the ball, she danced with Yuht, floating on sheer ecstasy. Her cheeks burned and her eyes filled with tears. She had been swept up in Yuht's embrace and attracted by his magnetism. She had been happy to see him, and he had said as much to her.

Then, there was her dream of Great-Grandmother Ethel reading her fortune, and Death deferred by meeting Yuht at the wrong time. What did this mean now that the Duke's Court had just announced her death sentence?

Filled with regret about past occurrences which were mirages of images, she questioned everything and left no memory unturned. Fate and destiny, chance and luck. Was her recklessness to be the death of her? Overcome by sadness and without hope for justice, she prayed.

"Is there any Remover of difficulties save God? Say: Praised be God! He is God! All are His servants, and all abide by His bidding!"[1]

Her prayer became a mantra. She repeated the words and phrases over and over until the syllables and sounds echoed through the foundation of the palace dungeon. She recited the prayer until her mind relaxed and her body slackened. Within ninety-five repetitions, she fell into an uneasy sleep.

She dreamed her great-grandmother's dream. It was a dream that had become a legend, as it was often recited around the evening fire. Grand Tock as a young boy was balanced on a round boulder; he ran atop the rock as it rolled across the land over the mountains and through the valleys to the land of the Giants. Pyrrha followed after, tracking the smooth path the stone had cleared. After a long march that flew by in the dream, she was at the edge of a deep pit in the ground. Looking in, she saw Grand Tock in old age happily sitting with a large calico house cat whose head rested upon his lap as he lovingly stroked its fur and told it tales of adventure. It changed. Grand Tock was now with the tiger. They both looked up and smiled at Pyrrha. The dream ended. She woke up.

It was a great comfort to awaken with the face of a loved one in her head, even with the tiger-cat haunting her dreams, but her reality had not changed. She was still imprisoned in a dark cell under the Copperton palace. She was still sentenced to death by Duke Yuddha's Court.

Time passed in a quick, quick, slow rhythm. She distracted herself by tracing lines on the rock wall. Sometime later, Sergeant Kyhn arrived with a fresh tray of food.

"Dear girl," she reprimanded. "Don't be stupid and starve yourself to death. The appointed hour will come soon enough."

She collected Pyrrha's untouched dinner and set a fresh breakfast tray on the table—a warm croissant, a bowl of fruit, and a cup of sweet milk tea.

"There is this, too!" Sergeant Kyhn waved a sealed scroll with the emblem of the Duke and placed it on the table next to the tray of food. Then, she exited the dungeon.

The smells of nourishment enticed Pyrrha to eat, but the sight of the official court announcement made the food edible only in small bites. The royal edict lay on the table untouched for some time. Somehow, she knew that what it contained would alter the course of her life and death, so she did not want to hasten the discovery of her future.

She procrastinated. She picked at her food, separating the croissant layers and peeling off any skin on the fruit. She washed her face in the sink, carefully massaging her cheeks and forehead with soap. She combed her hair, disentangling her braids and smoothed each strand from the roots to the tips. Then, she re-braided it again. She straightened the blankets on the cot and tidied the cell.

Finally, when there was nothing left to do, she mustered the courage to unroll the scroll and read its contents.

. . .

The Duke's Court
  Execution Warrant

Date: On the Ninth Day of the Eighth Month
  Year: In the First Year of the Reign of Duke Yuddha of Copperton
  Offender: Ms. Pyrrha Tock
  Crime: Guilty of Murder of an Endangered Animal & Worship of Old Religious Talismans
  Sentence: Death by Execution and Forfeiture of Dead Animal Parts
  Commuted: By the order of Duke Yuddha, Ms. Pyrrha Tock's sentence of execution is commuted to completion of three labors for the honor of Copperton.

The Duke's Court, under the auspices of Duke Yuddha, hereby charges Ms. Pyrrha Tock with the murder of a precious, endangered animal held sacred for its rarity. The penalty for this crime against the environment is death. As a token of the Duke's grace, an alternative enforcement of the death penalty has been granted. As humans are more sacred than animals, the execution of a human being is deemed just as unnecessary as the taking of a sacred animal's life.

To atone for her first crime, the wanton murder of a beloved tiger, Ms. Pyrrha Tock must face her death three times. Thus, Ms. Pyrrha Tock will be sent on three missions to prove her loyalty to the community and pledge her humility before its laws. If all three labors are successfully completed, Ms. Pyrrha Tock wins her right to life and freedom, but if she fails, she proves her guilt, and she is deemed, rightfully, to have been sentenced to execution.

To recompense for her second crime, the worship of dead animal parts and their use as religious talismans, the remains of the endan-

gered species killed unnecessarily will be confiscated by the Duke's Court Authorities for proper study and archiving.

Ms. Pyrrha Tock's first labor is to free Copperton's reservoir of the golden dragon which now pollutes the community's waters and poisons its inhabitants.

Ms. Pyrrha Tock will be released after this day of judgement to fulfill her first mission within one week. Upon completion, the Duke's Court will assign her second labor. The third of three assignments will be appointed at the successful fulfillment of the first two.

Upon penalty of punishment, the Tock family is responsible for Ms. Pyrrha Tock and the completion of her labors. Her actions are the family's actions; thus, another Tock member will be called upon to atone for her transgressions if she fails to complete all three labors successfully. In addition, if she is not successful, the property now called Tock's Land will be returned to the original owner—the Duke, the Royal Highness of Copperton.

By order of Duke Yuddha,
    Duke Yuddha
    High Judge of the Duke's Court
    Supreme Ruler of Copperton

May war be contained and peace prevail under the reign of Duke Yuddha of Copperton.

Pyrrha held the scroll in her shaking hands as tears streamed down her face. She read and reread the contents of her death sentence; she felt her life slipping from her control. Should she be thankful that she would not be hung in the public square nor poisoned with hemlock? Instead, she would face a millennium-old, fire-breathing monster who would not only take the breath from her lungs but the land from her family—land that had been given in thanks for Grand Tock's great legacy. Within her grandfather's lifetime, her actions would eclipse all he had done to rise out of poverty. The family would once again struggle as subsistence farmers. The dream of a proud family legacy would be snatched away like a piece of paper blown away in a storm.

THE BAG OF HOLDING

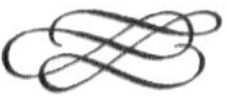

PYRRHA WAS CARRIED OUT OF THE DUKE'S PRISON UNDER THE cloak of darkness and a strong dose of sleeping drugs. She awoke in the morning in her bed in the little cottage on Tock's Land. Everything she had taken with her had been returned—passport, ID card, darts, silk pajamas and two pairs of woolen socks. It could have just been a nightmare. Except, Woods was sitting in her kitchen when she came out to make a cup of tea.

"Oh! Hiya!" Pyrrha mumbled.

"Where did you go?" Woods demanded. "Why did you just go off with those people in an unmarked car in the middle of the night?"

Pyrrha looked at him with tired eyes and a foggy head trying to make sense of it all. She puttered around the kitchen, setting the kettle boiling and looking through the cupboard and fridge for something comforting to nibble on.

When it became apparent that she was not yet in the mood to speak openly, Woods pushed forward with his one-sided conversation. "If you aren't going to tell me what you got up to, I'll, at least, tell you what I did while you were gone."

Pyrrha brought two mugs to the table—the delicate pottery

which had been spun on an artisan wheel and glazed with scenes of dancing waves; they were used only for ceremonies as they were so easy to break. She placed tea in each cup—not the normal teabags for everyday use but the delicate, aromatic leaves sent from her cousin on the other side of the mountains. This tea setting was used only for a special occasion like births, deaths, or weddings.

Woods took the selection of china and tea as a warning and changed his tone. "Auntie Farz went to see your mother yesterday at first light. She found her in the jing shed training her colony of ants to march in order as she tasted her latest jing concoctions."

Pyrrha smiled at the picture of her mother becoming the ant entertainer from old folklore. Her eclectic hobbies were never long-lasting, so everyone accepted them with humor. Usually, her experiments were academic in nature—What is the grain of truth in the old wives' tale or superstition? The fascination of the season was if ants could really be trained to follow instructions. Mama Jojo was having mixed success.

Woods continued, "Auntie told her about the people coming in the middle of the night, so they rushed home. When we met in the garden, Mama Jojo took my hands and looked me straight in the eyes and said, 'Don't you worry about Rrha! I had a dream last night that she was going to fight a dragon and that she would need you to carry a torch to light her way.' She got all misty eyed and emotional before Uncle led her back to a seat in the garden."

Pyrrha coughed out a laugh—trying not to make light of things. But, this was her mother. The world would fall apart, and she would have a dream that everything would be alright. There would be some mystical improbability, yet inevitably it would all come true, making perfect sense out of gibberish.

Woods kept talking, "I went and saw your father in the library too. He wanted to tell me all about Herculean mythology and how it was a metaphor for stages of spiritual enlightenment."

Pyrrha looked into the cup of dark liquid, still too hot to drink. She followed the wisps of steam floating heavenward. She put her head down on the table, closed her eyes and let silent, hot tears fall into her sleeves.

Woods was speechless, as tears always befuddled him. He sat next to her quietly in consolation, trying to show some respect for her sadness.

After a moment, he added one more thing to his report. "Your father did shout after me as I was leaving the library stacks 'tell her to pack wisely.'"

Pyrrha looked up and dried her eyes with a napkin on the table.

"What does wise packing even mean?" Woods questioned.

She glanced out the window and studied her tea before smiling at Woods. "Thank you!"

Then, she sipped her tea and nibbled on some biscuits and fruit while looking down at the table. Woods sat with her in silence. Pyrrha waited for her mind to stop spinning. She waited for the tea to awaken her senses. She waited for the food to settle her stomach.

"We are going on a journey, Woods," she stated matter of factly. "Today, pack a backpack, eat your fill of Auntie Farz's home-cooked food, and meet me at the jing patch after lunch. Pack only what is natural to carry for a day's outing so as not to look suspicious. Wear shoes that can walk a long way. Bring a bike. Don't tell Auntie and Uncle any more than they need to know."

"Do I get any more details than that! Why should I go with you?"

Pyrrha's eyes twinkled with her reply, "But my parents' prophesies! You haven't figured them out yet?"

Woods squinted and scrunched up his face at the thought of

Mama Jojo's gibberish and Dr. Rahd's riddles. "Ahhhh, does it always have to be like this?"

"Like what?" Pyrrha feigned innocence.

"Why do you think I will just go with you?"

"It is fated in the prophecies!"

"What?" Woods questioned this nonsense.

"Because, I need your help." Pyrrha said. Honestly, she did need his assistance.

"Don't I get more information before we leave?"

Pyrrha pushed Woods up and out the kitchen door.

"I'm sorry, but I just can't explain it right now. I'll meet you at one in the jing patch." Then, she went to prepare.

In her bedroom, she pulled out Grand Tock's old leather bag and dumped everything out on the bed to sort through it. This was the special pouch gifted by Jupiter the Giant that would always carry everything needed yet never weigh more than she could handle. There were more things in there than she had remembered from her last hike in the foothills beyond town. She had gone with some of her classmates in the village, but she had felt like she was hiking alone for how cliquish they were. They had whispered the whole way without including her, and they had hushed their gossiping when she was within earshot. That was the last time she had tried hanging out with other people—well, besides Woods.

On her bed lay all the contents from the bag of holding—

a comb and mirror set

several hair ties and barrettes

a light jacket

a few pairs of socks

an empty waterskin

her journal

a pencil case filled with colorful pencils

keys

a flint

a bar of soap in a pouch

Grand Tock's rope webbing

a waterproof tarp

a first aid kit with bandages

a replica of Uncle Marz's map

a warm and colorful scarf

She turned the bag inside out to shake out the messy bits found at the bottom—the pieces of lint, broken pencils, and crumbs from long-ago-eaten sachets of biscuits. Then, she repacked it, leaving out the keys and adding her throwing darts. She went to the kitchen to add fresh food and water. After more thought, she dropped in her passport and ID card as well as a sleeping bag, a small knife, a pouch of feminine items, and a towel. That should be enough to eat, drink, stay warm, be safe, and feel comfortable.

Once her bag was packed with supplies a plenty, Pyrrha got herself ready. She showered, washed her hair and braided it tightly around her head in the old style. She dressed in her softest and plainest clothes that would keep her cool in the day, by protecting her skin from the sun, yet keep her warm at night, by insulating her body from the wind. She picked out her favorite items to cheer her up—from rainbows on her socks to butterflies on her hair clips. All of this in an attempt to distract herself from thinking about her impossible challenge to scale Mount Omega in order to face the water dragon in the reservoir and avoid an imminent death. But still, her mind wandered.

She thought about Duke Yuddha, the Duchess Juno, and the trial. Pyrrha had prided herself on reading people and understanding her dreams, so the last few weeks confused her. It was clear that she had a magnetism with Yuht when they first met in the forest and again at the fair and the ball. They were drawn together when nearby—always standing a bit too close for respectable propriety. How confusing! He looked at her the way boys in school had ogled her when they had a crush. He should not have spent so much time admiring the curls around her face, her blinking eyes, and even how her dress hugged her form. Unlike the schoolboys, who had annoyed and angered her, his attention was confusing. She longed to see him again, yet she was uncomfortably awkward. He was married to the beautiful Duchess Juno, and they had two precious children together. Did he not love them? Never had an older, married man looked at her that way; it unsettled her. Excitement or terror? Every nerve was alivened.

Then, there was the conundrum with the dream—her lifetime flashing by as a motion picture before her death. Things had only just started; she was only fifteen; it was too early to die a natural death. Then, the last card in the deck was shown—meeting Yuht. Why was it so important for her to meet Yuht? How had it changed her fate? It could not be the usual love story with wooing, marriage, children, and blissful joy until their sunset years. They were not going to live some happily-ever-after fairytale.

This brought Pyrrha to the darkest memory and freshest wound. Yuht—or Duke Yuddha's Court—was sending her on a mission to battle a dragon living in the reservoir deep in the mountains far, far away. Death seemed inevitable.

These questions troubled her mind. She thought of Grand Tock's words—*What do I know? What is true?*

As Pyrrha's mind chewed on her predicament, she finished packing, wrote a note for her parents, and left for the jing patch. She took the way through the trees and stayed off the road. She ducked behind bushes and boulders when others were heard along the way. She arrived at the field and looked for Mama Jojo in the hut, but of course she was already gone, so she sat outside in the shade waiting for Woods. Her eyes settled on the bicycle that she was planning to ride leaning against the shack. There was a bushel of freshly hauled jing neatly packed in a burlap sack resting on the seat like a scarecrow. Mama Jojo had clearly set it on the bike in her line of sight for a reason. Without hesitation, she wrestled the bundle of jing into her bag of holding, even though she had no clue what her mother expected her to use it for.

The afternoon sun was warm as she laid on the bench of the picnic table, so she took off her jacket while she waited. She closed her eyes and looked at the apricot light coming through her eyelids. She traced the intended path, like veins in her skin, along a map in her mind.

"Hiya!" called Woods.

"You're early," replied Pyrrha.

"Well, I got out of the house before Auntie Farz could ask me any more questions."

"Didn't Uncle Marz pester you?"

"Nah! He knows too much. He knows what he doesn't want to know."

"Ha! True."

"So, where are we going camping?"

"The reservoir."

"Eh!" Woods coughed. "That's crazy."

"Yes—" Pyrrha replied.

"Let's not overthink this."

Pyrrha nodded. This was real trust. Woods would come on this journey, because he loved his cousin as much as he loved being a Tock. He would try to protect her as best he could—no matter the danger.

"Ready?" they asked in unison.

They looked up at the mountains. The distant hills and peaks looked like Gaea laying down. Somewhere in the rock formations was a once beautiful mountain lake, waterfall, and stream that used to flow down the hillside to the town. It was many years now since the reservoir had been dammed, the waterfall blocked, and the stream bed dry. Then, when the war started, a rumor had been circulated that enemy weapons had polluted the lake. However, secondary gossip spread in whispers. People said a man-eating-monster now lived in the mountains and nested in the valley behind the reservoir. Uncle Marz had hinted that Lake Omega was polluted with the sweat and blood of a dragon so fierce no one had survived to tell her tales.

Until a few days ago, Pyrrha had dismissed all of the rumors and gossip as hearsay. There were secrets, and then there were national secrets. She thought it ludicrous to state such fantastical truth, to hide such important information by talking of it openly. But then again, that might be the wisest thing to do. Pyrrha looked at the map with her back to the mountains, as just the sight of their curves and peaks might make her lose her resolve and contemplate running off to Jupiter's cave or sailing a homemade boat across the Ocean of Wisdom.

"We're going to ride our bikes as far as the abandoned logging road takes us today. Tomorrow, we'll walk to the Tree Fort," Pyrrha declared, as she rolled up her map and stuck it in her bag.

"It's about seven hours from sunset." Woods commented looking at the orange ball in the sky while counting the number of fists to the horizon.

"Let's go!" they whispered in unison as they picked up their packs, slung them over their shoulders, and headed with their bikes toward the overgrown trail at the corner of the jing patch.

Pyrrha's anxiety propelled her down the well-known ribbon of dirt. She moved like she was being chased by a swarm of angry gnats. She pedaled up the hills through the birch and maple until the incline finally gave her pause. Woods' long legs stretched to keep pace, so whenever Pyrrha cast a glance over her shoulder, she seldom lost sight of him among the green trees. The momentum of the adventure and the run of the wheels moved them farther from town and past the furthest fields. After two hours of solid biking on the back road, they stopped along a dry stream bed to drink from their waterskins and nibble on a few crackers.

"I was worried about you yesterday," Woods mustered, trying to start the conversation. "I was really worried after talking to your parents, because they didn't make any sense."

Pyrrha looked down at the ground and then at Woods and then at the ground again, not knowing what to tell him.

"Yesterday was yesterday. Today is today," she said simply.

"Don't tell me 'tomorrow will be tomorrow,' because I cannot deal with that ridiculous mantra right now," Woods interjected.

There was a few hours of daylight left, so Pyrrha put away her waterskin and snacks, dusted the crumbs off her lap, and stood up to ride again.

"Our adventure awaits!" Pyrrha nodded toward the road.

Woods followed her lead knowing the conversation was closed, for now. They must bike for as long as possible before cutting from the road and bushwhacking into the forest to find a hidden campsite for the night.

CAMPING WITHOUT STARLIGHT

THEY HID THEIR CAMPSITE IN THE SHADOW OF THE FOREST TREES. After sundown, the air was cool hinting at autumn weather yet to come. Pyrrha and Woods lit a small fire to warm themselves and keep the wild creatures at bay. This was not their first time camping alone together, but usually it was on Tock's Land, beyond the view of the houses but close enough to holler for help. Before the war, when they were still children, they had backpacked for weeks in the mountains with Grand Tock and Uncle Marz. However, after the escalating conflicts and Grand Tock being sent off on secret missions, they stayed much closer to home. It was just safer that way.

Pyrrha had pulled out dinner from the leather satchel that she had slung over her shoulder while she biked. Two meals of leftover curried rice with tofu and sides of pickled vegetables were packaged in silver roasting bundles. She placed the dinners on flat rocks among the coals in the fire to heat up, while she and Woods grabbed the tarp to construct a sleeping shelter.

They strung a rope up waist high between two trees and flung the green tarp over it to make a triangle tent with two open sides. On the forest floor, they found broken tree branches with bushy pine needles and bunches of brown leaves still attached to the twigs. These made shields over the openings. On one side, they stacked layers of branches to make a secure wall against the wilderness. On the other side, they made a door out of one cedar branch that had recently fallen in a storm. The fragrant needles made a covering which could be secured in place yet still brushed aside with relative ease. In the twilight, the shelter blended into the forest. Under the tarp awning, they rolled out their sleeping bags. It was a tight fit, but it would be safe enough for one night. They would be warm and dry. They would be out of sight from prowling animals.

When it was time to eat, they sat near the fire to eat their sizzling meals with chopsticks. They ate without reservation, as the bike ride had worked up their appetite.

Woods picked at his hot bundle of food and reopened their morning conversation. "So…we made better progress than I expected today."

"What do you think? Twenty miles?" Pyrrha asked.

"Yup, easily, on the bikes. And then, we hiked for another hour or more."

"Wow! We came farther than I expected," Pyrrha reflected.

"It's been years since we came out here to camp," commented Woods.

"Remember how Grand Tock would tell us stories?"

"Yeah! Uncle Marz is good, but he doesn't do the voices like Grand Tock."

"Naw, Uncle Marz doesn't have the flair for drama that runs in the Tock line," Pyrrha observed.

"Ha—well, someone had to be organized on the expeditions," Woods retorted.

"I'm glad Grand Tock adopted Uncle Marz as a godson. Imagine me growing up with just Mama Jojo and Dr. Rahd around?" Pyrrha paused and thought about that possibility. "I would have gone crazy by now, if I had even survived."

"I've thought that myself....Grand Tock knows people. He can read people....He wanted the best for you, so he was happy Auntie Farz would keep you fed and Uncle Marz would keep you safe—long enough to grow up, anyway."

"Am I grown up yet?" Pyrrha wondered aloud.

Woods had no answer for that question, so he looked at the fire. Pyrrha played with a long stick. Wherever she poked, a little flame would shoot up from the logs. If she rolled a log over, the fire would swirl up both sides reaching for the night sky, temporarily pushing back the shadows all around them. If she fanned the fire with a piece of bark, the coals would glow red hot and then happily envelop the uncharred bits of firewood.

The forest noises crescendoed as the daylight disappeared. The daytime animals settled, while the nocturnal species stirred. The crickets chirped far off, yet mosquitos buzzed nearby. Leaves rustled. Twigs snapped. The fire crackled. The wilderness was anything but peaceful and serene. Things unknown lingered out of sight just beyond the shadows of the night. Pyrrha and Woods sat close together. It was the farthest afield they had ever traveled without Grand Tock or Uncle Marz to wrap them in a cocoon of confidence. To keep the nervousness from building up, they continued their fireside conversation.

"So...do I get any more details about this little expedition before we head for the fort tomorrow?" Woods questioned.

"Hmmm..." Pyrrha started cautiously. "I thought about that as we rode today....I thought about mom's dream and dad's stories...."

"Me too! Any idea what they mean?"

Pyrrha did not respond in words. She just rummaged through her leather satchel that seemed too full of random objects to be light enough to be carried.

"Well…" Woods prompted.

"It's here…somewhere," Pyrrha motioned to the open bag.

"What?"

"This!"

Woods received the scroll humorously like a precious gift, a sacred offering—both hands outstretched before him, his head bowed low, and his eyes averted to honor the moment. The fine silk document was tied up with a golden ribbon. Woods jovial demeanor changed when he felt the heft of the scroll; its weight ensured that the contents were as serious as one's life.

"I'm going to share with you what happened—simply—". Pyrrha choked on her words for the fear of death was in the back of her throat. "I have a death sentence…"

"You can't…can you?"

"I don't know what will happen," Pyrrha stated plainly. "Just read it!"

Woods' head leaned close to the fire as he tried to angle the document just so to catch the light but not the shadows. With the light at his side, he moved his head and hands awkwardly to avoid dark spots obscuring the words. He took a long time to read, reread, and examine once more all of the markings on the scroll. There was the careful calligraphy written in ink so black it smelled of grief. There were the stamps and seals pressed upon the paper both embossing the lettering and staining them blood red. There was the scroll itself that exuded the formality of a royal decree.

"So… it says here… that you illegally killed the tiger…" Woods squeaked. "Is that true?"

"Maybe…I don't know…"

"Uh…but what about Grand Tock's order from Duke Zachariah?"

"I don't know… it was his task not mine…"

"Is that fair?"

Pyrrha didn't answer.

"Is there part of the story I don't know?" Woods pressed.

"Probably, but…"

"Uh…hmmm—" Woods acquiesced to the incomplete answer and moved on because there were so many other important questions. "So…the rumors about the dragon in the reservoir are true?"

"Hahaha…hehehe…hahaha…hehe…" Pyrrha cried out with a sidesplitting laugh. The stress of the kidnapping, imprisonment, trial, and journey rolled out of her like a croaking toad. Her laugh turned into hiccups, which turned into sighs.

Woods waited for the emotions to subside before he asked a follow-up question. "So…how are we supposed to kill the dragon?"

Pyrrha looked at him matter of factly, "We won't! You know I'm a vegetarian."

"You know eating meat and killing animals are not the same?"

"I already killed one majestic animal. I will not kill another!"

"Then, you will be executed, and another Tock will be sent in your stead."

"Exactly! I'm going to run away to Jupiter's cave," Pyrrha slurred sarcastically. "Then, I'll trek to the Ocean of Wisdom, make a boat, and sail to the lands beyond."

"Really?" Woods was skeptical of her sarcasm as the plan sounded plausible and, though dangerous, much safer than confronting the dragon in the reservoir.

"No! But I did consider running away—seriously."

"So…if we aren't running, what is the plan?"

"I don't want to kill the dragon," Pyrrha sighed. "I'm not sure how, but I want to get the beast to leave—to fly off—and never return."

"Great idea!" Woods exclaimed. "How do we do that?"

"I don't know."

"Oh."

Pyrrha and Woods focused on the flickering flames and thought about the flickering spirit of life. Here one moment and gone the next. Like the blink of an eye, a lifetime passes so quickly. That was the joy of mortality—each moment was precious as each human had only a limited number of years, months, days, and hours. The limitlessness of immortality was cause for procrastination. Why do something today when there was all of eternity yet to unfold? Time created impetus to make choices which propelled life forward.

Choices. To kill or not to kill the dragon—that was one question. To run away or to not run away—that was another option. Woods looked at the scroll again; he memorized its contents before handing it back to Pyrrha to put in her bag.

"So…" Woods started again.

"Just ask the question—you don't need to start with soooooooooo every time."

"Okay—so, I thought Yuht liked you!"

Pyrrha blushed. "You think he likes me?"

"That was as clear as the summer sun that day in the forest."

"Really?"

"Yup! He looks at you like you are the prettiest princess in the whole palace."

Pyrrha tried, without success, to suppress a smile. She gulped, "Uuuhmm…how can he like me when he is married?"

Woods squawked, "Oh Pyrrha! Are you so naïve?"

"Please don't!" she reprimanded. "Just cuz you're two-and-a-half years older than me doesn't mean you have the whole world figured out."

"Think about it Pyrrha—he's the Duke. He can do whatever he wants…at least he thinks he can do whatever he wants…he is the most powerful man in Copperton."

Pyrrha scrunched up her face like she was thinking through a trigonometry problem for the first time. She tried to make the ideas add up, but it seemed so much more complicated than it needed to be. Marriage was supposed to be between two dedicated souls who agreed to love each other for all eternity. Without that kind of commitment, it was another kind of relationship, not a true marriage—maybe a partnership, a friendship, or a business.

Woods continued, "I just don't get why he is sending you on this crazy mission." He paused mid-thought. "Unless…"

"Unless, what?" Pyrrha asked a little too eagerly.

"Juno doesn't like you," Woods mused.

"Well…yes…maybe…I think that is true…but…I don't know."

"Clear as the midnight moon!"

"Oh!…Well…That's unfortunate…I had hoped I had misread her," Pyrrha replied.

"Anyways, that is then and this is now. Reasoning out a motive won't help," Woods dropped that topic and picked up his previous train of questioning. "What do you think the dragon looks like?"

"It is hard to say if the rumors are true," Pyrrha mused. "They say he is a golden dragon, but that his skin is sometimes green and blue."

"I heard his wings are the size of the palace and he breathes fire bombs," added Woods.

"In my dreams—"

"Pyrrha! You are always having dreams—"

"Yeah, and they are often right!"

Woods chuckled at this truth. "Go on, tell me…"

"Recently…I often dream of dragons…One dragon changes shapes, sizes, colors, and even personalities."

"Maybe because you cannot picture what you don't know."

"Maybe…" Pyrrha mused. "Or maybe…golden dragons are special. Maybe golden dragons are like chameleons or octopuses constantly changing to meet the demands of the time."

"That's a terrifying idea!" Woods said. "That would mean that we have no idea what to expect."

"You're right. Just like our plans for tomorrow. Who knows what will happen on our hike to the Tree Fort?"

"We'll get tired. It's about fifteen miles from here. And uphill," Woods added.

"It'll be a hike! But, hopefully, we can spend the night there," Pyrrha said.

"Are you planning to dig up the rations we stored there during our school field trips?" Woods inquired.

"Yup! I packed enough biscuits to get us through, but if we raid the storage shed there, we will eat better on the climb up the mountain."

"I think there is climbing gear there too," Woods added helpfully.

"And, I'm hoping to find detailed maps of the best climbing routes," Pyrrha added.

"So…after a good night's sleep at the fort, we are climbing Mount Omega?"

"There is no other way up to the reservoir, is there?"

"How do you plan to scale those cliffs?"

"Carefully!"

"No, seriously!" Woods pushed.

"I don't know," Pyrrha sighed. "I can only hope the gear and maps are self-explanatory."

Woods sensed she had crossed over from tired to exhausted. There was no reason to push her to say more.

Woods acquiesced, "We have a big day ahead. Let's get some sleep."

"Can you rake the coals to put out the fire?" Pyrrha requested. "I'm going to string up our packs so that bears don't wreck our supplies."

"Sure," Woods agreed.

He took the long poking stick they had been using to tend

the fire and gingerly spread the coals around the pit. He moved the logs away from any hot embers and turned the charred undersides toward the sky so that the breeze would cool them down. With the thick bark fan, he scrapped up some dry, cool dirt and shoveled it over the hottest embers. He watched the dying smoke for a bit longer to make sure that nothing reignited unexpectedly.

While he was busy working, Pyrrha took out the webbing and wrapped a portion around their supplies, she swung the other end over a high, sturdy tree branch and lifted their bags twenty feet off the ground in the middle of a tree clearing. She took the remaining webbing and gently stretched it over their tarp tent to keep away any wandering animals.

Woods climbed into the tent and Pyrrha crawled in after. She moved the brush branch over the opening and secured the webbing in place. They slid into their separate sleeping bags and bunched up some extra clothing under their heads as pillows. Pyrrha's body willed her to sleep even as her emotions pestered her to stay awake. The bike ride and hike weighed heavy on her limbs, forcing the muscles to rest like rocks, while her thoughts about Yuht, the plans for mountain climbing, and meeting the dragon activated her mind with endless what-if situations.

Pyrrha listened to Woods regular breaths of sleep next to her. She focused on her own breathing to calm herself down. Sometimes the meditative rhythm of air going in and out of the lungs could short circuit the brain like gales of wind flicker the firelight. With a practiced long exhale, she could exhaust her lungs and trick her mind into turning off—just for a few hours of rest. She breathed in-and-out, in-and-out. She focused on the air as it flowed over the dimple in the top of her lip. Boredom from intense concentration lulled her body to finally sleep.

In the early hours of the morning when the need to get up and relieve oneself conflicts with the desire to stay under the warm blankets to get more sleep, Pyrrha awoke. There was movement outside their tent. The grunts and rustling confirmed that something big was prowling about outside of the thin walls of fabric and branches. Louder than the sounds was the foul, acidic smell of sour milk and rotten eggs that permeated their little shelter. Pyrrha elbowed Woods to make sure he was also awake.

"Is it a skunk?" Pyrrha whispered.

"I wish!" Woods replied. "It's a bear."

They both listened expectantly to the animal outside. He was nearby. Bears tread lightly on their large paws, so only an occasional snapping twig or snort could be heard.

"He's sniffing around the fire for some morsel of food, isn't he?" Pyrrha asked.

"Yup! But we cleaned up well," Woods agreed. "And you strung up the packs, eh?"

"They're high in the trees," Pyrrha confirmed.

Their ears were alert as they were effectively blind beneath the tarp and behind the cedar door.

"Twang!" the tent shook. The whole structure wobbled. "Crash!" a few sticks leaning against the tarp fell to the ground.

"That was the rope!" Pyrrha worried.

"The bear walked under the line and snagged it with his back," Woods guessed.

The bear odor was overpowering, like a pile of rotting dead animals with a whiff of pine needles. Faint morning light came through the open porthole created by the fallen branches. Woods looked out to see if he could spot the bear in the campsite. He looked around but could not see movement through that tiny corner view.

"I'm worried he'll storm the tent," Woods stated calmly, despite the inherent danger.

"We're protected!" Pyrrha smiled.

"Huh! With a prayer?!" Woods scoffed.

Before she could reply, the tarp moved in like the bear was headbutting the lean-to.

"Uh-aw-hu" the bear grunted.

Pyrrha and Woods were still as logs lying on the forest floor. They listened expectantly. The bear was pawing at the tarp but something else was getting in the way. They heard the swoosh of an arm batting at the air. Then, the bear swat the tent pushing it in at a precarious angle. It was only a matter of time before the whole structure came crashing down.

"Uh-aw-hu" the bear groaned again. It seemed that each time it touched the tent, it became annoyed by something on the tarp surface. Sufficiently irritated, the bear wanted nothing more to do with the campsite. He made off by circling the tent once more and grazing the rope with his backbone before strutting off in view of the porthole.

"He's leaving," Woods sighed with great relief.

"Are you sure?" Pyrrha asked wearily.

"See!" Woods pointed to the tail of the bear waddling away.

"Oh—thank God!" Pyrrha prayed.

Woods looked bemused and inquired, "Did you really say a prayer for protection over our tent?"

"Well, those are stronger than you think!" Pyrrha countered.

"Uh, but that bear was so close to tearing this tarp down."

Pyrrha smiled, "Can you keep a secret?"

"I guess."

"I put Grand Tock's webbing over our tent last night."

"That gauze helped us?" Woods sighed. "A prayer might have been better."

"Or both!" Pyrrha countered.

Woods knew it was no use arguing, so he did not respond. He did not know whether webbing or worship might have saved their lives; he was just grateful he was alive. He looked out the porthole for movement.

"I think the coast is clear," Woods said.

"Are you sure?" Pyrrha asked.

"We can take down camp."

"The sun is coming up."

They crawled out of the shelter and looked around. The bear was gone, but his tracks marked the ground. They examined the outside of the tarp to see what damage had been done.

"That webbing of yours annoyed him!" Woods confirmed.

He pointed to the area where the bear had been headbutting and pawing at the tent. There were porcupine quills—well that is what they looked like, but up close they were the webbing crystalized into five-inch-long spears that clearly had jabbed the bear and discouraged him from continuing to charge their shelter.

"Well!" Pyrrha smiled. "Grand Tock always said—'You only know the worth of things when they are tested.'"

Pyrrha and Woods wordlessly took down camp. They checked that the coals were cold and covered the fire pit with another layer of dirt. They deconstructed the temporary tarp tent and scattered the branches so as not to draw attention to their campsite. As they worked, they listened to the melody of woodpeckers and bluejays hammering and yammering among the trees.

Before they were ready to set off for the day's hike, they took a moment to drink and eat. The freedom of the wilderness was both liberating and inconvenient—that was generally how freedom felt, the rewards and consequences were two sides of the same coin.

A LONG WALK

IT WAS A COOL MORNING UNDER THE SHADE OF THE BIRCH AND maple trees. The path was overgrown from five years of disuse, but it was still well enough marked from all the years of scouts trekking to and from the mountains to town. Whenever Woods and Pyrrha felt lost, they spotted a blue trail marker painted on a tree or tagged on a stump. In fields where only grass and shrubs filled the landscape, a stone carrion built by their younger selves would highlight the way.

When they were children, backpacking with Grand Tock or following school guides, these paths were busy with other hikers on day trips or week-long expeditions. However, after rumors spread of a dragon in the mountain reservoir, no one dared stray too far from town for fear of being eaten as a snack. The natural beauty of summer should have been peaceful for Pyrrha and Woods, but it felt eerily quiet without other people on the trails.

As they walked, they chatted quietly. After sharing the contents of the scroll with Woods, it was only a matter of time before the rest of the details of the arrest, imprisonment, and trial came tumbling out. However, Pyrrha kept some secrets like her dream of Death and her feelings about Yuht, as she could not understand how Yuht's fate was connected with hers. It was a tantalizing and terrifying situation that was too complicated to explain—especially now that she was on a death march to slay a monster.

Yet, it was hard to feel distraught as they trekked through the summer flowers and twittering birds. The last several days seemed like another life. Pyrrha was swept in the flow of a strong-moving fate where her choices seemed limited.

"What a sham of a trial!" Woods affirmed.

"It is what it is..." Pyrrha sighed.

"The injustice!"

"And here we are..."

"Aren't you mad about it?"

Pyrrha looked confused. "Of course, I'm mad! I'm furious! But what am I to do?"

"We could run away."

"Where can we go?"

"To Jupiter's Cave and then over the mountains to the Ocean of Wisdom and Taiga Island beyond," Woods replied.

"Yes, but..."

"But what?"

"Tock has worked a lifetime to make Tock's Land what it is today. Uncle Marz, Auntie Farz, Mama Jojo, and Dr. Rahd would be kicked out of our homes and made the laughing stock of Copperton—and there still would be a dragon polluting our country's reservoir."

"This is still unjust!" Woods retorted.

"I know, but ..." Pyrrha paused her steps. "I cannot see another way forward." She continued walking as if to say—this is the way we shall go.

As the morning rolled along, the smooth dirt paths became bumpier terrain. Rocks and roots jutted out of the ground as tripping hazards. Woods and Pyrrha spent as much time focusing on where their feet stepped as they spent admiring the landscape. Here and there, every few miles, there was a burnt tree stump or a backend circle of grass. It looked liked the remains of a forest fire, yet it was localized in one spot several feet in diameter. It was like a fireball had incinerated one targeted patch of land while leaving everything else undisturbed.

"Should we be worried about the dragon?" Woods asked when they past a particularly large ashen stump that was charred black from fire.

In the distance, Mount Omega rose up ominously; it was all cliffs, crags, and caves.

"We're still so far away," Pyrrha sighed. "I guess if we get burnt to a crisp out here, we don't have to climb that thing."

"Ha! If only we're so lucky…" Woods replied.

Pyrrha nodded for Woods to look at the path ahead. "The turkeylings don't seem much bothered."

A family of birds sauntered across their way. The five brown balls of feathers—two parents and three poults—pecked at insects where dirt path met meadow grass. They fluttered into hiding in the bushes as Pyrrha and Woods neared.

"So…can I ask you about tiger stuff?" Woods inquired.

"Naw!" Pyrrha brushed off the question.

"Then, can we discuss strategies for approaching the dragon?"

"I guess…"

"So the dragon is in the reservoir, the one where we played and swam and canoed."

"Seems weird…it's hard to imagine a monster there….It's hard to imagine the lake is polluted. I have so many happy memories there of fun summer adventures."

"The last time we were there was for the music festival. Do you remember that?" Woods reminisced.

"Yeah, I remember eating cotton candy. There were so many

carts selling food along the pier. We ran the entire length of the lake sampling foods."

"Uncle Marz and Auntie Farz were dancing atop the dam in the pavilion."

"There was a band on that flat-bed barge in the middle of the water playing all those great hits," Pyrrha smiled at the memory.

"We must have run several miles going up and down the pier and back and forth across the dam crest before we sat down to see the fireworks that night."

"I remember sitting atop the dam looking down the wall at the old, dried up waterfall and riverbed. It was so high...I thought it was a thousand feet, but I think it is likely only a few hundred."

"Well, unfortunately, there won't be a party when we go back! Do you have some ideas?"

"We have two clues," Pyrrha began.

"You mean Mama Jojo's dream and Dr. Rahd's mythology?" Woods questioned. "How is that useful?"

"I don't know! But she had a dream I was going to fight a dragon, which has come true!"

"But what does it mean that I am going to carry a torch?"

"I don't know yet."

"Does Mama Jojo mean a flashlight or a burning stick?"

Pyrrha laughed, as her parents' clues were cryptic. "I don't know, but another thing, Mama Jojo put out a sack of jing for me to pack." Pyrrha tapped her satchel as she walked and talked.

"Huh... How can you fit a sack of jing in that little bag?"

"Oh, you haven't figured that out yet?"

"What?!" Woods was exasperated.

"This is a very special bag," Pyrrha whispered. "It's Jupiter's bag of holding."

"Huh!"

"Look!" Pyrrha stopped walking and opened the flap. "It holds everything I need but only weighs as much as I can carry."

"How is that possible?"

"Physics."

"Seriously."

"I don't know. It's Giant magic."

"Is that even real?!"

"You have heard the stories…" remarked Pyrrha.

"Yeah, but I have never seen that bag before," Woods retorted.

"Oh!… I guess not…Grand Tock and I kept it hidden."

"What other stuff in the stories is real?"

"Uh…all of it—"

Woods sighed. "Yeah, I guess I'm learning that since I saw the webbing stuff make those weird spike things."

The path dipped down toward a creek, where water splashed over pebbles making enough noise to distract them from their conversation. The stream was shallow enough that it would not be difficult to cross, yet it was deep enough in the middle that they would get wet up to their waists while wading. They stopped for a lunch break on the banks. There was an outcrop of rocks shaded from the midday sun yet close enough to a pool to take off their shoes and dangle their feet into the water. Occasionally, a minnow would wander by and nibble on a toe.

Pyrrha pulled out a small lunch bag and handed Woods one of the two sandwiches that she had packed the day before. They were simple—cheese with vegetables and some special sauce for flavoring—but they were satisfying after the morning's exertion. She also fished out a bag of nuts and some bubbly drinks to round out the meal. As they finished eating, Woods squared his shoulders and turned toward Pyrrha with all seriousness.

"Listen!" Woods started. "I'm not going any further until you answer my questions."

"Really!?" Pyrrha teased.

"Really! This isn't some game, some afternoon hike."

"You don't think I know that?"

"I could die. You could die."

"Yes! I know!"

"So, before I agree to take one more step, I need to know the whole story."

"Well, I can't tell you everything, but…"

"That's a start."

"You know the story of Grand Tock going to the mountains with Jupiter the Giant?"

"Yeah, we all know that story."

"Well, remember the second tiger that got away."

"Of course! The one who cried."

"So for many years, that tiger wandered throughout the Duke's View looking for Grand Tock and Jupiter the Giant. He wanted to avenge the death of the tigress."

"It's an animal. Is it so calculating?" Woods inquired.

"It's a majestic animal that is smarter than we imagine." Pyrrha gazed at the hills far off, as if scouting the shadows for something there. "Of course, at first, there was too much land and too few people for anyone to realize that the tiger was deliberately stalking humans."

"That's horrible!"

"Well, after a few deaths and more fearful complaints, Archduke Zachariah asked Grand Tock to the palace for a special favor. He requested Grand Tock's services to hunt and dissuade the man-eating tiger from attacking any more innocent people."

"Dissuade? You mean kill, right?"

"Well, yeah! Grand Tock thought the same thing. How do you dissuade a tiger from killing people except by killing the tiger? So Grand Tock went off to find and kill the tiger."

Pyrrha looked into the stream. The sunlight played on the water droplets making tiny rainbows that appeared and disappeared like fairies dancing in sunbeams. That was how reality was—it seemed constant but when she focused on the details, things could change and transform unexpectedly.

"So, I went with Grand Tock to find the tiger."

"Wait!? I never understood this part of the story. Your parents just let you go?"

"No, not exactly. They have always been distracted, but they aren't crazy. That, was my idea. I climbed into Grand Tock's bag—"

"You mean this bag?" Woods asked pointing to the bag of holding laying on the rocks with the remainder of their lunch spilling out.

"Yes, this very bag. It is much bigger than you imagine inside....It made me my own room....but that is a story for another time."

Woods smiled. "You have secrets!"

"I tell you a lot, but not everything."

"Do I even know you?"

Pyrrha winced, "Do I know you?"

"Fair point!" Woods frowned.

"Anyway, Grand Tock took me along for the adventure." Pyrrha continued. "At first he didn't know I was with him, but when he found me playing hide-and-seek in the bag, he brought me along just as Jupiter had carried him years earlier. Of course, he sent word home to Mama Jojo and Dr. Rahd that I was safe under his watchful eye."

"So, wait! Stop. Did your parents know you were going tiger hunting?"

"Of course not!"

"Did Grand Tock tell them?"

"No way—"

"When you came back, you wouldn't speak to anyone."

"Yes....So, to make an already long story short. Basically, that story of Grand Tock and Jupiter, well...that is the same thing that happened to me."

"What! Grand Tock tied you to a tree as tiger bait?"

Pyrrha looked toward the stream. "No, he is crazy, but not

that crazy. I asked to be tied to the tree to know what it was like for him." A cloud passed overhead and cast a shadow on the water making it appear opaque.

"But in that story, Jupiter killed the tiger," Woods said. "Grand Tock must of tried to kill the tiger, shooting it with a bow and arrow, right?"

"Uh…but…Grand Tock has always had bad aim. In the end, I was face to face with the tiger and used the darts to stab his heart."

"As a six-year-old!" Woods finally asked the question he had never known the answer to and which pushed him to keep talking. "How can you forgive Grand Tock?"

"Uhhh!" Pyrrha exhaled. "Can we not talk about this anymore? I'm going swimming."

She was hot from the hike and moody from the memory, so she stripped off her outer layer of clothing until she was in an undershirt and undershorts and jumped into the water. Her head submerged and re-emerged from the depth of the pool.

"AHHHHHH! It's cold! Come in, Woods!"

He, too, took off his sweat-soaked outer clothing and leisurely made his way into the cool spring. The liquid refreshed his tired limbs and invigorated his spirit. They jumped and played like brother and sister joking and laughing, splashing and diving with carefree abandon. For the moment, it washed away their frets about tigers, bears, and dragons; it cleaned away most of the dirt and sweat on their bodies, while diluting the fears in their hearts.

After their noonday swim, they rested a bit, collected their belongings, and crossed the river. They waded while carrying their packs and dry clothes over their heads, high above the water. On the other side of the stream, they dressed enough to continue trekking yet air dry in the breeze. As their conversation about the tiger was closed, Woods asked about the mission instead.

"So what do you think Dr. Rahd meant about Herculean mythology?" Woods asked.

"Ha! Who knows? Years ago, he told me that story about Hercules and Hera."

"Yeah! I know where Hercules goes crazy and slays his family. Then he needs to do all those labors to be forgiven."

"Well, in the beginning, before that, Hera made Hercules go crazy and slaughter his wife and children."

"So weird!"

"I know! And then she made him 'atone for his sins' as Dr. Rahd says, with the labors."

"What a horrible goddess!"

"Those gods of old were all like that," Pyrrha commented. "But, the point is, according to the learned Dr. Rahd, without Hera, there is no Hercules."

"Huh! What do you mean?"

"Look at Hercules name. It starts with Hera."

"So, how is that spiritual?" Woods asked with genuine curiosity.

"Dr. Rahd said, 'We need others to push us to be heroic.'"

"Uh! Your dad is so—"

"Fervent."

"Erudite."

"Yeah...but whatever my dad is, I sure wouldn't be doing this, whatever this is, without a death warrant hanging over my head."

"But, should we even be doing this?"

"It is what it is…" Pyrrha sighed. "What choice do we have?"

There is always a choice. Grand Tock's voice rumbled in their heads.

They both had decided what path they wanted to take. Pyrrha would follow the Duke's Court's order, and Woods would follow Pyrrha to protect and assist her in any way possible. Since their choices had been made, the only way was forward toward Mount Omega. Here and there along the path, they paused to examine the burnt trees and ashy patches of grass made by dragon's spit. The charred stumps and blackened earth attested to the creature's fiery temper. Pyrrha and Woods trudged along in silence, contemplating their fate and reluctant to disturb the peace. As afternoon turned to dusk and the sun cast long shadows beneath the canopy of trees, they approached their destination—Forest Fortress.

FOREST FORTRESS

High in the pine trees, at least fifty feet off the forest floor, the treehouse hid among the canopy of branches and needles. From memory, Woods and Pyrrha looked for signs of the large fort, as nothing could be seen from where they stood on the ground. Each tree housed cabins for sleeping, while each cluster of trunks supported pavilions for gathering. All were connected by a series of swinging bridges, rope ladders, and pulley elevators. They had built parts of these cabins, pavilions, and bridges during their young leadership retreats held every summer, so they tried to reconstruct a map of the floating fort in their minds.

However, in the low light of dusk, the massive hive of rooms and platforms vanished into the treetops like they did not even exist. All that could be seen from the ground was an obstacle course used for training youth to climb like mountaineers and solve problems like engineers, while working together in teams.

Woods and Pyrrha looked for the ladders and pulleys among the tall ferns, ivy, and saplings that had grown wildly since the dragon had taken up residence in the reservoir at the beginning of the war. Few people dared to come so close to

Mount Omega for fear of being seen by the monster, while out on an evening flight looking for a morsel of meat to eat. Their reticence was justified by the burnt patches of landscape that increased in frequency as they grew nearer to the mountainside.

Pyrrha and Woods searched their memories while they explored the larger trees for signs of a way up, but it was hard to make out details as dark descended.

"Where is my lantern?" Pyrrha said, rummaging through her overstuffed bag.

"Here! This might help," Woods replied.

He spotlighted her satchel with a head lamp he had pulled out of his pocket and strapped to his forehead. Before making another move, they stopped and listened. Twigs snapped, but the crackles were not from a quick rabbit. Leaves rustled, but the swish was not from a light breeze. Pyrrha and Woods turned defensive—they stood backs together to make a three-hundred-and-sixty-degree sweep of their position, looking and listening for danger.

"Who's there?" yelled Woods.

They waited silently, pushing their shoulder blades into each others' backs. A half circle of yellow lantern light illuminated the patch of ground in front of Woods as Pyrrha had no time to find her headlamp. They were being watched with sharp eyes. Pyrrha felt Woods push harder against her back, giving her a solid wall of strength to lean on as she tried to catch her breath and get her bearings.

He stood rooted as as a tree, only swaying with measured breaths. She caught Woods' pace of practiced inhales and exhales. Together they slowed their breathing. They extended the pauses before inhaling and exhaling to find as much silence as possible between each breath. They listened to the world. They relaxed into the moment. They scanned their bodies for fear as they scanned their surroundings for danger.

A whirl of dust and a swath of clothing passed near the circle of light cast by Woods' headlamp.

"We are here on official business of the Duke!" Pyrrha called out with serious candor.

"Cawcaw!" cried someone imitating a bluejay.

"Twang." A taunt bowstring went slack, but no arrow flew.

"We have not come to find failure," Pyrrha shouted into the darkness.

Everything was silent—the birds, the bugs, the rustle of leaves—the forest was unnaturally quiet. No one breathed.

"Trilllllllll-lil-lil-lil…." a morning bird serenaded them unnaturally at nightfall.

Woods and Pyrrha leaned into each other's strength. Their solidarity gave courage.

"I'm Ehn, the keeper of the fort," said a sweet voice nearby. "State your official business."

Pyrrha stepped forward toward the delicate voice. She curtsied deeply with a straight back.

"I am Pyrrha Tock," she announced hoping her family name would be recognized and respected. "We are here to complete a mission for Duke Yuddha."

"Show me your papers," Ehn requested. Her soft voice floated down like a feather falling out of the sky.

Pyrrha searched her bag for the scroll and handed over the rolled paper—ceremoniously—with both hands outstretched in a low bow. The keeper of the fort reached into the half moon of light to retrieve the document. Only a dainty hand and silk cuff could be seen for a second. Then, all was quiet again. Even the mosquitoes seemed afraid to buzz about their ears.

Pyrrha and Woods stood back to back, prepared for a fight. They dared not speak aloud as eyes and ears were all around them, so they resorted to an old childhood game they had played—hand-to-hand sign language. To anyone more than a foot away, it might have looked like they were fidgeting while holding hands, but it was anything but a romantic gesture. Woods held his hand flat as Pyrrha made various shapes and drew different patterns on his palm.

What? Do! Pyrrha signed.

How many? Woods asked.

Three? Five?

Five plus more.

What? Do! Pyrrha signed again.

Woods did not reply, because they had only learned hand signing as a simple game long ago. They had never learned the complex grammar to explain detailed ideas.

Woods waited awhile and then signed, *Run?*

No! Pyrrha replied, *Wait.*

They did not need to wait long. Something flat and solid slid under their feet—the reverse of how a magician pulls a tablecloth out from under a tea set. They felt a small jerk of a rope and they began to sway from side to side. They were on a lift ascending toward the canopy.

Pyrrha signed, *Jump!*

But when they both moved out toward the edges of the platform, they hit an invisible wall of webbing that softly bounced them to the center of the elevator contraption. They lurched higher and higher toward the treetops. The platform swung from side to side as it moved up toward the sky. After several minutes of upward movement, they went sideways before settling down.

Pyrrha and Woods had reached the balcony, where the platform settled. They sat down on the floor of the lift and used Woods' lamplight to explore their surroundings and assess what they knew. The Tree Fort was intact and operational, as it was inhabited and guarded by a band of people who were led by a seemingly delicate individual named Ehn.

However, as sweet as her voice sounded, her fellow guards were well-trained to protect their space. They had captured

Woods and Pyrrha in a trap without much effort, and they had quickly escorted them onto a deck in the treetops without even revealing themselves. The webbing that contained them was a finer version of Grand Tock's spider cloth from Jupiter the Giant. It was something similar in function but worlds apart in quality. Whoever these people were, they were stealth in the wilds, comfortable in quiet darkness, yet respectful of the Duke enough to not attack someone bearing a scroll with his seal.

Woods and Pyrrha sat trapped on the deck of the fort. They pulled at the fabric admiring its fineness even as they were frustrated by being imprisoned. They sat. They waited. Their fear cooled as the chill of evening in the hills embraced them. Pyrrha took her coat from her bag and gave Woods a scarf since he rarely got cold.

"What now?" Woods mumbled under his breath.

"We have to wait," Pyrrha replied.

"For what? How long?"

"I guess they are taking counsel to decide if they are going to help us or not."

"Did you know this was going to happen?"

"No!" Pyrrha sighed. "I wasn't given detailed instructions."

"What did they tell you?" Woods inquired.

"Nothing more than the scroll, and you read that." Pyrrha said no more. She waited and listened.

A light in one of the cabins had come on some time ago and low voices drifted on the wind. Nothing made sense, as the words were too faint and muffled to be understood. Only the rise and fall of an argument could be inferred from intonation. After a time, it seemed the disagreement had resolved into a kind of plan and the sound of toasting and the smell of food wafted down.

"That food smells good," Pyrrha whispered. "I'm hungry."

"Me too," Woods replied.

"I have some biscuits in my bag if you want."

"No need!" Ehn's lilting voice interrupted their conversation.

Both Pyrrha and Woods jolted to attention at the sound of another person nearby.

"We mean you no harm Lil' Tock," said Ehn. "And your friend is safe too."

Out of the darkness stepped a young warrior dressed in silk gowns with her hair braided into a crown. Her fierce demeanor contradicted her slight figure and melodic voice, so it was hard to know if she was as compassionate as she sounded or as severe as she stood. Next to her, Woods' headlamp caught the outline of a guard standing at attention with his hand on the hilt of the knife in his belt.

"This is Vahid, the head of the fort guards," Ehn nodded in his direction, and he stood at attention. She nodded again.

Vahid stepped forward and dropped his hands to his sides. "Welcome to Forest Fortress," he said. He looked anything but welcoming standing six feet tall and half as broad at the shoulders. His face remained blank, yet any expression looked fierce with the symbols of battle shaved in his hairline.

Ehn lit a kerosene lantern on a picnic table on the deck of the fort revealing a small meal of cheese, dried fruit, pickled vegetables and crackers. It was a well-chosen assortment of delicacies that could easily be preserved for travel. She stepped toward the elevator and released the gauze netting which had contained them. With the wave of her hand, Ehn beckoned them toward the table. Woods sat unmoved, distrusting this contradictory creature before him and her armed guard.

"My dear lad," Ehn encouraged. "What can I tell you that will allow you to trust us and the food I have placed before you?"

"What is the name of the mountain with five peaks?" Woods asked.

"Mount Gaea," Ehn replied without hesitation.

"What is the river which can go everywhere and nowhere?"

"River Libertad."

"Where can you find both black pearls and red coral?"

"The Ocean of Wisdom."

"Have you seen Grand Tock?"

Ehn paused before answering. "Yes, a year before I was stationed here—

"What!" Pyrrha squeaked. "Where? Why? How?"

"Unfortunately, I cannot disclose more," Ehn replied. "At the time, I did not know who he was. We were on different missions, so…"

Pyrrha understood. She had heard this line before, and when people did answer her questions, the stories often left her sick with worry about what precarious obstacles her grandfather must overcome to avoid death. Long ago, she had learned not to ask questions she did not want answers to.

"Who are you?" Woods asked.

"I'm Ehn, the keeper of the fort. Who are you?"

"Uhhhh, Woods."

"Come eat, Woods!" Pyrrha motioned him to the table. "If they call me Lil' Tock, then by the honor of Grand Tock they have agreed to help us."

"How can you trust them?"

"The food tastes good," chirped Pyrrha. "And since I can tell you that, I have not yet been poisoned."

Woods and Ehn chuckled uncomfortably at her observation and the reality of trust—only through trust can one discover if someone is trustworthy or not.

Woods sat down at the table of snacks and began eating. It had been many miles and a great deal of effort to get this far, so he set aside his worries and enjoyed the food in front of him despite Vahid the guard's uneasy gaze scrutinizing his every move. Ehn sat nearby, as they nibbled on this and that. She watched patiently as they ate their fill.

"We have much to discuss," Ehn said, as they wiped crumbs from their mouths. She snapped her fingers and a boy about eleven sauntered forward balancing a carafe of warm liquid on a tray with a handful of mugs. "This is Tabor," she nodded in his direction.

The bubbly youngster tiptoed around the table placing cups and pouring hot apple cider. With every sashay and splash, he flipped his wheat-colored hair out of his sky-blue eyes.

Everyone watched the two boys. Woods put a hand on Tabor's shoulder to stop him when he was served. "You're from Ironweald, eh?"

Tabor nodded his head as they locked eyes.

"How did you get here?" Woods questioned.

Tabor looked to Ehn and only spoke when she winked her approval. "The same way you did, sir."

Woods cocked his head to one side. "Adoption?!"

Tabor shrugged. Then he skittered off into the darkness with the empty tray.

Pyrrha was as surprised as Woods to see another person who openly showed their light hair, which singled them out as a stranger from Ironweald. She followed the sound of the boy's footsteps as he pranced across the decks out of sight. When all was quiet again, Pyrrha turned back to Ehn with newfound respect and courage.

"Let's begin," Pyrrha said.

"Why have you come here?" Ehn asked.

"We must climb Mount Omega to Lake Lotanna," Pyrrha replied.

"So will you attempt to slay the dragon behind the reservoir dam?" Ehn asked incredulously.

"Yes! That is the plan," Woods interjected.

"Well…not exactly," Pyrrha interrupted. "I don't want to kill it. I just want to encourage it to go away."

"How?" Ehn inquired.

"We don't know," Pyrrha replied honestly.

"Many a warrior much more experienced than you has failed this task," Ehn stated. "Why do you think you will succeed?"

Pyrrha looked at Woods before replying.

"I don't."

"Then why continue?"

"I have no other good choices."

"There are always choices."

Pyrrha did not want to cry, so she looked down at her hands and then off into the darkness. She avoided the gazes of Woods and Ehn until she regained control of her emotions.

Ehn spoke instead, "From where I sit, your insistence on coming this far is proof of your choice….And…I think you have a chance to succeed."

"Really?!" Woods exclaimed.

"Yes.…It's statistically slim, but…" Ehn stopped.

"Please…tell us…" Woods urged.

"The prophecy says, 'No man may kill the dragon,'" Ehn explained. "As you are not a man, Pyrrha, and you do not want to kill the dragon, so you have a chance."

"Ahh-hhemm!" Pyrrha coughed. The statistically slim chance of success stuck in her throat and made it difficult to formulate a reply.

"We have been listening," Ehn said. "We have followed you since you hid your bicycles along the roadside and entered the forest."

"Oh!" Pyrrha finally spoke up. "So, you will help us?"

"I will make a trade. My help for your help."

"What help?" Woods asked. "How can we possibly help you?"

"See, I can be your guide up the mountain. I know the fastest and quietest ways to the top and down again without disturbing the beast," Ehn explained. "Then, if you are successful, I will ask for your help on my own future assignment from the Duke."

"Oh!" Woods could not contain his disgust. "So he likes you too."

"Woods—" Pyrrha exclaimed.

"I don't know," Ehn replied. "I've never met him."

"Yes," Pyrrha interrupted. "We need your help—"

"No," Woods said. "What is your task from the Duke? It must be worse than this."

"It isn't," Ehn stated flatly. "It couldn't be...but, honestly, I don't know yet."

"What do you mean?" Woods demanded.

"My current task is to monitor the dragon from this station, so if you are successful, I will be reassigned."

"Oh! So you don't even know what this future task is yet?" Woods fumed. "How can we trust you?"

"Trust is something we do, so there is nothing that I can say to convince you that I am trustworthy." Ehn replied. "But...I guarantee the dragon will kill you if I do not guide you up the slopes of Mount Omega and advise you on some kind of strategy."

"And with your help," Pyrrha interrupted their argument. "Do you think we have a chance to succeed?"

"Yes..." Ehn changed her tone. "I think you are lucky, Pyrrha —you survived that tiger attack as a little thing, so you are luckier than most."

"What are our chances with the dragon," Woods asked a little less defensively.

"Fifty percent," Ehn said. "Maybe better...And, I think fate is on Pyrrha's side."

Woods and Pyrrha looked at each other. The possibility of having a guide up the mountain was a relief, notwithstanding that the weight of the odds were not strongly in their favor. However, the requirement to assist Ehn with her own unknown task from the Duke was a bit disconcerting. Ehn stood up and left them to their thoughts.

A few minutes later, Ehn returned with mugs of hot

chamomile tea, while Vahid brought fuel for the brazier. A few minutes later, Tabor came and started the fire.

"We will have a fire to take the chill out of the nighttime air," Ehn said. "Vahid, will you tell us a story about the dragon to prepare us for this mission?"

Everyone got comfortable in their seats. A hush fell over Pyrrha, Woods, Ehn, and Tabor, who settled in, ready to listen.

"Years ago, in a place far away, there was a war," Vahid began in the low, raspy voice of a warrior. "During the war, the soldiers dug deep into the earth to mine things yet unknown to help win any sort of advantage over their enemies.

"As they dug deep into the earth, they unsettled things that they did not know hid in the depths. Among the many secrets that came out from the crevices was Her Highness, the Dragon. She had a multifarious coat of scales and a mood that was just as temperamental. When she stirred from her comfortable cave, she was unhappy to be awoken from her dreams and flew far and wide, breathing fiery destruction wherever and whenever she was perturbed.

"Alas, five years ago, she settled here in Lake Lotanna on Mount Omega. She came for the ravine filled with fresh water high in the mountains, as it was the perfect cool nest for a hot-tempered dragon. As she snuggled in, the water warmed around her, making her fall asleep and dream again.

"However, it was an uneasy sleep. The sound of the war reverberated throughout the land and troubled her rest. So, as she slept, she sweat out all of the anxiety and sadness she heard in the world. This caused the once pure, spring-fed reservoir to become a toxic pool of dragon soup.

"From time to time, the Archduke Zachariah's Court requested teams of surveyors and soldiers to visit the reservoir to make a plan to slay the dragon, so that the country could once again have a plentiful, clean water supply. Yet, it was to no avail. Several brave individuals met their death trying, while the rest gave up, cowed by fear.

"The Archduke sent for a sorceress who was fluent in the ways of old magic to find what ancient knowledge could be resurrected to assist with the problem of the golden dragon in Lake Lotanna. After praying, chanting, and offerings to the gods of old, the oracle spoke: 'Death shall come to any man who tries to kill the dragon in this nest.'

"Thus, it came to be that everyone believed no one could chase Eruliaf away." Vahid stopped the story abruptly, and an uneasy quiet settled around the fire.

Woods broke the silence. "We all heard rumors, but we never knew what was true."

After a pause, Pyrrha piped up, "So, how will I succeed? Is it even possible, if no one before me has come close?"

"Pyrrha, you are a woman," Ehn said matter-of-factly.

"But what about me? Should I expect to die now?" queried Woods.

"I don't know," she said. "I don't think so…"

"That doesn't give me much confidence!" Woods said with exasperation.

"I don't think so, because of the dream," Ehn said reassuringly.

"You mean Mama Jojo's dream about Woods carrying the torch?" Pyrrha asked.

"Yes," Ehn said.

"You're asking me to trust that Mama Jojo's dreams are right," Woods sighed. "That's a lot of trust!"

All seated by the fire looked from one to another trying to make sense of things.

"Tonight, you will rest," Ehn said, breaking the silence. "Tomorrow, we climb Mount Omega to the Penultimate Ridge."

The seriousness of her words rang out. The food felt heavy in their guts.

"In the morning, we'll discuss the plans in more detail," Ehn stated. "I will give you the Elder's best advice to assist you with this task."

Woods and Pyrrha looked surprised, as they had not voiced their agreement, but the long walk and chamomile tea had began to press on them. They became too sleepy to protest or question Ehn's proposal. They rolled out their sleeping bags on the the deck and crawled in. Ehn, Vahid, and Tabor tidied up the area and went off to their own quarters. All were set for a good night's sleep.

- - -

Morning in the forest started a little before sunrise. The activities rose with the dawning light. Small rodents and birds scampered and flit about looking for their morning meal while avoiding becoming a snack themselves. As the day warmed, the sunlight filled the air with a refreshing hope to be alive and stay alive. The rejuvenation of a good night's sleep outdoors was only dampened by the reality of the task that lay ahead.

Pyrrha prepared for the day. She performed her morning ablutions, said her prayers, and sat in her meditation. This was her mantra.

"I adjure Thee by Thy might, O my God! Let no harm beset me in times of tests, and in moments of heedlessness guide my steps aright through Thine inspiration."[1]

She vowed not to let the Duke's death sentence hang over her like the stench above Bowen's Bog. Gently, she pushed the distasteful smell away like blowing out ninety-five birthday candles, one at a time. She slowly breathed in and out—controlling her wandering mind with strict inhales and exhales. Optimistic courage was necessary for this journey, so no extra energy could be sapped away by wishing things were different than they were.

Just as she finished, a youth who looked like the younger brother of Vahid approached with Ehn. He was strong like an elm tree with the same intricate shaved patterns throughout his short hair.

"Roman, thank you for the breakfast," Ehn said as she motioned to the table.

Roman set down the two bowls of hot oatmeal topped with simmered apples and maple syrup. Then, he left without a word —only sneaking a few extra glances at the two guests to the fort.

Oatmeal was not Pyrrha's favorite meal, but the comfort of warm nutrition encouraged her to eat her fill. Woods spooned in his breakfast without complaint. As they sat drinking breakfast tea, Ehn unfolded the map of the mountain terrain across the table between them. They would discuss the plan for the day.

"We will climb Mount Omega to the Penultimate Ridge," Ehn explained. "There is an old, hidden path that cuts through the hill along this steep rock face."

She pointed to lines on the map as she talked.

"You and Woods will make camp there at Hallowed Nest on this side of the final crest. There are short paths over and through this last ridge to Lake Lotanna. Tomorrow, you will meet the dragon."

"That sounds like a deceptively simple plan," Woods remarked.

Ehn continued unamused. "Hallowed Nest is an old campsite used by generations of travelers, so simple provisions for food and shelter are stored securely in the cave behind the ancient pine. We will travel light today."

Ehn looked from Pyrrha to Woods and back again to ensure that they were both listening carefully.

"There are a few rules while we are on the mountain: We must be quiet. We must be more careful as we climb higher. Unnecessary, unusual noises could awaken the sensitive creature, though recently she sleeps soundly. We won't make a fire or bring any fragrant foods. Any smells of smoke or delicious desserts will rouse her for sure. We mustn't do anything that will attract her attention."

"The dragon is a her!" Pyrrha repeated.

"Yes!" Ehn nodded. "She hates men. That is why she will kill any who annoy her."

Pyrrha smiled. This tiny detail had not seemed important before, yet now it made sense like the sun shining in the summer sky. "So will Vahid, Tabor, or Roman join us?"

"No, they will monitor our progress from the plain," Ehn replied. "It's safer that way."

"What about Woods?" Pyrrha asked. "Is he climbing the mountain?"

Ehn looked at Woods. "Against my better judgement…but he was foretold as the light-bearer in your mother's dream…as you remember…so…"

Pyrrha and Woods exchanged a nervous frown between them.

"Woods!" Ehn emphasized. "No matter what happens, do not cross over the final ridge as the dragon will surely try to incinerate you with her fiery breath if you encroach upon her territory."

Then, she looked at Pyrrha and added, "Yes, the dragon may try to kill you too, but only if she feels threatened. She seems to always be kinder and gentler to fellow females, of any species, so she may first play with you to discern your intentions. She usually only attacks if you annoy her."

Pyrrha and Woods stopped eating as the somber reality of their journey set in. Ehn noticed the end of breakfast and stood up.

"Ready? Take the lift down. We're heading off."

"We haven't packed our bags yet," said Woods.

"We took care of that last night," replied Ehn.

She pushed Pyrrha's satchel and water bottle toward her and gave Woods a new backpack empty of most provisions.

"Where is my stuff," Woods huffed.

"Don't worry, it is safe in storage. By tomorrow night, you will be back here celebrating with us, or we will send it to your family as a keepsake."

Woods nodded. Pyrrha sighed. For what Ehn said was true. Where they were going, they did not need everyday necessities. They needed all of their lived experiences—knowledge and skills, plus a great deal of luck—to succeed. It was better to leave quickly and not ruminate on their predicament, or courage would seep away with every passing breath.

SCALING MOUNT OMEGA

THE EARLY MORNING HIKE FROM THE FORT TO THE BASE OF THE mountain was deceptively simple. They trotted at a good pace up the leisurely incline along the base of Mount Omega, heading to the back of the mountain. Ehn led Pyrrha and Woods along the main path while Vahid, Roman, and Tabor took alternate routes in parallel, scouting the surrounding areas for unusual signs. They traveled lightly, each carrying only enough food, water, and supplies to last a day. Pyrrha carried Grand Tock's special satchel, as it was always only as large and as heavy as she could handle.

It was a hike very similar to the previous days—trees interspersed with meadows, sunshine warming the skin and light breezes cooling the body. Yet, the signs of the dragon's activities were omnipresent. Instead of a single bush or a small patch of grass being burnt black, swaths of the forest and fields had been ravaged by fires. If they had not known it was the dragon's work, they would have assumed a wildfire had caused so much damage. They trekked through the charcoal landscape stepping lightly and talking little. Few birds or animals disturbed the uneasy peace.

They stopped to rest and drink water in a grove of trees that were remarkably green and fragrant among the blackened char. Vahid, Roman, and Tabor stayed at a distance, monitoring the horizon for movement.

"These are quaking aspen, aren't they?" Woods remarked.

"Ha," Pyrrha smiled putting on a brave face. "Are we supposed to be afraid?"

"No, the trees are said to quake when the slightest breeze makes the leaves shiver," Woods explained.

As if on cue, a light gust lifted the leaves making them chatter and shuffle like a group of nervous children telling ghost stories.

"This close to the mountain, this is the last enclave of green untouched by the dragon's temper," Ehn commented. "Beyond this point, the mountain will be different than you remember."

"So what does the reservoir look like now?" Pyrrha asked.

"Well, it is no longer crowded with boats and sunbathers, ice cream vendors, and juggling clowns," Woods mused.

"No! That's for sure," Ehn agreed. "Unfortunately, the once green landscape is brown. The plants are wilting from the toxic fumes emanating from the water."

"Why is it so polluted?" Pyrrha asked.

"Her Highness has been nesting," Ehn explained. "All her sweat and tears go into the water, making it an acidic stench pool." Ehn looked up at the mountain as if worried that just talking about the dragon would bring her out of hiding. "They say that the deep reservoir is perfect for her kind. The top water is warmed by the sun and the spring at the bottom of the lake is eternally cool. She can swim up and down to easily regulate her body temperature."

"Who knew dragons were so sensitive?" Woods said.

Pyrrha took in the information trying to make heads or tails of the story. Then she asked, "Have you ever seen the dragon?"

"I don't know," Ehn answered matter of factly. "It is hard to know if what I saw swimming in the lake were fish or the tips of a dragon's tail. You know she can change shape like an octopus and change color like a chameleon."

"So that's true!" Pyrrha worried. "How can I face a constantly changing creature?"

"Unfortunately, dearest Pyrrha," Ehn frowned. "You know 'Life is change. There are no constants.'"

They all sighed. There was no reply to the truth. They wordlessly ended their rest stop, stood and packed up. They trudged the last steep hillside to the base of the mountain cliffs. Here Vahid, Roman, and Tabor bowed goodbye before trotting off in different directions on a choreographed patrol.

Mount Omega's Foothills had been named for their remarkable resemblance to a foot. The terrain of the forward facing hills gently rose out of the ground much how a foot slowly develops from the pinkie toe to the big toe—each rounded mound larger than the last. From the toe-like hills on the plain, the foot arched skyward to finally plateau at the ankle where the reservoir filled with rains from on high and a spring down below. Everyone imagined that this large foot joined the leg of the invisible goddess who towered in the sky. With surprising accuracy, even the back of Mount Omega resembled a heel that vertically rose out of the ground, standing strong and stout to support the weight of the goddess. It was this cliff face that they endeavored to scale.

All morning, Pyrrha, Woods, and Ehn silently made their way up a grey wall of granite. It was extreme hiking with a bit of rock climbing. They crawled up steep inclines using knee and finger holds for leverage. One misplaced foot would send a cascade of pebbles and dust down on those below. Ehn led them with grace, Pyrrha followed, and Woods was the fall guy—if anyone or anything fell, he was there to pick up the pieces. Woods tried to contain his frustration when a rock hit his head or he breathed in a cloud of falling dirt. Thus, they ascended the steep base of Mount Omega's Heel.

"My arms are a little shaky," Pyrrha signaled to Ehn.

Ehn looked at them, looked at the sun, looked at the slopes above, and frowned. However, it was clear that they could not keep going at this pace without a break, so she acquiesced.

"We'll rest on this landing," Ehn signed back.

She took out some dried apricots and passed around a water bottle to replenish their strength. On this part of the mountain, they were still far enough from the dragon to speak cautiously in small voices.

"This is not the traditional path up to the reservoir," Ehn explained. "In the days of old, we could take a leisurely stroll up the moderate incline over Mount Omega's Foothills and across the arch to the lake. However, that path has been closed ever since the dragon took up residence behind the dam. Any talking or scuffling along that way can tickle the tender eardrums of Her Highness. Your scratching at the rocks and this pit stop would have aroused her suspicions if we were on the other side."

"But, we can talk here?" Pyrrha asked.

"For a little bit longer we can whisper," Ehn replied. "The rock is thick here and the wind blows our words in a circle making it seem as if they come from the plain below."

Woods asked, "Where did the dragon come from? Why is she here?"

"That's a good question," Ehn sighed. "She arrived at the start of the war. Likely, she was rooted out of her den deep underground with all of the mining in those distant parts. No one knows why she took to this mountain and this reservoir, but once she snuggled into the water, she seemed content to nest for awhile."

"How am I to rid her from the lake?" asked Pyrrha.

"That is a question for tonight," Ehn replied. "You should not be thinking about tactics while scaling the mountain. It will only make it more likely that you will fall."

"So you have ideas?" Woods was hopeful.

"Yes, but that is for later." Ehn looked at the path ahead and the distant goal far up the slope. "First steps first."

Pyrrha and Woods were quiet. Instead of looking awkwardly at each other, they returned to the climb toward Hallowed Nest in the Penultimate Ridge.

Ehn gave them instructions. "For this next bit, cover up and wear your gloves."

They took a moment to roll down shirt sleeves, tuck in pant legs, put on gloves, tie handkerchiefs over their mouths, put on sunglasses, and secure hats on their heads. All that could be seen was a bit of skin beside the eyes not covered by their glasses.

Before they set off, Ehn gave further instructions, "We have to harness up. For this part, we'll have a cord to guide us. Hold on tight, and attach your harness to the wire line. And, no matter what, do not get distracted and do not let go." She looked Pyrrha and Woods in the eyes and gave them one last command, "Even if you get scared, do not scream. Control your body and your emotions."

Pyrrha, Woods, and Ehn stepped into harnesses and tightened them around their legs and waist. They checked the rope and knots to make sure that everything was securely fastened and would not slip if it had to hold their weight. Ehn examined and tested Pyrrha's and Woods' mountain climbing gear to make sure it was ready for the worst case scenario—a fall from the cliff.

The snaking path up the rock became thinner and thinner. At first, the path could fit two people abreast. Next, it narrowed to only fit one person walking along the cliff edge. Then, it became a spaghetti strip only wide enough to place one foot in front of the other. To make this walk possible for amateurs, a network of wires with harnesses had been constructed. Woods and Pyrrha secured their belts to the wire roping with carabiners. The carabiners were wrapped in yarn to muffle any scraping and clicking that would echo louder than necessary.

The mountainside grew steeper as they ascended. Every few dozen feet, there were small passes where it was essential to hang onto a rope handrail while crossing narrow ledges along the cliff face. Pyrrha edged her feet gingerly across. She watched dust fall down, down, down in a never-ending descent.

The sunlight glinted off the rocks. The glare was temporarily blinding. The path moved about uncertainly in the changing light. Looking up, there were only trees hanging precariously off ledges and blue skies appearing pleasantly nice. While looking down, there was nothing but rock for a thousand feet, then the blackened earth stretched out for miles across the once green plains. Without sharp concentration, vertigo was inevitable.

Slowly, inch by inch, they walked the minuscule ledge with their harnesses sliding along the rigging. Every fifty feet or so, they met a piton, a spike driven into the rock, that secured the wiring to the cliff face. At each of these bracings, they had to unclip and re-clip their carabiners, so for a split second, only firm footing and strong grip held them to the mountainside.

Ehn, Pyrrha, and Woods shuffled single file along the path. They were evenly spaced more than fifty feet apart so that no two people were ever on the same section of wiring. This kind of climbing required a special kind of concentration—feet on ground, hands on rope, muscles engaged, body balanced, mind focused. There was no time to think about scratching a fly bite or swatting away a gnat. With attention on the immediate task, Pyrrha calmed her anxieties about meeting the dragon in the future and quelled her anger about the Duke's Court in the past, as she could only focus on the here and now. Future and past cannot exist when one lives in the present moment.

A blob landed on Pyrrha's sunglasses. Its eight legs scurried across from one lens to the next. She momentarily panicked about the tiny insect, but she did not remove her hands from her lifeline. She took a deep breath and blew upward toward her eyes. The spider glided out of view on the wind, and she hoped it had not landed in her hair.

Pyrrha's foot slipped. She felt the harness tighten around her waist. The wire handrail bowed low with her weight dangling off the cliff. She suppressed a scream as she looked down at the nothingness below. The landscape and air blurred into shades of grey. She swayed like a pendulum. "Breathe," she whispered under her breath. "Calm!"

Pyrrha tried to focus her mind as she dangled precariously off the cliff. She willed her fear to stop spinning. She reached for the harness, the rope, the rock face. She waited for the movement of the world to slow around her.

That moment of distraction had cost her a foothold and caused her to fall off the path, but the precautions had worked. She was alive. The harness had protected her from tumbling off the mountain.

Pyrrha looked up and saw Ehn twenty feet away, just on the other side of a secured piton. She threw a cord to Pyrrha. Slowly, they worked together to move Pyrrha to an outcropping where she could find handholds and footholds to climb up to the ledge again. Once her footing was securely on the path, Ehn wordlessly urged them on with her eyes.

To regain concentration, Pyrrha began to hum under her breath a prayer sung to young ones to help calm disquieted nerves and lull a crying baby to sleep.

"Alláh-u-Abhá, A—lla—ooooo—ahbha—A—lla—ooooo—ahbha—A—lla—ooooo—ahbha—Alláh-u-Abhá."[1]

This song consisted of a single phrase repeated over and over again with ever-changing pitches and rhythms. It was like a brook washing over rocks as it flowed toward the sea. The simple song settled Pyrrha's nerves.

Step after step along the mountain ledge, click after click with the carabiner on the wire roping, verse after verse of the lullaby, Pyrrha, Woods, and Ehn inched their way along the cliff face. As they moved, they gathered dust. Tiny red dots speckled their clothing. The flecks of dirt danced lightly in the breeze pulsing with their anxiety as they crossed the narrower expanse. Their once black clothing turned the color of clay, moving like a living creature. Pyrrha wanted to wipe away the hairs that tickled her cheek and neck, but the vertical drop one thousand feet down to the base of the mountain kept her eyes focused on the path and her hands gripped to the wire.

At long last, the spaghetti ledge widened to a single foot path and then to a double-wide road. As the extreme climbing became moderate hiking, less focus was paid to each step and more attention was given to other details. Pyrrha, first, caught her gasping breath that had run wild like a dog off its leash. Then, she watched her feet on the path to maintain her footing on the ledge that plummeted to the plains far below. Finally, she focused on their destination, a round castle-like tower with a flat expanse where they could sit down and rest.

Pyrrha stifled gleeful giggles when they reached the wire's end and unhooked their harnesses from the network of ropes securing them to the mountainside. Pyrrha looked to Ehn and then to Woods with elation at their success crossing the high wire. As she calmed, her attention focused on Woods' clothes— he was covered in red, throbbing dust. Then, she looked at herself to see the moving blobs on her clothes.

"Don't scream," Ehn quietly ordered. "The spiders are harmless."

Pyrrha and Woods frantically brushed the small spiders from their clothing. Every clot of dust was wriggling with excitement. The eight-legged dots hopped, leapt, skipped, and crawled haphazardly en mass.

Ehn hurried the two terrified souls to the small pool carved into the stream flowing down the hillside. She pushed them fully clothed into the deep tank of water. The shock of the cold liquid and the joy at seeing the spiders scurry to the safety of dry land was more than Woods and Pyrrha could handle. Both squealed with joy as they splashed water over their heads. Only a few deathly glares from Ehn could hush their noise and contain their outbursts.

Ehn calmly collected their bags and dusted them off. She removed the remaining spiders with sprays of water. Then, she tossed the bags across the stream and eased herself into the cool water for a fully-clothed bath.

The long walk in the hot sun, the intense concentration on the rope ledge, and the fear of spiders was soaked out of them as they sat in the pool.

Pyrrha turned to Ehn and whispered, "Why didn't you say anything about the spiders?"

"You didn't need to know," Ehn mouthed.

What?! Woods shrugged his shoulders gesticulating his disagreement.

"Think about it…" Ehn murmured softly above the sound of flowing water. "The cliff was bad enough, if you knew it was covered in spiders it would have been that much harder to cross." She let the impeccable logic of her words sink in. "Anyways, they are quite harmless. They don't like biting humans. We're too bitter for their taste."

However, instinctive fear of insects sent a shiver down Pyrrha's spine. The feeling of something crawling through her scalp made her take off her cap and dunk her full head of red hair into the water again and again. Woods did the same. All were grateful to cool off after the long climb.

"We have about two more hours to walk the final leg up to the fortress," said Ehn softly, "so we will stay here for a short rest. After we cross the next ledge, we cannot talk at all until we enter the cave at Hallowed Nest as we'll be too close to Her Highness."

They each got out of the water in drips and drabs. They stayed on the far side of the stream away from the cliff face of spiders. They snacked and drank fresh water to refresh themselves. They lay across the rocks drying out in the warm sun.

Pyrrha tried not to think too much about the path ahead. She tried not to imagine what obstacles Ehn had not yet told them about and what challenges they had yet to face. It was easy to get trapped in a web of unending what-if problems with impossible solutions that just encourage hyperventilation.

She could not control the future, nor could she change the past, so she had to focus on the things she could do in the here and now. Conquering her fear, one breath at a time, was her wisest course of action. That, and sending out a prayer to the universe, her ancestors, or whoever would listen—"Help! Please help me!"

These two tactics might aid her to learn the secret that would push Her Highness, the Dragon out of nesting in Copperton's reservoir—Lake Lotanna.

THE PENULTIMATE HIKE

WHEN THE SUN WAS THREE QUARTERS OF THE WAY ACROSS THE sky, Ehn signaled that it was time to pick up, pack up, and move on. They were nearly dry and well rested from the soak in the water and naps on the rocks. Their limbs had stopped trembling from scaling the cliff and their minds had relaxed when they knew the spiders were no longer a threat. Ehn signaled it was time to put on their backpacks and hit the trail.

"Headlamps out and on your head," Ehn whispered. "Hopefully, we'll arrive before sunset, but we should be ready just in case we need them for the last bit of the hike."

"Won't the light bother Her Highness?" Pyrrha asked.

"Not really," Ehn replied. "She should be sleeping underwater. Plus, the setting sun and moonlight should make our flashlights inconsequential."

They dug around in their bags and pulled out their lamps and strapped them on their heads. They checked that their lights were working and set them to turn on easily with a single click of a button.

"From here, we must be perfectly quiet," Ehn whispered as

they readied to leave. "We must even walk softly, muffle all coughs, and suppress any sneezes."

Okay! Pyrrha and Woods signaled.

"No eating either," Ehn continued. "And, if you need water, no gulping. Drink quietly."

Got it! The two nodded.

Together, they started the final hike up to the Penultimate Ridge. Ehn led, Pyrrha followed, while Woods was the tail. No one talked. No one coughed. No one clicked their heels on the rocks. They crawled up the steep inclines at a snail's pace. Their methodically slow movements ensured a soft step across the gravel trail. Each snapping twig or crunching rock seemed to echo loudly up and down the mountain.

As they ascended toward the top of Mount Omega, the trees became shorter, seeming to hunker down in fear of the higher elevations. The signs of animals and birds became scarce. All that moved was the wind rustling the grassy patches and bushy branches. Ehn, Pyrrha, and Woods trekked the dirt ribbon into the sky. On one side, the wall of granite towered overhead, while on the other side, the rock escarpment fell steeply to the plains below.

Step after step, they snaked their way up the goat path toward the summit. The sun fell lower in the sky. Their shadows lengthened. Dusk filled the ravines between boulders. Yet, they marched on toward their goal. They were silent as mice climbing walls. Only once they stopped under a rock overhang to rest a moment. They paused to take in the view of the sun dipping toward the horizon. It illuminated the valley in golden light. Each took a silent sip of water. Then, they carried on, hoping to make Hallowed Nest before dark.

This hiking was not hard. It was not particularly treacherous. The morning's rock climbing had been far more physically demanding. Yet, this last part of the trail was tedious. The quiet scrapes of their boots on gravel or across roots were a constant reminder that they were disturbing the peace —too loud, too foreign, too unwelcome. The dramatic cliffs were claustrophobically close on one side, and on the other side, the open vista gave even steady minds agoraphobia. Then, there was the omnipresent fear of the dragon—the unseen and unknowable essence that could decide to wake and strike unexpectedly. Her Highness could fly out of her nest and set them afire with one breath. It all coalesced into too much to think about and too much time to think about it all.

Pyrrha paid extra attention to her body and her breathing. However, that could not divert her attention enough, so she added an observation game to distract herself. She took mental pictures of the trail, the view, the plants, her shoes. She captured the colors and textures of the world around her. This forced her to stop thinking in words and to only see what was actually present.

Orange lichen clung for dear life to the grey rock face. The sky turned aqua, amber, fuchsia, then navy as the sun neared the horizon. The wind tickled her face with stray wisps of hair that had fallen out of her braids. The cedar bushes piney citrus aroma wafted invigoratingly over the trail.

Yet, indifferent to all the beauty corralling her attention, her mind wandered off. Yuht's features were outlined in the rock face. Dragon wings wearily beat in the rustling leaves. Grand Tock rode a chariot of clouds across the sky. Her stomach growled like the bear attacking their campsite. Mama Jojo's sack of jing slapped against her hip in the satchel. These dizzying thoughts raced around as distractions from the task at hand— quietly climbing Mount Omega.

In the distance, amongst the clouds, a black form soared in the sky. At first, it was small: an insignificant blur, an impression of sunlight and shadows. Yet as they ascended the path, the black silhouette seemed to regularly reappear.

Pyrrha tapped Ehn on the shoulder, pointed and signed, *Is it the dragon?*

Ehn shook her head, *No!* But, her expression was worried.

The three stopped under an overhang. Ehn took out her binoculars and shared them with Pyrrha and Woods in turn. At first, all they could see were wings. With a second longer look, they saw a strong beak and sharp talons. Fortunately, it was not the dragon, but they were not out of harm's way. Soaring high above was a bald eagle whose white head and tail caught the light in turns.

We must hurry, Ehn mouthed.

"Cleek—cleek," the eagle screeched as he circled lower and lower, nearer and nearer. "Cleek—cleek! Eek, eek, eek!"

The noise made Pyrrha jump, Woods freeze, and Ehn cringe. The sound was deafening as it echoed off the mountainside. There were few trees to hide amongst, there were no caves to dive into. At attention, they moved purposefully toward their destination ever more aware that the eagle's calls might rouse the dragon.

"Cleek—cleek," the eagle sounded an alarm. "Cleek—cleek! " The bird soared in ever tightening circles over their heads swooping closer with talons out and beak ready to attack.

Hurry! Ehn beckoned to Pyrrha and Woods. She pointed to the rock at the top of the next incline.

"Cleek—cleek! Eek, eek, eek!" His wings whipped by Pyrrha's ear.

Pyrrha shifted her bag and unzipped her windbreaker. She faced the eagle and opened her coat wide like she was spreading her wings to fly. Instantly, she had the wingspan of a mountain raptor, a viable opponent in battle. The eagle gave pause.

"Cleek—cleek," the eagle retreated to a slightly higher elevation.

Ehn and Woods followed her example. They shifted their backpacks and opened their clothing to look like winged creatures ready to flock together for an attack. Their colorful clothes flapped convincingly in the mountain breeze. They were a gaggle of adventurers.

"Cleek—cleek! Eek, eek, eek!" the eagle warned as he landed on an upper cliff ledge. There, above his head, was a large nest in a tree with his partner roosting on some eggs.

Move! Ehn encouraged them up the mountain path.

Ignoring the sounds of the crunch of their heels, they made haste over and around the next switchback. While they scurried ever higher up the rocks, they watched the sky for signs of the dragon stirring from her nest in the reservoir. They hoped and prayed that the eagle had not awoken her from her rest.

Finally, they arrived at a small clearing, a dead end. The path stopped at a gnarled pine tree standing resolutely in front of the cliff. It seemed there was nowhere left to go. Ehn dashed forward and they followed close behind, trying not to step on her heels. She stretched up and placed her palm upon the tree trunk and worked her hands up to a broken branch just above her head. When the tree moved, a deep crevice emerged in the rock face. Ehn slid next to the mountain and pushed on the crack. A door swung in, revealing a room. They all entered. Ehn turned on her headlamp and shut the rock door behind them.

Before Ehn, Pyrrha, and Woods was a cavernous cave decked out as a house. To the right was a row of bunkbeds, to the left was a kitchenette, and in the middle was a seating area. It looked like the interior of an old wooden cabin with all of the curtains drawn for the night. Nothing was ornate or embellished. All of the furniture and decor was simple, sturdy, and utilitarian.

"Welcome!" Ehn said in her normal voice.

Pyrrha and Woods shuffled to the armchairs in the center of the room and sat down heavily. The day's climb had drained them more than they had known. Ehn walked into the kitchen and began opening and closing cupboards looking for supplies. She found a lantern and placed it in the center of the cave.

"Here!" Ehn gave them each a premade camping meal. "Eat, I'm sure you are hungry."

With individual heating devices activated with water, the meals were warm and ready in minutes without the use of fire or smoke. However, despite the convenience, the hot dinners did not taste like much, as they had little aroma.

"How is the meal?" Ehn asked Pyrrha and Woods as they quietly devoured their food.

"Good, but what happened to the taste?" Woods mused.

"I wasn't kidding when I said Her Highness has a sensitive nose, so even fragrant meals in here would be too tempting to her when we opened the door and the smells wafted out."

Pyrrha looked down at her empty bowl with a sheepish smile and said, "I guess it wasn't that bad."

"Well my time is almost done here," Ehn smiled at them. "Before I leave, I must give you some instructions."

"What, you are not staying to help us?" Pyrrha asked.

Ehn waived off her question and continued on, "Everything you need, we have packed in the bags. The books will be especially helpful."

"Can you give us some more details?" Woods begged.

"Try to match the stories with your supplies..." Ehn said cryptically.

"I don't think I understand," Pyrrha sputtered.

"This is your quest," Ehn insisted. "If I tell you more, it might ruin your chances."

"How can helping us hurt us?" Pyrrha asked.

"This is what the council decided," Ehn said. "I must go before it is too dark to descend."

"You are climbing back down now?" Woods remarked.

"I'm going down," she said with a wink.

Ehn stood up and nodded a goodbye to both of them. She

slipped on her rock climbing harness and secured her backpack around her waist and chest. Then, she opened the cave door and strode out past the old pine tree on the small nesting ledge that gave the site its name. Woods and Pyrrha stood in the doorway of the cave watching the pink, orange, and purple clouds from the sunset.

Ehn did not walk toward the trail head. Instead, she ran toward the edge of the cliff and soared off the ledge into thin air. As she jumped, she pulled a cord on the side of her backpack. Pyrrha and Woods ran to the mountain's edge to watch a dark kite open from her backpack and catch the wind. The final rays of light from the sun glinted off the broad wings that glided soundlessly through the descending darkness.

They stood on the lip of the cliff squinting to see Ehn's flight path down the mountain and across the plain to the forest where the fortress stood amongst the trees. However, the kite quickly camouflaged into the ground below, making it nearly impossible to spot except when a tiny glint of light here or there showed its track to the ground. As the last light of the day disappeared, Woods and Pyrrha returned to the pine tree and closed the cave door.

There was much to do before tomorrow. The preparations must begin.

THE DARK NIGHT

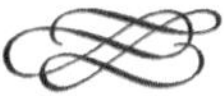

THE CAVE WAS DARK, COOL, AND DAMP LIKE THE INSIDE OF A cellar. It was silent—the kind of quiet that buzzes in the ear and strains the eardrum to hear any noise at all.

"Hmmm…" Woods cleared his throat.

Pyrrha moved to an armchair and sat down. "I suppose it's time to plan this thing."

"Humf…you got any ideas?"

"Well, we should see what they packed us in our bags as it should give us some clues about where to start."

Pyrrha opened her satchel and began removing items one by one and lining them up on the rug in the center of the room.

Woods examined inside his own backpack, only to be surprised. "Guess what, Pyrrha?"

Woods had unzipped the back flap of the backpack to reveal a row of a perfectly tucked feathers.

"I have my own set of wings!" Woods exclaimed with terri-fied excitement.

"That means…you are going to need to jump off the cliff just as Ehn did," replied Pyrrha.

Woods stared at the bag with awe, then he carefully tucked

the feathers in exactly as he had found them and re-zipped the bag to ensure it would work properly when he needed it.

Pyrrha continued to unpack her own satchel and place each item in rows on the floor. Each line included different kinds of things.

Clothing—a light jacket, a few pairs of socks, a colorful scarf;

Personal—a comb and mirror set, several hair ties and barrettes, a journal, a pencil case, a passport, an ID card;

Health—a bar of soap in a pouch, feminine items, a towel, a first aid kit with bandages;

Food—a waterskin, some crackers;

Tools—Uncle Marz's handmade map, a flint, Grand Tock's webbing rope, her throwing darts, a small knife;

Sleep—a tarp, two sleeping bags—both Pyrrha's and Woods' bedding rolls;

Other—a bushel of jing.

There was one final pile of things on the floor. It consisted of all of the new things in the bag that did not belong to Pyrrha or Woods and must have been packed by Ehn as they slept the night before.

Woods and Pyrrha looked at the items, trying to make sense of the supplies. There were two books—a basic chemistry textbook and a collection of fairytales. There was a topographical map of the mountaintop which showed the paths in and around Hallowed Nest, the reservoir, and the dam. There was a hatchet whose small size concealed its fierceness. Finally, there was a small, wooden box with Woods' name on it containing four things—binoculars, a slingshot, a handheld lighter, and a string of festive red firecrackers typically lit during New Year's celebrations.

"So, should we start with the books, Pyrrha? Which one do you want to read?"

"Fairytales, please. Woods, you get the chemistry book."

"I'm guessing you should look for stories of dragons—" Woods mused.

"I'm guessing you should look for jing concoctions," Pyrrha quipped.

They both were too tired to continue being snippy, so they read for awhile in silence.

"I found something," Pyrrha said raising her head from her storybook.

"I think I found some things too."

"Should we switch books?"

"Sure," Woods agreed. "Here I've turned down a few pages that I think might be of use."

"There is only one story in here about a water dragon who breathes fire," Pyrrha shared. "It's on page ninety-five."

"I'll read it after I get some tea," Woods replied. "I need to get up and stretch."

Woods left Pyrrha to prepare. He took the two sleeping bags and rolled them out on two different bunkbeds on opposite sides of the sleeping quarters. He puttered in the kitchen cleaning the dinner dishes and boiling some tea. With two hot cups of bland flowers and herbs, he came back to the armchairs.

"Here's some tea." Woods set the steaming mugs between them.

"Thanks," Pyrrha smiled. "I was looking at this map, and it is very curious." As she spoke, she laid the topographical map on the tabletop and started pointing at the legend.

"See these marks?" She waited for Woods to follow her finger snaking across the paper. "These grey lines are internal tunnels inside the mountain." Then, she pointed to a second set of thick, black lines. "These darker lines are trails that go over the mountain."

Woods studied the map. Clearly, this cave had been the site of a major reconnaissance mission. There were lookout points in eight directions that could easily be accessed without leaving the cave. In addition, outside trails led to several secret entrances, so someone could quickly disappear into the cave or appear outside on a trail.

"Well, this makes Ehn's instructions for me to 'not go over the summit peak' much easier to follow. But...these tunnels are confusing. Hopefully I don't get lost inside the dark passages in the mountain and never find my way out again."

They both studied the map together. Pyrrha focused on the outside paths that went down toward the dam while Woods paid close attention to the tunnels that had secret entrances and exits by the reservoir.

"There is a lot of information here," Pyrrha mused. "I think that this was used as the maintenance station or headquarters for the dam."

"Huh! That's an idea," Woods said. "What have you found?"

"Look at the notes on the dam wall," Pyrrha pointed to several penciled additions on the map. "It seems that they were planning some major renovations to reinforce the rock face."

"This hints that the mortar holding the dam together has been weakened by something."

"What could have done that?" Pyrrha thought back to her geography lessons. "Do you think it's just normal wear and tear?"

"Yeah, I imagine the dam needs some attention as no one has been able to fix anything for the last five years."

"If there were problems from before the war, then they would have just gotten worse."

"Remember the dripping faucet the week we went camping?" Woods recalled. "The floor boards in the bathroom had to be completely replaced."

"Grand Tock always used to say, 'Water looks deceptively nice, but it is a powerful force.'"

Woods frowned at the truth. "Well, some of this is making sense, but I'm still not sure what this box is about." He looked at the firecrackers by his feet. It was a piece that he could not yet place with the other parts of the puzzle.

"There are many things that don't yet fit together," Pyrrha sighed. "I wish that Ehn would have told us more of their ideas about what to do."

"We should get some sleep," Woods mumbled. "Hopefully, our sleeping minds will figure this stuff out." The exhaustion of the day had hit him. "I'm off to bed."

"I'll follow soon," Pyrrha said looking up from the chemistry book.

"Good night. I'll leave the kitchen light on as a nightlight. Is that okay?"

"Yes, please! It is too dark in here." Pyrrha called after Woods as he walked toward his cot on the far side of the cave. "Good night!"

After a good hour of quiet reading and contemplation, Pyrrha got up to go to bed. The day's hike and the burdens of tomorrow weighed on her soul. She washed her face and went to lie down in her cot. Woods was fast asleep, gently snoring. His regular breathing was a comfort in the quiet cave. The kitchen light was a welcomed flicker of illumination in the darkness.

Pyrrha was tired, but sleep did not come, so she rested on her back and placed a small pillow on her stomach to feel the comforting pressure hugging her belly as it rose and fell in time with her breathing. She thought about the dragon, the lake, and the supplies, but that just made the pillow wobble and shake as she panted with fear and anxiety. At times like these, the only thing capable of clearing her mind was prayer—not a simple verse or two that she could repeat as a mantra, but it was time to recall one of the long tablets she had memorized as a girl in preparation for adulthood.

She got out of bed and found a meditation rug leaning against the wall. She rolled it out on a clear bit of floor. She sat;

she breathed. She waited for a prayer to come to mind to recite. She inhaled and exhaled in-and-out, in-and-out, in-and-out. Her favorite tablet rolled out of her in a low rumble. She enunciated the words silently so as not to disturb the quiet cavern.

"In the Name of God, the Most Ancient, the Most Great.

"Indeed the hearts of the sincere are consumed in the fire of separation: Where is the gleaming of the light of Thy Countenance, O Beloved of the worlds?

"Those who are near unto Thee have been abandoned in the darkness of desolation: Where is the shining of the morn of Thy reunion, O Desire of the worlds?"[1]

This prayer was like none other. It's power emanated from the first line calling those who recited it to be inflamed with love. The verses spoke of the trials and tribulations of a seeker on the path to enlightenment. Pyrrha chanted the tablet from memory, concentrating all of her thoughts on the next word and the next phrase so her mind would not wander overwhelmed by tomorrow morning's tasks. The prayer calmed her as she followed the memorized script; it was like floating down a deep river channel carved from her head to her heart. When she came to the end of the tablet, she took a moment of pause to be enwrapped in solitude, but when the worries flooded in again, she started reciting the tablet once more from the beginning.

"In the Name of God, the Most Ancient, the Most Great."

The second time through, she slowed her pace to stretch out the recitation. She concentrated on each syllable and sentence, pronouncing them softly and absorbing their meaning deeply in her soul. She let the rhythm of the prayer wash over her in waves of clear water that cleared away the stench of visions of destruction and death. The tablet was medicine easing pain as it absorbed into the blood to circulate around the body. It filled Pyrrha with peaceful pulsing health that helped her muscles relax and her mind focus. However, when she came to the end for a second time, anxiety crept into her thoughts once more, so she began the same prayer again.

"In the Name of God, the Most Ancient, the Most Great."

"…Coldness hath gripped all mankind: Where is the warmth of Thy love, O Fire of the worlds?"[10]

The third, fourth, and fifth time chanting the prayer ran together in a blur, but with each repetition, Pyrrha became calmer and slipped deeper into a meditative space somewhere between waking and sleeping where she could hear the noise of Woods' gentle snoring a few yards away, but she could not quite feel the floor she was sitting on or keep track of time and space.

"In the Name of God, the Most Ancient, the Most Great."

"… The lamps of truth and purity, of loyalty and honor, have been put out: Where are the signs of Thine avenging wrath, O Mover of the worlds?"[10]

At some point, she moved from the floor to her bed and fell asleep with the words from the tablet ringing in her ears like a throbbing heartbeat.

Then she awoke.

She opened her eyes; she gazed into the face of the tiger sitting on the foot of her bed. His fur was ruffled; his brown eyes gazed deeply into hers; his warm body emanated strength. The majestic countenance of this endangered animal, in all of his power and wisdom, sat with his claws gently tucked into her bedding. Then, he roared. He roared displaying his teeth and the inside of his jaw; the reverberations shook the bed and echoed off the cave walls.

Then, the tiger was gone and so was Pyrrha.

Inky silence absorbed her. She was no longer in the cave, nor was she anywhere else. She had entered nothingness, a vacuum void of everything. No sight. No sound. No smells. No tastes. Only oblivion—a leaf floating in a starless night far from anyone or anywhere she knew. Darkness surrounded her—loneliness, sorrow, grief, fear. In this emptiness, she languished for what seemed like years without hope of rescue. Yet, all things must come to an end.

She landed in a garden. The flowers had sprung open to reveal their vibrant colors and blossoming forms. Roses, violets, hyacinths, tulips, and geraniums sat side by side accentuating each other's beauty within a diverse display. The sun gently played on the scenery, so everything danced and sparkled. In the center of the garden, was a stone fountain with a bubbling spring cascading down the carved layers into a large collecting pool at the base. Around the fountain stood four distinguished personages whose long, silk robes billowed in the breeze. They emanated light and certitude as if all knowledge and wisdom streamed from their beings. Pyrrha bowed deeply, embarrassed that she had disturbed their peaceful moment in heaven. As she looked down at the ground, her eye caught one detail—there among the tulips, perched on a flower stem, sat a large black spider ominously staring her way.

Pyrrha awoke shaking from her visions. It was morning. She had been in bed for many hours. She had not slept well, but she was not tired. A calm resolve animated her. She was pessimistically optimistic—it would eventually turn out alright in the end, but it was going to be difficult between now and then. This day, she would face the dragon. She would face her fears. She would prevail, or maybe she would return to that garden of her dreams.

HER HIGHNESS

Pyrrha got out of bed to find Woods already awake. He had scrounged the kitchen cupboards looking for a suitable breakfast. At the kitchen nook, he had placed two bowls of oatmeal and two steaming cups of brown liquid resembling coffee but without any flavor or smell. Pyrrha found him sitting on one of the benches reading while nibbling at the food. She splashed her face with cold water before finding her way to the table.

"I don't know how I slept last night, but I fell asleep right away," Woods said.

"I don't know how I slept either. I mean, I slept, but I had so many dreams that I might as well have lived through the nightmares," Pyrrha replied.

"Hm, you really don't look well rested…but you still seem in good spirits…which is great… considering."

Pyrrha laughed at the truth of the comment. "Any new ideas since last night? Anything in the fairytale or chemistry book?"

"Actually, yes!"

"Really?"

"There is one story about Hercules and the Hydra in the

fairytale book, and, in that story, there is only one detail that stands out." Woods pointed to the book and read the line. "The water smelled of rotten eggs."

"Sulfur?" Pyrrha asked.

"Yes, so I looked in the chemistry book to see what combinations could create a sulphur-like reaction."

"Did you find anything?"

Woods grinned. "Of course."

Pyrrha looked at Woods with a glint of hope in her eyes. They had discussed the issue last night, but they had not found anything very useful. Woods moved Pyrrha's half-empty bowl of oatmeal out of the way and placed the chemistry book in front of her. The section title read—"Bio-Chemical Reactions for Powerful Plant Concoctions."

Pyrrha read and reread the few paragraphs on the open pages. The answer was there in black and white text.

"How did we miss this last night?" Pyrrha asked.

"Actually, I read it last night, but..." Woods commented.

"What! Why didn't you share it with me?"

"It didn't make sense until I reread it this morning," Woods protested.

"I'm glad you made heads and tails of it after sleeping," Pyrrha sighed. "You know I'm slow when it comes to working out the chemical reactions, especially...look at how many compounds are involved."

"Hm, yeah, I know..." Woods agreed. "Good thing, I found these notes in the back."

"What?!" Pyrrha grabbed the notes and slumped back in her chair. "Ehn is a funny one. She made this into a kind of treasure hunt."

Woods agreed with a nod. "I don't get it! Is there a difference if she tells us or we read it from the book ourselves?"

Pyrrha shrugged. She smiled. With this new understanding

of the task that lay ahead of them, the anxiety of failure seemed to melt away.

They finished their breakfast and coffee before leaving the table to make their final preparations. Pyrrha straightened her clothes and put on her jacket and shoes. She checked her bag and made sure all of her supplies were secured and that anything she would need for the day was placed at the top of the bag, ready to grab immediately. She stood near the door and watched Woods at the kitchen sink washing out their bowls and cups and putting them on the drying rack.

"Are you ready?" Pyrrha asked Woods.

"As I'll ever be," he said as he escorted Pyrrha to the entrance and hugged her goodbye.

Their embrace was a little too long and a bit too strong, but both of them held each other for one last moment of comfort before the trials of the day began. Before they both lost the courage to carry out the plan, Pyrrha pulled away, opened the cave entrance, and strode up the mountain in the evanescent darkness of dawn.

Pyrrha looked back one last time to see Woods standing by the pine tree, watching her stride up the path over the hill to the lake. He would wait in the cave for a bit and then follow another route to the reservoir—never crossing the summit, just tunneling through the mountain. He would watch her progress through the binoculars until it was his time to act. When the dragon flew off, and Pyrrha was safely down, he would soar to camp as Ehn had done the evening before.

Pyrrha ascended toward the crest with deliberate steps and careful attention. She was aware of her surroundings and hyper alert to each movement. In her mind, she played through the plan and thought about the contingencies. It was not a long or challenging hike, but the burden of her task slumped her shoulders like a boulder in her bag. She was hunched in determination. The sun was rising in front of her, so when she crested the mountain, it glinted off her full body casting a spotlight on her before she descended into the reservoir valley still shrouded in shadows.

On a flat landing along the path down to the head of the lake, she stopped to take in the vista before her—green water, brown trees, and grey rocks under a red morning sun. The mountains curved and plunged down into the ravine filled with liquid stench. Once this lake had been so pure that it was clear to the bottom several hundred feet below. Now, the valley of spring water reeked like a skunk.

Her breath caught in her throat as she drew in the sulfurous smell of the dragon's noxious outgassing for the last five years. The rotten-egg odor wafted up as billows of pernicious fumes. Thus, she took out her handkerchief, which she had dosed in a special film, and tied it around her face for protection. Pyrrha peered from the mountainside into the dark waters looking for movement—signs of Her Highness, the Dragon. The water was flat except where a breeze touched the surface, sending rippling waves. The few trees and bushes that spotted the landscape looked sick from lack of proper hydration; their bark peeled exposing naked smooth spots where rugged toughness should be. The gravel path down to the water's edge was uncertain from disuse. Yet, she pressed on.

The sun rose higher each moment illuminating more of the valley with each passing minute, so Pyrrha did not tarry long. She could not risk daylight exposing her position; she continued her trek down the mountainside to the banks of the reservoir. She padded softly, minimizing the scratch of her soles on the gravel path. As she descended the hillside and neared the water's edge, the sulfurous odor increased in magnitude. She concentrated on breathing so as not to choke on the foul air.

She thought of Woods alone in the confines of the cave. He should be consulting the map and following the snaking passageways through the mountain. He might soon be watching her from one of the handful of lookout points over the reservoir. She would not glance in his direction, as she did not want to give away his position if the dragon was eyeing her.

After what seemed like an hour of trudging, Pyrrha reached the manmade cement embankment that stretched all the way to the dam wall. In years gone by, it had been the landing pier for small boats that paddled and sailed on the lake. During festivals, vendors sold refreshments and souvenirs while performers spun and sung. The long, flat expanse was a good place to begin her labor.

Pyrrha reached into her saddle pack and hustled out the bushel of jing from Mama Jojo. She cut the knots which sealed the burlap sack closed. Then, she opened the mouth and wrestled it to the water's edge. She dragged the bag along the cement shoreline, slipping chunks of jing into the water as she moved. Though she wanted to run quickly down the expanse of pavement dumping all of the clots of root into the water, she knew she must move deliberately to minimize noise and reduce the splash that each nugget made as it broke the lake surface. As she slid along, she studied the water; she peered into the depths of the reservoir in search of movement, color, shape—anything to hint at the whereabouts of the dragon. As Pyrrha walked the embankment foot after foot, the sack kept providing a seemingly endless supply of jing. The bushel held its own surprise; it seemed to contain an unlimited store of roots. As she approached the dam face, the bag finally emptied the last nugget into the water.

The morning light sparkled on the surface, activating the jing and causing it to fizz and bubble. As it reacted with water and heat, the liquid changed from green to turquoise to aqua to clear. The jing purified the putrid toxic mass into something resembling water, yet a bit more acidic. The transformation was subtle at first, looking only like the trick of the eye in the play of the light. However, it was a chemistry marvel. The reaction moved out from the shoreline into the center of the lake. A shadow like a cloud moved across the water. The jing transmuted the dragon sweat into something not entirely toxic, merely astringent.

To get a better view of things, Pyrrha made her way to the center of the dam wall, where the stone pavilion crowned the engineering enterprise. The domed canopy was supported by nine pillars each carved with unique elegance to represent the diversity of the peoples served by this water supply. In times of old, grand summer events would have been held here with big bands, dance parties, and picnics. This pavilion was where Uncle Marz and Auntie Farz loved to waltz together. It was a place for glad tidings and joy as it celebrated water and life.

As she moved along the top of the dam crest, a school of golden koi swam next to her, flashing their yellow and orange tails out of the water. The fish played happily in the sunlight, seeming to enjoy the cleaner water. They followed her like puppies begging for a treat—their mouths opened wide with anticipation. Eerily, their synchronous jumps matched her pace.

Ehn's warnings rang out—*Beware! The dragon can shape shift and change color.*

Were these fish really dragon tentacles eyeing her movements? Pyrrha prepared herself for an attack. She cleared her mind and thought of peace. The steam from the chemical reaction was rising from the water, making a low-hanging mist over the valley. She sent up a prayer that Woods was already in place, so he could spring into action as soon as he was needed.

Pyrrha focused on the green island which rose in the center of the lake. The fish flailing nearby transformed into a spiked tail. A head emerged from the depths on the far side of the lake —yellow eyes glared and golden teeth gleamed. Her Highness, the Dragon had awoken from her nap. The water parted and the wind stilled. Putrid stench filled the air.

Pyrrha corralled her wits and summoned her courage. She

secured Grand Tock's webbing to one of the pavilion pillars and spun around to face the dragon who was churning up the waves.

Dear lady! Whose daughter do we have the honor of hosting? The dragon's wild eyes—even at a great distance—looked into her soul and asked her this question.

I am Pyrrha of Tock's Land. Pyrrha focused on communicating her thoughts with every fiber of her body. She summoned the wherewithal to make eye contact and stand resolute.

Who? Who do you think you are? The wild beast's temper hissed.

Pyrrha held her ground. She looked into the fathomless eyes and communicated through her soul. *I am Pyrrha of Tock's Land. Grand Tock's granddaughter.* As she engaged the dragon in pleasantries, she tested the strength of the rope webbing to make her escape over the lip of the dam and down the dam face.

You have caused me great disrespect by disturbing my sleep. As Her Highness spoke, the island of a body moved closer and closer to the pavilion. The swirling of the water seemed like a whirlpool as the dragon shifted and turned to face the trespasser.

Forgive me my intrusion. I was sent by the Duke. Pyrrha momentarily broke eye contact to bow respectfully. She hoped good manners would flatter the great monster and smooth communication.

The dragon stopped moving toward her. *Has he sent you to kill me?*

Pyrrha looked deep into Her Highness' face and answered truthfully. *Yes.*

"YAHHHHHHHHHHHHHH!" The dragon screeched. Her wings emerged out of the lake and slapped the surface. Waves rippled outward splashing the shorelines with angry whitecaps.

"But, I will not kill you!" Pyrrha yelled. The words tumbled out of her mouth and poured out of her soul. *I will not kill you!*

Even if I attack you? Her Highness insisted. She was playing to buy time. The dragon had been moving steadily across the lake toward the dam wall. In the short amount of time that they had been speaking, the dragon had closed the gap. Her tail was encircling the pavilion, inching ever closer to Pyrrha's legs.

I have come in peace. Please let me leave in peace.

"HyaHyaHyaHyaHyahhhhhhhh!" the dragon cackled.

Pyrrha tugged on Grand Tock's webbing then jumped from the pavilion down the vertical dam face. The old spillway had once been a waterfall bricked over in the name of innovation. Now, the wall was a matted tangle of weeds and crumbling rocks holding back a reservoir of rancid water.

Pyrrha swung side to side looking for the weakest link in the masonry, trying to remember the map's notations and translate them into real positions. She worked quickly, eyeing the ledge above her, expecting the dragon's face at any moment to be peering down on her.

You cannot escape Her Highness Eruliaf! The message reverberated through liquids and solids in a tidal wave of energy. She was moving out of the water, shaking off the droplets, preparing to take flight.

There, perched on the ledge of the dam, in all her magnificent glory, was the golden dragon, radiant as a rainbow and channeling the strength of the moon. Pyrrha shielded her eyes and focused on the dam face. She scanned the brickwork looking for discolored, rough patches that would signal water damage. Applying minimum pressure to the right place would provide maximum results. A green twig caught her eye. A rooted sapling had grown into the rocks softening the wall with its insistence to live.

Your Highness Eruliaf! Pyrrha called to the dragon using her name. *You must leave. Copperton needs fresh water to survive.*

"Ehhhrrrr!" The dragon huffed. Warm air swirled around Pyrrha. Her Highness perched on the pavilion clutching the lip of the wall with her talons. She was not yet breathing fire, but her temper was rising along with the temperature of her exhales.

Stop! No fire. She willed herself to be understood. *Stop! No fire. We will both die.*

"Ehhhrrrr!" Eruliaf huffed. Pyrrha sweated. Hot air shot down in gusts. As the dragon's anger rose, so did the temperature of her breath. At any moment, she would be exhaling fire.

Stop! The jing vapors will explode.

"Ehhhrrrr!" Eruliaf was panting. Her yellow eyes had turned a furious red.

The moment of reckoning had come—Pyrrha grasped the sapling with both hands and tried to pull it out like the weed it was. Yet, this green rooted plant clung to the dam face. It held fast. The small tree did not budge.

I will kill you. Eruliaf puffed. She used her claw to bat the rope webbing and swing Pyrrha from side to side, yet her first attempt was foiled. Her talon caught the webbing and was ensnared in the mysterious netting.

Pyrrha was not deterred. She took out the hatchet and started wailing at the wall. She focused on the brickwork a few feet above and beside the tree roots trying to loosen the hold in a circle. Once again she braced both legs on either side of the sapling and pulled with all her might. This time, she had help from Eruliaf, who swatted at the rope again. It jerked from side to side. The momentum pulled Pyrrha with the tree. The sapling came out along with its roots. This tore the crumbling brickface off the dam wall. A trickle of water spouted out of the opening made by the missing tree. More water followed.

The majestic being took flight. She pushed off the wall and beat her wings against the air. She dove toward Pyrrha, who was hanging by a thread next to a geyser of toxic liquid.

My life or yours! Eruliaf shrieked as she dived down into the valley to attack Pyrrha.

Bang! Pop! Clap! Snap! BOOM! Firecrackers ignited the gaseous mist hanging above the reservoir. The world exploded. A fireball raced toward the peaks of the mountains and down toward the surface of the lake. The noxious liquid burst out of the breach in the dam like it had been detonated by a bomb.

Pyrrha swung violently against the rock wall. Black, pain, sorrow closed her consciousness. The shadow of Eruliaf in flight crossed the sky.

A LAUREL'S WELCOME

Pyrrha felt gentle scratching on her wrist where her pulse should be. Fingernails bit her skin systematically from elbow to fingertip. The therapeutic massage enlivened her nerves like tickling pins and needles. Chanting enveloped her in waves of healing from deep within the earth. The words were foreign; the tone was low; the rhythm was steady. The prayer called Pyrrha back to this world, coaxing life into her chilled body.

""Yá Alláhu'l-Mustagháth…Yá Alláhu'l-Mustagháth…Yá Alláhu'l-Mustagháth…"[1]

Tears flowed from Pyrrha's closed eyes as she lay upon a cot in a warm room flooded with sunshine. Blood streamed through her veins and vessels. Slowly, the color of life returned to her skin; her breathing became calm and stable. She felt safe and cared for by this stranger, who summoned her soul to reconnect with her body. The powerful song and the doctor's medicinal touch pulled Pyrrha back to consciousness. Yet, she had no energy to awaken.

Time passed as the shadows danced across the walls; the warm of day and cool of night breezed through the room. On the third day, Pyrrha awoke to herself in stages, noticing her senses one at at time—sight, hearing, smell, touch, taste. She studied the pink lines in her eyelids, listened to the birds laughing in the trees, smelled the rose oil used on her skin, felt the scratching of the massage, and tasted the bitter medicine dripped on her tongue.

Speech had eluded her until she uttered in a hoarse whisper, "Where am I?"

The doctor looked up from her work, with a glint of hope. "You are in a fortress in the trees," she said simply.

"Who are you?" queried Pyrrha.

"I'm Jesyka from Lan Daifu."

Pyrrha frowned at the incomprehensible responses. She was back at the start of her journey. She was being treated by a disciple of a legendary, mythical doctor named Lan. This news was too much for her to understand, so she closed her eyes to sleep again.

When she stirred again it was because she smelled onion soup with rye bread and heard the familiar lilt of Woods' voice nearby. She smiled her first smile in many days and opened her eyes to see her friend comfortably settled in an armchair, sipping a bowl of soup and chatting with Jesyka about herbs, crop yields, and rain predictions.

"Hi!" Pyrrha coughed.

"Eh! The dragon princess stirs," teased Woods.

"She is looking more lively today," said Jesyka. "Are you ready for some food?"

Pyrrha nodded. Woods and Jesyka came to her bedside and helped her sit up; they adjusted the pillows behind her back, so she would not need to use her little strength. They brought a tray of food and placed it on her lap. Then, they put a cup of clear broth in front of her, guiding her hands to the handles on both sides. Pyrrha cautiously brought the cup to her lips as her arms felt weighted down by invisible chains; she gingerly sipped the fragrant liquid. The soup did not disappoint. It warmed her lips, mouth, throat, and chest on its way to her stomach. It continued to warm her body as its nutrients entered her bloodstream and reached her toes.

When she had finished the small cup of broth, she looked up at Woods to examine her dear friend. He was frazzled and worn with a small cut on his face and a bandage on his arm; however, he smiled down on her like sunshine on a meadow, content and peaceful.

"What happened?" Pyrrha asked looking from his face to his arm.

"Just a few cuts and scrapes from our adventure," Woods replied.

"I'm all ears," Pyrrha sat up straighter to give her friend her full attention.

"The short story is that I was rattled from seeing the dragon, so I landed a little hard in some bushes after soaring gracefully down the mountain."

"All said! He did miraculously well," Jesyka interjected. "Considering it was his first flight with wings."

Woods blushed at the doctor's praise, "Anyway, my cuts and bruises are nothing like what happened to you."

"What did happen?" Pyrrha inquired.

"That's a good question. Even I haven't heard the whole story of how you got down from the dam and back here before me," said Woods.

"Ah," Jesyka sighed. "That is a long story, which both of you can hear around the table tonight. Let Pyrrha rest for awhile longer, and then she can get cleaned up and dressed for a proper meal with Ehn and the others."

Pyrrha obeyed Jesyka's request by setting her empty cup of soup on the side table and nestling into the pillows for another nap. Woods acquiesced by clearing up the dishes with his good hand and shuffling out of the room. Jesyka also picked up her materials, but before leaving the room, she lit a lavender candle to encourage a soft afternoon nap.

"I'll wake you when it's time to get ready for dinner," Jesyka whispered to Pyrrha as she closed the door.

When Pyrrha awoke two hours later, Woods was contentedly siting in the corner chair reading a novel. His feet were on a stool and his book was propped on a cushion in his lap.

"Hiya!" Pyrrha croaked in a barely audible voice. "You still here?"

"Hi!" Woods set down the book on the lamp stand, and shuffled over to the bedside. "I'm here." He smiled. "How you feeling?…You know we can have dinner here if it is too much to get out of bed."

"I'd like that…" Pyrrha looked up into Woods' eyes. "But I'm stiff from all of this rest." She furrowed her brow almost as if she was relearning how the muscles worked. "It's not like me to pass up a few extra hours of sleep."

"Ha!" Woods laughed. "What happened to the girl who sleeps til noon every chance she gets?"

"I'm still here," Pyrrha frowned. "I think I'm still here."

"You are going to be alright," Woods said emphatically as much for his sake as for hers. "Well, I'll get Jesyka to help you change."

"Kind of you!…You know me well, but some things should remain hidden," she grinned wryly at her feeble attempt at a joke.

"Ha!…Honestly…you are nicer to strangers."

This made Pyrrha chuckle at the truth of the statement. Woods knew her almost as well as she knew herself. He studied her for a long moment, nodded his head goodbye-for-now, and made a graceful exit to find Jesyka, who would help her clean up and dress for dinner on the deck.

The long table was wrapped in colorful cloth and covered in fragrant food in preparation for a banquet. Roman and Tabor happily hummed as they haphazardly set plates, dishes, cutlery, and goblets around the dining table. Vahid called after them to remind whoever would listen of what was still needed to be brought to the table before they could sit down to eat. Pyrrha stood, supported by Jesyka and Woods, at the entrance to the dining deck. The three looked on with bemusement at the hustle and bustle typical of any communal meal at Forest Fortress. With an assortment of people in attendance, and no single chef to coordinate, it was a happy potluck of cakes, chickens, couscous, carrots, and an uncut watermelon. None of the dishes fit together to make a typical meal, but each sparkled as a delicacy all its own.

Jesyka found Pyrrha and Woods seats in the middle of the table, where they could easily enjoy the food and where they would be surrounded by merriment. The others made their way to the table. Ehn sat at one end and Vahid, the guard, sat at the other head of the table. Across from Pyrrha sat Tabor and Roman. The meal started with a frenzy of re-introductions to the new faces. It was not easy for Pyrrha to follow exactly what each person said. Woods, who had a knack for names and a few more days of interactions under his belt, kept up with the conversations that volleyed all around. Jesyka was one to watch, observe, take note, and ponder, so she ate quietly by Pyrrha's side.

As everyone devoured their fill and spoke their piece, a calm chatter settled over the table with a few different discussions—a sweet reminiscence, a lively debate, and a philosopher's corner. Eventually, Ehn called the group back together with a toast.

"Eh-he-he…" Ehn cleared her throat to bring everyone back to cordial attention. "I would like to raise a toast to Pyrrha, the dragon's freedom fighter!" Everyone raised a glass of clear water and clinked them together in the air above the center of the table. It was like a large embrace.

Vahid stood to speak, "I would like to raise a toast to Pyrrha for emancipating our water supply and clearing the reservoir of that poisonous liquid."

Everyone rose from their seats and cheered again.

Tabor clamored onto his chair and raised his glass high in the air and said, "We cannot forget Woods! He was a great help setting off the explosion of stinky air."

Woods cleared his voice and announced another toast, "I would like to thank Jesyka for her healing ways. She cleaned up all our scrapes and revived Pyrrha."

When everyone settled back into their seats, Pyrrha, whose face was burning with embarrassed glee, raised her timid voice to ask, "Can someone please tell me what happened? I remember being face to face with Eruliaf and pulling the tree from the dam, but it was all black after that."

The table settled into an uneasy silence. Several individuals began talking at once, and then they each hushed. No one really knew where to start or how to tell this tale.

After a long, uncomfortable pause with many knowing looks cast back and forth and here and there, Ehn spoke. "Well, it is a shame you did not see the spectacular multifarious dragon as she alighted from the reservoir wall and glided out over the land toward the North Sea. She was terrifyingly beautiful on the wind with her scales reflecting a million colors in the morning light."

Roman, pragmatically broke in, "We should start at the beginning, don't you think?"

"That is the beginning after the end for Pyrrha," said Tabor emphatically.

Simultaneously, everyone began talking around the table.

Finally, Jesyka's sweet voice called the group back to order with two simple words, "Long ago..."

Everyone paused their talking spellbound by the beginning of a great story.

"Long ago, in a place far away, there was a fifteen-year-old warrior who climbed a mountain with two friends to slay a dragon—"

Everyone burst into laughter.

"Don't make her into a legend yet!" Woods chided.

Pyrrha interrupted, "No really! What happened next?" She looked from Ehn to Tabor to Roman to Vahid for answers. "We know the beginning, but no one has told me how Eruliaf the Dragon left—or how I survived."

Vahid's low voice rumbled, "Four days ago, you and Woods ascended the mountain with Ehn. From this valley, we watched your progress up Omega's Heel as you hiked and climbed the cliffs. We also watched the dam and what we could see of the reservoir hoping that Her Highness Eruliaf slept undisturbed. Throughout the day, we signaled to Ehn. We were all relieved when you made it safely to Hallows Nest, and Ehn glided back to camp without incident.

"That night, most of us felt too anxious to sleep, so we sat around drinking tea and telling stories, waiting for the morning light. However, somehow, each of us, one by one, fell sound asleep and slept with vivid dreams. When the roosters crowed at dawn, we were shocked to find ourselves well rested.

"As the sun rose, we each took turns watching the mountain, reservoir, and dam. Truth be told, we just waited to catch a glimpse of you as the view from here is not clear. To venture closer would risk awakening the dragon too soon and put you in more danger. We were amazed to see you repel down from the pavilion and start tearing at the dam wall. Then, we saw Her Highness perched above you on the lip of the dam. We couldn't tell from here what exactly happened as water and fire exploded out. The light could be seen for miles. We think the force of the gushing water blasted the rock face and knocked you to one side. You hit your head on the dam wall.

"A waterfall of dragon sweat mixed with jing juice flowed down the dam spillway and into the old riverbed that weaves its way through the valley to the moat around the Duke's Palace and Newcomen. The smell of the putrid water clouded the entire valley and made us all a little weak in the knees. But, we quickly regained our senses as Her Highness Eruliaf took flight out over the plains.

"She flew low and awkwardly like an old woman awoken from a long nap who just stumbled out of bed. Her wings touched the air making a low thud like a mallet hammering a tree in the forest. Fortunately, the fire distracted her. She focused on the distant horizon and followed the water as it flowed down from the mountains, out to the plains, past the palace. She turned and flew out toward the northern sea. Eruliaf followed this course shrieking curses with spouts of fire. She shimmered like a crown of magnificent jewels in the morning light.

"Her shadow glittered as it swooped over this fort. We all hid out of sight under the foliage of the trees as she went north. When the sound of her wings stomping the air and the pitch of her fiery breath descended octaves with distance, we regrouped to access the damage.

"Pyrrha, you were still hanging by a thread from the dam wall. The waterfall was still pouring down the spillway toward town. A small forest fire had broken out at the base of Mount Omega where Eruliaf had vented her anger on some innocent trees.

"We divided up into teams—one to rescue you and another to check on the flood and contain the fire."

Pyrrha was speechless as she listened to the story and heard about the destruction she had caused by awakening the dragon and releasing the water from the reservoir. She was also weak with gratitude to know how close she had been to Eruliaf's temper but had been spared a toasty death by dragon fire.

Roman spoke up, "So I guess you are wondering how you got down from there?"

Pyrrha nodded her head as no words would come to her lips.

"Pyrrha, you were really high up there hanging from such a fine thread of a cord that we were all worried about the line fraying and you falling to your death. We wondered if we should climb up Omega's Heel, cross the summit, and reel you up and over the top of the dam, but that would take a full day. So, we decided to take the riskier route of rock climbing the spillway and lowering you down on a repelling line."

"It seemed like a simple plan," Vahid chimed in. "But, we didn't know how stable the dam face was after all the breakage."

"It's my story, so I'm going to tell it," Tabor interrupted from across the table.

"Alright! Alright!" Roman and Vahid acquiesced.

"Good thing that I'm an ace free climber," Tabor boasted. "I threw rope and gear over my shoulder and scaled the cliff face, setting anchors and bolts along my path. Roman then followed."

Roman did not want to be forgotten, so he added his piece, "I was second, carrying the stretcher and securing the lines to lower you down."

"It wasn't hard," Tabor cut in, "climbing up the dam. The hard part was reaching you as you were hanging twenty feet out from the wall. In the end, I had to climb all the way to the crown of the dam and lower myself down from the pavilion just as you had done. Then, when I was next to you, I could pull you back to safety with the help of Roman."

Roman took his cue to keep the story going, "Once we secured you to the stretcher, we rappelled down and brought you back to camp where Ehn took over caring for you until Jesyka arrived."

Woods spoke, "I arrived shortly after that. You were already cleaned up and tucked into bed by the time I soared down off the mountain and walked back to camp."

"Yes, what an entrance!" Ehn said. "You winged your way down from the cliff like a pro. We were all worried you would get stuck in the trees, but you glided safely to the clearing and only picked up a few scratches on the landing."

Woods blushed, "Yah, the ground comes up fast. Ehn you made it look so easy, but it's hard to slow down without breaking a bone."

"You didn't break your bone…it is just a sprain," Ehn teased. "But you tasted more dirt than you wanted."

Everyone around the table who had cliff jumped nodded. Vahid reached across Jesyka to pat Woods' good hand.

"Not dying is the best part," Vahid winked at Woods.

The table fell into quiet conversations as clumps of friends chatted about other stories that had occurred in the last few days. The lilting voices with the clinking of plates, bowls, forks, and knives hummed along as the evening descended into night. Then, an unexpected rustling in the forest brought everyone to attention.

"Oye-hey! It's Ramy. Please release the ladder and let me up. I have news from Duke Yuddha."

Vahid and Roman went to the edge of the deck and flashed their spotlights on the ground where Ramy stood. He looked haggard, like he had run the full path from town without rest.

"Bring him up," Ehn ordered.

The young man was escorted by Tabor and Roman to a small room. Ehn and Vahid left the table to debrief him on his news.

Despite everyone's curiosity, they did not eavesdrop on the hushed conversation in one of the tree cabins. Instead, they busied themselves with cleaning up dinner plates, preparing chamomile tea, and putting out a light dessert of cookies, chocolates, and berries. Tabor and Roman worked on making an evening fire in the brazier.

Pyrrha and Woods sat at the table feeling too unfamiliar with the routines to be of help. They sat in silence expectantly. After awhile, Ehn, Vahid, and Ramy emerged and joined them by the table.

"We have news," Ehn said in a flat tone. She was completely devoid of the lightness she had shown at dinner. "Ramy will share what he knows."

"I have run since this afternoon to make it here before the soldiers. They have a warrant out for your arrest, Pyrrha," said Ramy, who was still hoarse from the marathon.

"Oh?" Pyrrha gasped.

"You have flooded the palace and destroyed thousands of priceless items which were in storage there," Ramy explained.

"How could she have done that?" exclaimed Woods. "She has been here for the last week."

"Yes, but the dam waters flooded everything—the town, the palace, the road, and much farmland," Ramy said. "Pyrrha broke the dam when freeing the dragon, so they are holding her responsible for the damage."

"But!" Pyrrha sighed. "Is that fair?"

Ramy replied, "Fair or not fair? Just or not just? That is for the Duke's Court to decide. I can only tell you what I know."

"Well, please tell me all you know, so I am not ignorant when they come." Pyrrha squared her shoulders and faced the messenger to hear his story.

"When you broke the dam wall, a waterfall sprung out releasing the reservoir into the old stream bed that flows to the town and fills the moat around the Duke's Palace. That old river fed a system of cisterns under the palace so that there would always be a wellspring of water accessible from wellheads within the palace walls. This old technology was made before pipes and pumps delivered water to every room installed with a faucet and drain."

As Ramy spoke, Woods and Pyrrha imagined in their mind's eye the extent of the disaster.

"When the water rushed through its old course, it gushed into the old cisterns which were unable to contain the volume of water emptied from the reservoir. So, all the wellheads within the palace burst open, shooting out geysers of water. It sprayed the secret inner chambers of the palace with an ammonia-like liquid."

Ramy paused his story and looked from Pyrrha to Woods to Vahid to Ehn before continuing.

"The basements and ground floors of the palace flooded. Many of the forgotten items in storage in the unused wellhead rooms were destroyed—chairs, tables, chests, and robes were saturated with the water and left in ruins.

"The last I saw of the damage was the Duchess running from room to room ordering the attendants to clean up the mess. It seems that the Duke's prized library used for harvesting the wisdom of the ages was also flooded out. The Duke looked devastated as he stood knee-deep in water. A red-headed servant girl had to escort him out to the courtyard to get some air. Before I left, I heard Duchess Juno shouting your name, Pyrrha!, and demanding additional punishments. I took the fastest path here to warn you."

Ehn turned to Pyrrha and Woods, "Are you ready to travel?"

They looked at each other.

"Yes!" said Woods.

"No!" said Pyrrha. "There is nowhere to go."

"I can lead you to Grand Tock's cave in the Duke's View," said Ehn, "And from there, you can follow the old maps and flee north across the ocean."

"No!" Pyrrha reiterated her point. "I will not flee like a highway robber."

Woods admired Pyrrha in the firelight with both fear and awe, with sadness and understanding. It was little use arguing with Pyrrha when she had stubbornly articulated a decision.

"I will support your choice," Ehn acquiesced.

"Let's enjoy tonight around the fire," Pyrrha said as she raised a mug of warm cider to her friends who had helped her scale the mountain and return safely again.

"Hear, hear!" Woods exclaimed, raising his cup. "Let's cele-brate this night in peace."

"Let's keep tonight, and in the morning we can start a new day," Vahid raised a glass.

Around the brazier, the small band of warriors all toasted to one last night at Forest Fortress, one last night before the new summons from the Duke would arrive. They drank and chatted; they told stories and cracked jokes. They spent this last evening before the Palace Guard would arrive as if it was their last night of freedom.

When the revelry died down, Pyrrha was left alone with her thoughts in her room in the Tree Fort. The nightlife twittered outside her open windows. The owls hooted. The mosquitoes buzzed. The grasshoppers chatted.

Two paths opened before Pyrrha. She had chosen to go right and await the Duke's Guard that would soon arrive with the scroll containing the next labor assigned by the Duke's Court. However, she could still change her mind and turn left to escape through the mountains and across the Ocean of Wisdom to the land of Taiga. Both paths held their own punishments and rewards; neither was without sacrifice and punishment. What was her fate? She would exercise her own freewill to choose her own destiny.

To be continued...

Pyrrha's Journey is a trilogy. The second and third books continue Pyrrha's journey through more Herculean adventures.

ABOUT THE AUTHOR

Rehema Marie Clarken, Ph.D.

Rehema was born in Tanzania, raised in the U.S. Virgin Islands, and educated in Michigan, U.S.A. As an adult, she traveled to Asia, where she lived and worked for fifteen years. She has been writing stories and journaling since childhood. Wherever she goes, she always keeps a pen and notebook as her closest confidant.

After years of globetrotting, Rehema has settled in Hancock, Michigan, where she runs the Keweenaw Learning Center and Hyacinth Publishing House. She teaches middle school math through engaging hands-on activities, and she mentors young writers to craft their own stories to become the authors of their own lives.

FIND OUT MORE...

For more about Rehema Marie Clarken and her other projects, visit https://rehemathewriter.com

Follow her on Facebook and Instagram @Rehema.the.Writer

To contact Rehema Marie Clarken, email rehema.the.writer@gmail.com

To learn about Rehema's professional experience for speaking and teaching engagements, look her up at https://www.linkedin.com/in/rehemaclarken

For more information about Hyacinth Publishing House and their other authors and books, visit https://hyacinthpublishinghouse.com

To contact Hyacinth Publishing House, email hyacinthpublishinghouse@gmail.com

ACKNOWLEDGMENTS

This book could not have been written without the support of many dear souls. First and foremost, I must thank my dear husband, Jeff, for loving and supporting me through all the ups and downs of our life together. His confidence buoys me even in the most challenging of difficulties. Without his encouragement, I would not be the person I am today. I would not have finished my doctoral dissertation, nor would I have finished this book. He is my Woods; he is the one I want to accompany me on this lifelong adventure.

I must also thank my family. My parents have given me a life that allowed me to grow up to become the adult I am today. It was natural to follow in their footsteps; they were my first educators and were role models as writers. My sisters have encouraged my creativity; they read my early drafts and gave me gifts that brought many hitherto fantastical details into reality. My brother, nephews, and grandparents inspired characters in the book. Without their presence in my life, this narrative would not have been as rich with personality.

Many believe that writing is a solitary endeavor, but that is not completely true. Much appreciation goes to the many individuals who taught me how to write and to think deeply about the world. In particular, I would like to thank Louise Bourgault, Kim Douglas, Karla Saari Kitalong, Paul Lehmberg, Z.Z. Lehmberg, Jon Saari, Jaspal Kaur Singh, Mark Smith, and Ray Ventre. In addition, I appreciate the dedicated help of Darcy Greenwood, Cora Thiele Hays, Andrea Hope, and E Olson. Your attention to detail has made my books so much richer.

Finally, I would like to thank Bahá'u'lláh and the Bahá'í Faith. Belief in something greater than myself and guidance from One wiser than me has enabled me to survive and prosper. Spirituality has been a solace and inspiration in my life and as I wrote this book.

GUIDE TO NAMES AND PLACES

The names of people and places in the story are alphabetized. They were chosen to represent the diversity of people in my life —friends, family, acquaintances, colleagues, and students. All characters are fictional; they are from my imagination even when they are named after real people. No character should be confused with any real person who happens to share the same name or similar traits.

Auntie Farz (FARz): Auntie Farz is an immigrant to Copperton, who fled her homeland because of war. She is mild-tempered and pragmatic. As youth, Uncle Marz and Auntie Farz married and adopted Woods. Together, they live in a matching cottage on Tock's Land next to Grand Tock's family homestead.

Captain Mahoney (MA-hone-ee): Captain Mahoney is a member of the Duke's Guard. She commands Sergeant Kyhn and Officer Stone. She arrests and imprisons Pyrrha. She is precise and severe in her commitment to the Duke's Court's orders as a Captain in the Palace Guard.

Copperton (COP-per-tun):
Copperton started as a frontier mining town in the northern

mountains. As more copper was found, more people came to live in the area. Copperton grew from a town to a city-state and then a territory that gained recognition as an independent country. Long ago, Copperton and Ironweald developed on two sides of a mountain range. Their histories of mining once united them, but as time went by they grew apart. Copperton is a dukedom, which means that the ruler is a duke. Duke Zachariah establishes a Duke's Court to assist with the governance of the country. In Chapter 8, Duke Yuddha, the only son of Duke Zachariah and Duchess Zaynah, is crowned ruler.

Death: Death is the personification of death, a shadow hooded in mystery that comes to take Pyrrha away in her vision-like dream in Chapter 4.

Dr. Rahd (doctor ROD): In real life, the author's father is named Rod. This character is loosely based on her parent who was a university professor. After he retired, he survived a stroke which enabled him to see differently and become a prolific artist.

Duchess Juno (JOO-no): Juno is another name for Hera, the queen of the Olympian gods, who is the goddess of empires and is known for her jealous temper. In the beginning of Pyrrha's Journey, Duchess Juno is Marchioness Juno, the wife of Marquess Yuddha (Yuht). Together they have two sons, Sir Ian and Sir Jacob. In Chapter 8, Duke Yuddha ascends the throne, and Juno is crowned Duchess of Copperton.

Duchess Zaynah (ZAY-nuh): Duchess Zaynah is the younger wife of Duke Zachariah. She is the mother to Duke Yuddha, her only child. In Chapter 8, she becomes Archduchess Zaynah when her husband retires.

Duke Yuddha (YOU-duh): Yuddha means war in Sanskrit. At the beginning of the story, he is Marquess Yuddha, who is married to Marchioness Juno and is the father of their two sons, Sir Ian and Sir Jacob. Duke Yuddha is the formal title for Yuht when he becomes the ruler over the Dukedom of Copperton.

Yuddha and Yuht are two different names for the same person; this represents two different sides of the same individual. The two names highlight how he changes personalities based on given circumstances and required roles.

Duke Zachariah (ZACK-uh-rhye-uh): Zachariah is an old name which means God has remembered. Duke Zachariah married Duchess Zaynah. Together they had one child, Yuddha. During the period of this story, he is aged and suffering from the onslaught of dementia. Duchess Zaynah has become his full-time caregiver, and the Duke's Court tries to compensate for his inability to rule by assuming more responsibilities among themselves. In Chapter 8, the Duke and Duchess retire and leave public responsibilities behind when they become the Archduke Zachariah and Archduchess Zaynah.

Duke's View: The Duke's View is the land north of what was the original valley of Copperton, where the majority of citizens live in and around the capital, Newcomen. The Duke's View stretches north over the mountains to the Ocean of Wisdom. The land was charted by Grand Tock with the assistance of the map gifted to him by Jupiter the Giant.

Ehn (EN): Ehn is the leader of the band of warriors who are stationed at Forest Fortress to monitor Mount Omega, Lake Lotanna, and Eruliaf the Dragon nesting behind the dam. Ehn is a Chinese name that means kindness, favor, and grace. She is both fierce and feminine—balancing male and female energies to solve all problems in her path.

Emerson of Riverside: Emerson is a soldier of Copperton who is returning home from the war with Ironweald. He stops by the Tock's family campfire for hospitality before walking the rest of the way home.

Eruliaf (ERre-leaf) **the Dragon**: Her Highness Eruliaf is a golden dragon who, during the war-time fighting between Ironweald and Copperton, was scared out of the mines deep under the mountains that divide the two countries. She has taken up residency on Mount Omega in Lake Lotanna, because the water is cooled on the bottom by a spring and warmed on the top with sunshine. Eruliaf is FAILURE spelled backward—it represents the opposite of failure, but it also something that is not quite success. She is the embodiment of the struggle between success and failure that preoccupies the warrior's mindset.

Farmer Saari (SAHR-ee): Farmer Saari is a kind citizen of Copperton who sells vegetables to make a living. He is a generous friend of the Tock family. Saari is a common Finnish last name that means living near an island. More importantly, it is the family name of two great professors from two different universities in the Upper Peninsula of Michigan. Both were always kind and generous with their wisdom, so I immortalized them with a nod to their humility.

Forest Fortress: Also called the Tree Fort. It was constructed from a series of tree houses connected together with hanging decks and swinging bridges. It is the headquarters for Ehn, Vahid, Roman, and Tabor who have been sent to guard Mount Omega and monitor Eruliaf the Dragon. Originally, it was built as a camp for school children to enjoy nature and learn about wilderness survival. Pyrrha and Woods went their on school field trips.

Grand Tock (Grand TAH-k): Grand Tock is the patriarch of the Tock family. As a young boy, he was kidnapped by Jupiter the Giant, who took him deep into the mountains and shared a vast bit of knowledge about the lay of the uninhabited lands on the northern border of Copperton. This event changed the fortunes of Tock—he no longer was a poor farmer; instead he became a brave explorer who expanded the dominion of Copperton to include a huge swath of uninhabited mountains named the Duke's View.

Great-Grandmother Ethel: She is Grand Tock's mother and Pyrrha's great-grandmother. In her youth, she had fiery red curls like Pyrrha. Ethel was a great apothecary and seer. She specialized in brewing jing concoctions using the family farm to create many healing medicines. The Tock family continued to brew her recipes that were handed down through the generations.

Great Hall: The Great Hall is located in the Duke's Palace. It is the room where the Coronation Ball is held.

Ironweald (I-ron-wheeled): Ironweald is the name of the country that borders Copperton to the south. Long ago, the two lands were very similar sharing many cultural traditions. They both had developed as outposts that became city-states and then independent countries. Their original wealth was derived from minerals and trees. Ironweald had a weak democracy that was hijacked by strong leaders who ran the country for their own profit. Ostensibly, the war was sparked by violations of mining treaties. However, most believed it was the inevitable outcome of many years of growing tensions.

Jing (GING): Jing is a mythical root that can be used as the foundations for an assortment of medicinal concoctions. The inspiration for it comes from traditional plant-based medicines that are used around the world; it could be something similar to ginger or ginseng.

Jupiter the Giant: Jupiter is another name for Zeus. Grand Tock's fortunes change dramatically the day that Jupiter the Giant kidnapped him in the family jing fields. He was forced on an expedition into the northern mountains to restore Jupiter's jing fields and to help him slay a tiger. Jupiter gives Grand Tock many gifts that allow his family to prosper—like the map, bag of holding, and darts.

Jesyka from Lan Daifu (Lan DIE-foo): She is a practitioner of ancient medicine from the order of Lan Daifu. Lan is a Chinese surname that means plant or orchid, while Daifu is a Mandarin term for doctor. Through the years, the author has always had a friend named Jessica, Jesse, or Jess, so she added this sympathetic, nurturing character to her novel to immortalize their generosity.

Lady Eliza (eh-LIE-za): Lady Eliza is the wife of Lord Yuri. She is a friend and royal companion to Marchioness Juno (Duchess Juno) and a member of the Duke's Court. During the time of Marquess Yuddha's absence due to the war with Ironweald, Juno, Eliza, and Yuri become the only active members of the Duke's Court. Eliza means pledge of God.

Lord Yuri (YOU-ree): Lord Yuri is married to Lady Eliza. He is a member of the Duke's Court. He is a friend of Marquess Yuddha and Marchioness Juno. During the time of Marquess Yuddha's absence because of the war with Ironweald, Juno, Eliza, and Yuri become the only active members of the Duke's Court, thus gaining immense power. Yuri means light of God.

Mama Jojo (MA-ma JOE-joe): In real life, the author's mother is named Mary Jo. This character is loosely based on her parent, who has a touch of the mystic and a bit of the eccentric about her.

Mount Omega (OH-meg-ah): Mount Omega is a special mountain that is at the edge of the central valley of Copperton. Old folklore tells how Mount Omega is the last physical remnant of a great goddess' foot standing upon the earth before she stepped into heaven. The mountain, which is shaped like a foot, also starts the foothills to larger mountains to the northwest. The front of the mountain has five hills that look very much like toes while the back of the mountain rises up as a steep cliff, not unlike the heel of a foot.

Neema the Tiger (Nay-AY-ma): Neema is a Swahili name with personal family significance. In addition, it eludes to the Nemean Lion in Hercules' legend, which is one inspiration for this story.

Newcomen (NEW-com-mon): Newcomen is the capital city of Copperton and the site of the palace which houses the Duke's family and the Duke's Court. The city is divided in half by the river, which runs from the reservoir through the center of town and the main valley of the Dukedom of Copperton.

Neilson of Riverway: Neilson is a soldier of Copperton who is returning home from the war with Ironweald. He stops by the Tock's family campfire for hospitality before walking the rest of the way home.

Officer Stone: Officer Stone is the young driver in the Duke's Guard. He is under the command of Captain Mahoney. He helps escort Pyrrha to the palace dungeon and to the trial at the Duke's Court.

Old Snark: Old Snark is an unaffectionate nickname for Uncle Duceau. He is an apothecary who sells used medical supplies. He mixes unorthodox concoctions (like Joy) that could be considered an unethical application of a doctor's medical training. He is an acquaintance of the Tock family through Great-Grandmother Ethel, who was a great apothecary and teacher.

Palace: The palace is where the Duke's family resides. It is the seat of power for the country of Copperton. It sits on the northern side of the capital city of Newcomen, nestled into the mountainside. It has a large room for entertaining, called the Great Hall. It is also where the Duke's Court takes council. Underneath the palace is a dungeon where Pyrrha is imprisoned.

Pyrrha (PEER-ah): Pyrrha is the main character of the trilogy *Pyrrha's Journey*. The story starts with her fifteenth birthday—the age of maturity in Copperton. The name Pyrrha originates from Greek myth; she is the daughter of a Titan, Epimetheus, and Pandora. She is the wife of Deucalion, the son of Prometheus, who could see the future and foretold the coming of a great flood. In Greek myth, Pyrrha is similar to both Noah's wife and Eve, because she is cast out on a boat with Deucalion during a great flood that covers the known world in water, and when they land, they become the parents of the new race of humanity that is made of material strong enough to resit the misery that escaped Pandora's box. Pyrrha comes from pyro, fire (but it is not pronounced the same), because, it is said, Pyrrha had hair the color of flames.

Ramy (RAY-mee): Ramy is the town crier and an ally of the band at the Forest Fortress. He brings news from Newcomen to the fort.

River Libertad (Lib-er-TAD): This is the river of freedom that flows through Copperton.

Roman (ROW-men): Roman is a member of the band of warriors at Forest Fortress. He is the younger brother to Vahid and assists Tabor to bring Pyrrha back to safety.

Sergeant Kyhn (KIN): Sergeant Kyhn is a young, new member of the Duke's Guard. She directly reports to Captain Mahoney. She escorts Pyrrha to prison and is one of the guards to take her to trial in the Duke's Court.

Tabor (TAY-bor): Tabor is the youngest member of the band of warriors at Forest Fortress. He is an adopted child from Ironweald. He free climbs the dam to reach Pyrrha after she is knocked unconscious.

Tiger Valley: Tiger Valley is where Tock went with Jupiter the Giant to slay the first tiger. It is the same place where Grand Tock returned with Pyrrha to slay the second tiger.

Tock's Land: The Tock family's homestead. It has two cottages—one for Grand Tock, Dr. Rahd, Mama Jojo, and Pyrrha, and the other, newer cottage for Uncle Marz, Auntie Farz, and Woods. They have a deep, fresh well and acres of forest and farmland. The land was gifted by Duke Zachariah for service to the country.

Tree Fort: See Forest Fortress.

Uncle Duceau (DO-so): See Old Snark.

Uncle Marz (MARz): Uncle Marz is the adopted son of Grand Tock. They met on the expeditions to chart the lands on Jupiter the Giant's maps. Grand Tock took Marz under his wing and brought him back to Tock's Land when they returned to Newcomen. Marz is an exceptional artisan who carves wood, creates mosaics, copies maps, and makes art.

Vahid (VAH-heed): Vahid is a member of the band of warriors at Forest Fortress. He is second in command after Ehn, who is the leader of this group. Vahid is a family name which means one, nineteen, or unique.

Woods (WOODz): He is the adopted son of Uncle Marz and Auntie Farz who came from Ironweald. He has grown up living in the cottage next door to Pyrrha. He treats her like his little sister—watching out for her and protecting her from the world. Woods is down-to-earth and dependable. In many ways, his consistency fuels Pyrrha's energy (fire for life), which makes them a dynamic duo.

Yuht (YOUt): Duke Yuddha and Yuht are two different names for the same person. Each name represents a different aspect of his character and highlights how he changes personalities based on given circumstances and required roles. Yuht is his nickname and the name of his inner self that he does not show to the public. Yuht comes from Ute, which means mountain.

NOTES

1. FINDING YUHT

1. This is one of the morning prayers revealed by Bahá'u'lláh. The full prayer reads:

   "I have wakened in Thy shelter, O my God, and it becometh him that seeketh that shelter to abide within the Sanctuary of Thy protection and the Stronghold of Thy defense. Illumine my inner being, O my Lord, with the splendors of the Dayspring of Thy Revelation, even as thou didst illumine my outer being with the morning light of Thy favor."

   (*Prayers and Meditations by Bahá'u'lláh*, no. CLVIII)

3. FINDING THE WAY HOME

1. This is an excerpt from a prayer for aid and assistance by 'Abdu'l-Bahá. The full prayer reads:

   "Lord! Pitiful are we, grant us Thy favor; poor, bestow upon us a share from the ocean of Thy wealth; needy, do Thou satisfy us; abased, give us Thy glory. The fowls of the air and the beasts of the field receive their meat each day from Thee, and all beings partake of Thy care and loving-kindness.

   "Deprive not this feeble one of Thy wondrous grace and vouchsafe by Thy might unto this helpless soul Thy bounty.

   "Give us our daily bread, and grant Thine increase in the necessities of life, that we may be dependent on none other but Thee, may commune wholly with Thee, may walk in Thy ways and declare Thy mysteries. Thou art the Almighty and the Loving and the Provider of all mankind."

   ('Abdu'l-Bahá, in *Bahá'í Prayers: A Selection of Prayers Revealed by Bahá'u'l-láh, the Báb, and 'Abdu'l-Bahá* (Wilmette: Bahá'í Publishing Trust, 2002) p. 23)

2. This is an excerpt from a prayer written by Bahá'u'lláh that is often read in the evening. The full prayer reads:

   "O my God, my Master, the Goal of my desire! This, Thy servant, seeketh to sleep in the shelter of Thy mercy, and to repose beneath the canopy of Thy grace, imploring Thy care and Thy protection.

   "I beg of Thee, O my Lord, by Thine eye that sleepeth not, to guard mine eyes from beholding aught beside Thee. Strengthen, then, their vision that they may discern Thy signs, and behold the Horizon of Thy Revelation. Thou art He before the revelations of Whose omnipotence the quintessence of power hath trembled.

"No God is there but Thee, the Almighty, the All-Subduing, the Unconditioned."

(*Prayers and Meditations by Bahá'u'lláh*, no. CLXXI)

3. This is a short excerpt from a prayer for protection written by 'Abdu'l-Bahá. The prayer, in its entirety, is included below:

"O my Lord! Thou knowest that the people are encircled with pain and calamities and are environed with hardships and trouble. Every trial doth attack man and every dire adversity doth assail him like unto the assault of a serpent. There is no shelter and asylum for him except under the wing of Thy protection, preservation, guard and custody.

"O Thou the Merciful One! O my Lord! Make Thy protection my armor, Thy preservation my shield, humbleness before the door of Thy oneness my guard, and Thy custody and defense my fortress and my abode. Preserve me from the suggestions of self and desire, and guard me from every sickness, trial, difficulty and ordeal.

"Verily, Thou art the Protector, the Guardian, the Preserver, the Sufficer, and verily, Thou art the Merciful of the Most Merciful."

('Abdu'l-Bahá, in *Bahá'í Prayers: A Selection of Prayers Revealed by Bahá'u'lláh, the Báb, and 'Abdu'l-Bahá* (Wilmette: Bahá'í Publishing Trust, 2002) p. 154)

4. THE DREAM

1. This prayer is taken from a Tablet of Bahá'u'lláh. Reportedly it is to be said after a troubled dream, or at other times of difficulty:

"O Thou by Whose name the sea of joy moveth and the fragrance of happiness is wafted!

"I ask Thee to show me from the wonders of Thy favour that which shall brighten mine eyes and gladden my heart. Thou, verily, art the All-Bounteous, the Most Generous."

(*Additional Prayers Revealed by Bahá'u'lláh*, no. 1)

6. MARKET DAY

1. This is an excerpt from a healing prayer written by Bahá'u'lláh. The full prayer reads:

"Praised be Thou, O Lord my God! I implore Thee, by Thy Most Great Name through which Thou didst stir up Thy servants and build up Thy cities, and by Thy most excellent titles, and Thy most august attributes, to assist Thy people to turn in the direction of Thy manifold bounties, and set their faces toward the Tabernacle of Thy wisdom. Heal Thou the sicknesses that have assailed the souls on every side, and have deterred them from directing their gaze toward the Paradise that lieth in the shelter of Thy shadowing Name, which Thou didst ordain to be the King of all names unto all who are in heaven and all who are on earth. Potent art Thou to do as pleaseth Thee. In Thy hands is the empire of all names. There is none other God but Thee, the Mighty, the Wise.

"I am but a poor creature, O my Lord; I have clung to the hem of Thy riches. I am sore sick; I have held fast the cord of Thy healing. Deliver me from the ills that have encircled me, and wash me thoroughly with the waters of Thy graciousness and mercy, and attire me with the raiment of wholesomeness, through Thy forgiveness and bounty. Fix, then, mine eyes upon Thee, and rid me of all attachment to aught else except Thyself. Aid me to do what Thou desirest, and to fulfill what Thou pleasest.

"Thou art truly the Lord of this life and of the next. Thou art, in truth, the Ever-Forgiving, the Most Merciful."

(*Prayers and Meditations by Bahá'u'lláh*, no. XIX)

13. JUSTICE WITHHELD

1. This is a prayer by the Báb that is to be said in times of great difficulties. Bahá'ís often refer to it as the "Remover of Difficulties" prayer:

"Is there any Remover of difficulties save God? Say: Praised be God! He is God! All are His servants, and all abide by His bidding!"

(The Báb, in *Bahá'í Prayers: A Selection of Prayers Revealed by Bahá'u'lláh, the Báb, and 'Abdu'l-Bahá* (Wilmette: Bahá'í Publishing Trust, 2002) p. 226)

17. FOREST FORTRESS

1. This is an excerpt of a prayer for tests and difficulties by the Báb. The full text of the prayer reads:

"I adjure Thee by Thy might, O my God! Let no harm beset me in times of tests, and in moments of heedlessness guide my steps aright through Thine inspiration. Thou art God, potent art Thou to do what Thou desirest. No one can withstand Thy Will or thwart Thy Purpose."

(The Báb, in *Bahá'í Prayers: A Selection of Prayers Revealed by Bahá'u'lláh, the Báb, and 'Abdu'l-Bahá* (Wilmette: Bahá'í Publishing Trust, 2002) p. 227)

18. SCALING MOUNT OMEGA

1. The Arabic phrase "Alláh-u-Abhá" means "God is Most Glorious" or "God is All-Glorious." It is often used as a salutation, but more importantly, it is an obligatory prayer to be recited ninety-five times a day. Many people also use it as a mantra in times of great need, as it can be a quick prayer to God asking for assistance without distracting from the task at hand.

(The Kitáb-i-Aqdas, note 33)

20. THE DARK NIGHT

1. This is an excerpt of the Fire Tablet by Bahá'u'lláh. This tablet is to be said in times when the trials and tribulations that one faces are beyond what can be endured. It references the great atrocities that have befallen the Prophets of the world as well as many martyrs and saints. It asserts that through suffering, we know joy. This is not just an esoteric concept, but it is also a practical matter as joy and sorrow are relative terms, much the same way that hot and cold are on a continuum. Thus, the trials individuals endure are also relative to the depth to which one feels. This tablet is a bounty of metaphors and a door to spiritual understanding. To better understand it, one can read and meditate upon the full tablet in *Bahá'í Prayers: A Selection of Prayers Revealed by Bahá'u'lláh, the Báb, and 'Abdu'l-Bahá* (Wilmette: Bahá'í Publishing Trust, 2002) p. 312. An electronic version is available at bahai.org/library.

22. A LAUREL'S WELCOME

1. The Arabic phrase "Yá Alláhu'l-Mustagháth," has been translated as "O Thou God Who art invoked" or "He Who is invoked for help." Like the phrase "Alláh-u-Abhá," it can be said in times of great need to ask for aid and assistance. It can be chanted as mantra to beseech God for immediate help.

   (From a memorandum dated 28 December 2001 from the Research Department to the Universal House of Justice)